THE DOCTOR AND THE ROUGH RIDER

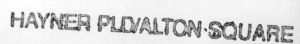

Also Available by Mike Resnick

Ivory: A Legend of Past and Future

New Dreams for Old

Stalking the Dragon
Stalking the Unicorn
Stalking the Vampire

Starship: Mutiny
Book One

Starship: Pirate
Book Two

Starship: Mercenary
Book Three

Starship: Rebel
Book Four

Starship: Flagship
Book Five

The Buntline Special—A Weird West Tale
The Doctor and the Kid—A Weird West Tale

MIKE RESNICK

THE DOCTOR AND THE ROUGH RIDER

A WEIRD WEST TALE

an imprint of **Prometheus Books**
Amherst, NY

Published 2012 by Pyr®, an imprint of Prometheus Books

Cover illustration and interior illustrations © J. Seamas Gallagher
Cover design by Nicole Sommer-Lecht

Inquiries should be addressed to
Pyr
59 John Glenn Drive
Amherst, New York 14228–2119
VOICE: 716–691–0133
FAX: 716–691–0137
WWW.PYRSF.COM

16 15 14 13 12   5 4 3 2 1

Library of Congress Cataloging-in-Publication Data

Resnick, Michael D.
    The doctor and the Rough Rider / by Mike Resnick.
        p. cm. — (A weird west tale)
    ISBN 978–1–61614–690–0 (pbk.)
    ISBN 978–1–61614–691–7 (ebook)
    1. Holliday, John Henry, 1851–1887—Fiction. 2. Geronimo, 1829–1909—Fiction.
3. Roosevelt, Theodore, 1858–1919—Fiction. 4. West (U.S.)—Fiction. I. Title.

PS3568.E698D635 2012
813'.54—dc23

                                                                    2012027522

Printed in the United States of America

To Carol, as always,

And to Gio Clairval and Sabina Theo,
a pair of gorgeous European ladies who are
truly fine writers as well as my good friends.

PROLOGUE

From the pages of the August 19, 1884, issue of the Leadville Bullet:

First Electronically Published Issue

*T*his is the first issue of the Bullet *to be published, which is to say powered, entirely by electricity, thanks to the help of Mr. Thomas Alva Edison and Mr. Ned Buntline. The electronic genius and the inventor have essentially re-invented the publishing business, because now the presses can run night and day without anyone manually working them. We've no idea why Messrs. Edison and Buntline have chosen to set up shop in our town, but we are incredibly grateful. First electric street lights, and now this!*

Gambler Sells Interest in the Monarch

Famed gambler John H. "Doc" Holliday has sold his share of the Monarch Saloon and Casino, though he will still be retained as a dealer for poker and faro.

Buntline Sells Brass Mole

Ned Buntline, claiming that the local silver mines are played out, has sold his Brass Mole, the remarkable machine that can dig through solid rock, to the McGraw Mining Company of Northern California.

Baseball Draws Crowd

Yesterday's baseball game against Denver drew almost two thousand spectators, a truly remarkable total given the heat and most people's unfamiliarity with the game.

From the pages of the August 19, 1884, issue of the Medora Times:

Theodore Roosevelt in Altercation

Young Theodore Roosevelt, formerly the Minority Leader of the New York State Assembly and currently the owner and resident of Elkhorn Ranch, was involved in an altercation last night in the town of Mingusville, some 35 miles west of here.

Mr. Roosevelt was after some lost horses and stopped at Nolan's Hotel at nightfall. He was in the restaurant when a local bully began teasing him, calling him "Four-Eyes" because of his eyeglasses, and challenging him to a fight, little knowing that he was challenging the lightweight boxing champion of Harvard University. Mr. Roosevelt made swift work of the bully and summoned the sheriff to take testimony as to what had occurred before the diners and drinkers dispersed. The bully broke loose from the sheriff and his deputies and was last seen clambering onto a moving freight train that was headed for Chicago.

Marquis de Mores Sues

The Marquis de Mores had gone to court, claiming that he is in fact the owner of Elkhorn Ranch, and that Theodore Roosevelt has no title to it.

"This could take months to resolve in a court of law," said the Marquis to your reporter, "and while I have no doubt as to the outcome, if Mr. Roosevelt would like to settle the matter sooner on the field of honor, with either pistols or swords, I stand ready and willing."

From the pages of the August 19, 1884, issue of the Tombstone Epitaph:

Apaches on the Move

Observers report that Geronimo, the leader of the Apaches in the Arizona Territory, has broken camp and is headed in the general direction of Tombstone. There is no evidence that Tombstone is his destination, or that he is on the warpath, but former Sheriff John Behan has been placed in charge of preparing our defenses, just in case.

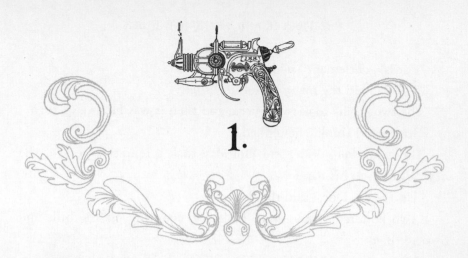

1.

"I EXPECTED THIS WEATHER IN TOMBSTONE, but not up here in Leadville," said Texas Jack Vermillion as he fanned his face with his cards in the Monarch Saloon. "I do believe it's hotter than hell today."

"I expect I'll find out soon enough," replied Holliday. He pushed some cash to the middle of the table. "I'll open for fifty."

Three men matched his money. Vermillion looked at his cards once more, then laid them face down. "Too damned hot for me to think," he muttered. "I'm off to get another beer."

"Why?" asked Holliday. "The beer here's as warm as the water you shave in."

"Then I'll pretend it's cold. I just can't think straight in this heat." Vermillion got up and trudged over to the bar.

"Pity," remarked Holliday. "There goes some easy money. He's not much of a poker player even when he's thinking." Suddenly he reached into a pocket, withdrew a bloodstained handkerchief, held it to his mouth, and coughed into it, covering it with even more blood. It was such a common occurrence that no one paid any attention to it.

"Cards, gentlemen?" said the dealer.

"Three," said the man on Holliday's left.

The two others took two apiece, and then it was Holliday's turn.

"Just one, I think," he replied.

The cards were dealt, and Holliday took a tentative peek at the new addition to his hand.

"Up to you, Doc," said the dealer.

"Two hundred," announced Holliday, counting off the bills and tossing them in.

Two men immediately folded. The third studied his cards, frowned, stared long and hard at Holliday, and finally cursed and tossed his cards onto the table.

"Okay," he said unhappily. "It's yours."

"Thanks," replied Holliday.

"So did you pull your full house, or was it a bluff?"

"Full house?" repeated Holliday. "Maybe I was drawing to an inside straight."

"Were you?"

Holliday shrugged. "Anything's possible."

"Aw, come on, Doc," persisted the man. "I'm tapped out. At least let me know what you had."

Holliday allowed himself the luxury of a small smile. "Tapped out? What were you going to bet with if you'd pulled whatever it is you'd hoped to pull?"

The man grinned. "I thought I'd borrow it from you."

Holliday laughed—or at least it began as a laugh, but ended as a bloody cough. "You've got a fine sense of humor, Mr. Richardson. I'll give you that."

"Show me your cards so I can see whether I had you beat or not," said Richardson. He reached his hand toward Holliday's cards, and an instant later Holliday jerked at the knife he wore on a string around his throat, broke the string, and brought the point of the knife down hard into the table, just between Richardson's index and middle fingers.

"*After* you pay to see them," said Holliday. His voice wasn't raised, his smile wasn't hostile, but there was something in the tone of his voice that said that this wasn't a party trick, that he was fully prepared to kill any man who tried to see his hand without paying the price.

Richardson pulled his hand back quickly.

"All right, Doc," he said quickly. "Whatever you say. No offense meant."

"None taken," replied Holliday, pulling his knife out of the table with an audible grunt.

"Maybe I'll see you at Kate's one of these days," said Richardson, getting to his feet.

"Better be soon," said Holliday. "I'll be moving into the sanitarium any day now." He grimaced. "And once I move in, I'd give mighty long odds on my ever moving back out."

"Soon, then," promised Richardson and headed out into the street.

"So he's too broke to call, but he's not too broke to rent one of Kate's metal chippies for the night," announced Holliday with an amused smile. "I'll offer three-to-one that he stops to make a few bets at the Silver Bullet along the way."

There was general laughter, and Vermillion returned to the table, carrying two beers and placing one of them in front of Holliday, who gingerly touched the glass.

"Hot," he remarked.

"I don't recall Tombstone ever being any hotter," agreed Vermillion.

"Not only that, but the air there was thick enough to breathe," added Holliday. "Up here in the mountains, even the birds have to walk."

"Maybe you should have stayed in Tombstone," said a man at the bar.

Holliday shook his head. "I should have stayed in Georgia."

"Why the hell didn't you?"

Holliday turned to see who was speaking to him, and his gaze fell on two young men in nondescript clothing, neither cowboys' nor miners' outfits.

"Do I know you?" asked Holliday.

"Indirectly," said the younger of the two men. "You knew some friends of mine."

"Oh?" said Holliday, refusing to ask who the friends were, since the young man seemed so eager that he *should* ask.

"That's right," said the other man. "At least we'd like to think you knew them. We'd hate to think you gun strangers down in cold blood."

Sounds pretty damned tempting, thought Holliday. Aloud he said, "I take it that whoever we're talking about were friends of yours?"

"Frank and Tom McLaury. You killed them at the O.K. Corral."

"May I suggest that you have very poor taste in friends?" said Holliday.

"*We* liked them well enough," said the younger man.

Holliday shrugged. "*You* were welcome to."

"I don't like your attitude, Holliday," said the younger man.

"A lot of people share your opinion of it," agreed Holliday with a pleasant smile. Suddenly the smile vanished. "And it's *Doc* Holliday to you."

The younger man tensed, and his fingers poised over the handle of his pistol.

"Don't do that, son," said Holliday, still not raising his voice.

"Or you'll make me regret it forever?" came the sarcastic reply.

"Try it, and your forever ends in about half a second."

The young man's friend grabbed him by the arm and tried to lead him away.

"Come on, Billy!" he urged. "Look at him, nothing but a skinny old lunger. He's not even worth a bullet."

"Listen to your friend," said Holliday. "He makes sense."

The young man pulled back for a moment, then uttered an obscenity and pointed his finger at Holliday. "I'll see you again!" he promised.

Holliday pointed back, and pretended that his finger was a gun and he was firing it. Most of the gamblers laughed, and finally the two men left the saloon.

"You know who they were, don't you?" asked Vermillion.

"Sure," answered Holliday. "But I wasn't going to give them the pleasure of saying I knew. The kid's Billy Allen, and the bigger kid is Johnny Taylor—and I'll lay fifty-to-one that neither of 'em ever saw either McLaury brother or got within two hundred miles of Tombstone."

"Then what was that all about?" asked one of the poker players.

"Just a couple of kids looking to make a reputation," said Holliday.

"Happens a lot," added Vermillion. Suddenly he grinned. "Never the same kid twice, though. Doc keeps his fair share of undertakers in business."

There was general laughter, and then Holliday announced that he was there to play poker, cards were dealt, and a moment later bets were made.

The game continued for another hour. Then Holliday was seized by another coughing fit, and it left him weak enough that he relinquished his seat and walked slowly to the bar, accompanied by Vermillion.

"I'd go outside for a bracing breath of cold, clear air," he muttered, "but . . ."

"I know," agreed Vermillion.

"Sometimes I wonder why the hell I ever left Arizona," said Holliday.

Vermillion grinned. "It just might have had something to do with those arrest warrants that were issued against you and Wyatt."

"They were sworn out by Wyatt's political enemies," said Holliday. Then he grinned. "And all the men I beat at poker."

"Then why *don't* you go back?"

"You know why," replied Holliday. "This is where I've chosen to die of this damned consumption. They've got the best facility west of the Mississippi, and I didn't live in this airless town for two years so I could go back down the mountain now that it's time to die."

"*Is* it time?" asked Vermillion.

"It's getting close. I'm coughing up more blood than usual, and even the whiskey doesn't kill the pain. And when you drink as much of that poison as *I* do . . ." He let the sentence trail off.

"I'm sorry, Doc. I thought you had a few more years."

"I thought so too," said Holliday. "Oh, well, I've only got a couple of regrets."

"That you didn't marry Kate?"

Holliday chuckled. "Hardly. She's made my life a living hell for more than ten years. Think of what she could do if I married her."

"She broke you out of jail, though," noted Vermillion.

"Couldn't nag and badger me in jail," said Holliday. "No, my greatest regret is that Wyatt and I aren't friends any longer."

"I know you're not, but I don't know why."

A self-deprecating smile crossed Holliday's face. "Blame it on my aristocratic upbringing. I said a few things about Josie I shouldn't have said."

"His wife?"

"His *Jewish* wife," answered Holliday, emphasizing the subject he should have avoided. "I loved her like a sister. I was just drunk, and drunks say mean, stupid things that can't be taken back."

"And your other regret?" asked Vermillion quickly, trying to change the subject.

"That it's going to be the consumption that takes me, slowly and inch by inch, instead of a bullet."

"I could backshoot you right now if you'd like," said Vermillion with a smile.

"You're all heart, Jack."

"That's not what Kate's chippies say," laughed Vermillion.

"And they'll keep saying it as long as you keep paying them," said Holliday. He straightened up. "Well, I can lean on the bar all night, or I can go home and cough myself to sleep. See you tomorrow, Jack."

"I'll be here," said Vermillion.

Holliday walked out into the sweltering heat of the night. His instinct said that he should be able to take a deep breath of cool mountain air, but his brain told him that there simply wasn't any cool air to be had within a hundred miles, even at this altitude.

He stood in front of the Monarch for a few moments, hoping for an errant breeze that never came, then turned and headed off toward Second Street, where he shared living quarters with Kate Elder at the back of her brothel. A small prairie dog suddenly blocked his path, which was more than passing strange since there were no prairie dogs at this altitude or in these mountains. Rather than walk around it or trying to scare it away, Holliday stopped.

"You know they lie in wait for you?" said the prairie dog in a familiar voice.

"I figured it was a strong possibility," answered Holliday.

"You are not afraid," observed the prairie dog.

"Why should I be? I go up against kids trying to make a reputation from time to time. But I'm the first shootist they've ever faced."

"Why should you think so?"

"They're still alive," said Holliday with a grim smile.

"Do not be careless," said the prairie dog. "We have things to discuss—important things."

"Now?"

"Soon," said the prairie dog, and vanished.

Holliday had gotten about halfway to Kate's brothel when Billy Allen stepped out into the street about twenty feet away from him.

"Been waiting for you, Doc," he said. "It's gonna be a pleasure to kill you."

"Be more of a pleasure if both of you faced me like men," said Holliday with no show of alarm or concern. "You can come out of hiding, Johnny. I can see you over there in the shadows."

Johnny Taylor walked out into the street and stood about fifty feet away from Billy Allen. "How are you going to handle this, Doc?" he asked with a smile. "Which one are you going to try to shoot while we're both drawing on you?"

"You think this is a contest?" said Holliday, pulling out his pistol, instantly putting a bullet between a startled Billy Allen's eyes, and turning to aim at Taylor. "You think I'm going to wait for a referee to ring the bell? You came here to kill me, son. I'm going to let you in on a little secret. The graveyards are full of kids like you who thought they could kill men like me."

Johnny Taylor went for his gun, but it was too late. Holliday fired another shot before his gun had cleared his holster, and he was dead before he hit the ground.

"Damn!" muttered Holliday, holstering his gun and pulling out his handkerchief as he felt another coughing seizure coming on. *Isn't one of you ever going to be good enough to put me out of my misery?*

"Don't turn around, Doc," said a deep voice from behind him.

"Hands in the air. Reach for your gun and you'll still have one hand left to vote for me come reelection time."

Holliday tensed.

"Don't even think of it, Doc. I'm not one of those kids you just killed."

Holliday raised his hands and turned to face his newest antagonist, a tall man with a gun in each hand.

"Sheriff Milt Andrews," he introduced himself. "And you, sir, are under arrest for murder."

"If you're here this quick, you saw what happened," said Holliday. "Those two were waiting for me."

"No question about it."

"They were here to kill me, not talk to me," continued Holliday.

"Anything's possible," agreed Andrews. "But neither of them pulled a gun, and we got enough people coming out now because of the sound of the gunshots that I won't be the only one to testify that they both died with their guns in their holsters."

"You *saw* it!" said Holliday angrily. "You *know* it was self-defense."

"I saw it," echoed Andrews. "And if I wasn't Billy Allen's uncle, I might even agree with you. Now let's go on over to the jail." Holliday coughed again. Andrews waited until he was done and then shot him a cold, humorless smile. "I'll have Kate Elder send over a supply of your handkerchiefs, since I don't figure you're getting out anytime soon."

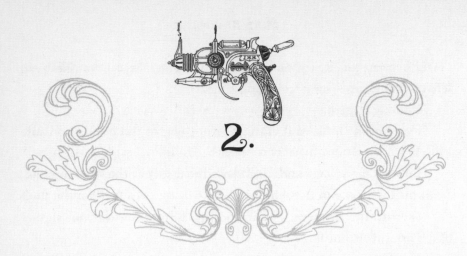

2.

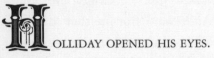OLLIDAY OPENED HIS EYES.

He was lying on his cot, it was still dark out, and the deputy who'd drawn the graveyard shift was two rooms away, snoring peacefully. He swung his feet to the stone floor, massaged the back of his neck with his long delicate fingers, and blinked his eyes a few times. He started to reach inside his coat for his flask, then remembered that it had been taken from him, along with his gun, when he'd been arrested.

He pulled his watch out of a vest pocket by its gold chain and opened it. It was four thirty in the morning, and as far as he knew the whole damned town was asleep. So why the hell was he awake?

He felt very uneasy, finally got his eyes to focus, and studied his surroundings—and then he saw it, perched between the iron bars on the ledge of his window.

"Don't you get tired of pretending to be birds and animals?" he said.

The bird spread its wings and leaped lightly to the floor. By the time it landed, it had morphed into an Indian—a very familiar Indian.

"I hope to hell you didn't come to gloat," said Holliday. "I've got a hangover and my head's splitting open."

"Your head is intact," announced the Indian with certainty.

"Figure of speech," said Holliday. He stared at the Indian. "Well?"

"We have serious matters to discuss, Holliday," said the Indian.

"Lower your voice," said Holliday. "If the guy at the desk hears us, he's going to come over to see who I'm talking to, and when he finds out it's Geronimo himself, he'll blow you to Kingdom Come."

Geronimo shook his head. "He will not awaken."

"You killed him?"

"No. But he will sleep until we are through with our business."

"I thought we were through with our business a year and a half ago," said Holliday.

"No," said Geronimo. "That was *your* business; this is *mine*. Do you remember that I told you there was one White Eyes among your race that I could treat with?"

"Yes."

"He has now crossed the great river, which you call the Mississippi."

"And now the medicine men will end their spell or curse or whatever the hell it is and let the United States expand to the Pacific?" said Holliday.

"It will not be that easy," said Geronimo.

"Somehow it never is," said Holliday with a sigh. "Damn! I wish I had my flask." He stared at Geronimo. "I don't suppose the greatest of all the Apache medicine men would care to magic it to me?"

Geronimo shook head. "You will have access to such things soon enough."

"You're breaking me out of here?" asked Holliday eagerly.

"I will break nothing."

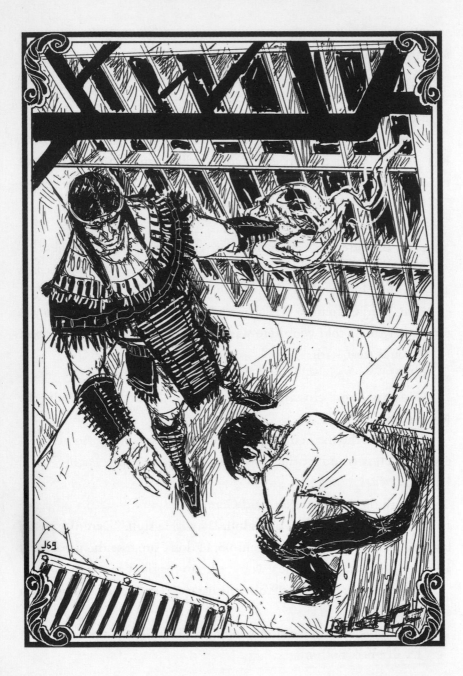

"You know what I mean," said Holliday. "Don't play word games with a man who's got a hangover."

The Indian stared at him expressionlessly for a moment, then walked over and sat down at the end of the cot. "Holliday, I am willing to make my peace with the White Eyes."

"Good," said Holliday, certain that nothing was quite that easy.

"There is one man, a man of courage and character, that I will treat with, and no one else."

"So you said."

"He will not come because I ask him," continued Geronimo.

"Do I know him?" asked Holliday.

Geronimo shook his head. "No. I doubt that you have ever even heard his name mentioned."

Holliday frowned, trying to follow the Indian's line of reasoning. "Then why should he come for me any more than he'd come for you?"

"He will not."

"Then—"

"But he will come because your friend asks him, and it is not in his nature to refuse a challenge."

"My friend?" repeated Holliday, frowning.

"The man Masterson."

"Bat Masterson?" said Holliday, and Geronimo nodded his head. "We're not exactly friends, him and me. We just find ourselves on the same side most of the time, thanks to Wyatt Earp. He and Wyatt are lawmen, or at least they were. And Wyatt and I are friends." *Or at least we were*, he added silently.

"Nonetheless, it is he who knows and has befriended the man I seek, and he who will convince that man to come to my lodge."

"Bat's not out here any longer," said Holliday. "He gave up being a lawman to become a sportswriter—a newspaperman. He's up in New

York, covering horse races and boxing matches and this new baseball game."

"That is where he met the man I must speak to," said Geronimo with absolute certainty.

Holliday was going to ask how he knew that, and then realized the silliness of doubting a warrior who could change into an animal or back into a man on a half second's notice. Instead he said: "Who is this miracle man? Grant and Sherman are dead, and George Custer turned out to be a fool."

"He is a very young man, but he is already the most accomplished of the White Eyes."

"If he's *that* accomplished, what if he's too busy to come?" asked Holliday.

"He will come because his curiosity will overwhelm his reluctance. He will want to see all the wonders that Edison and Buntline are famous for. Further, he has forsaken the crowded cities of the White Eyes to live on this side of the river, and he will realize instantly that to refuse my offer is to keep his country forever confined to the other side of the river."

"If he's all that special, maybe I've heard of him after all," said Holliday. "What's his name?"

"Roosevelt."

"Is that a first or a last name?"

"It is his name."

"Thanks," said Holliday sardonically. "I've never heard of any Roosevelt. How many men has he killed?"

"None."

"What is he, some kind of preacher or religious leader?"

"No," said Geronimo.

"A scientist like Tom Edison?"

"No."

"And he's the only one you'll treat with?"

"That is correct."

"Must be a hell of a man," said Holliday. "What's he done?"

"Masterson will tell you," answered Geronimo.

"Why not you?"

"I know his aura, not his accomplishments."

"His aura?"

Geronimo nodded. "All men have them. Yours is black, for the death you bring and the death that awaits you."

"And his?"

Geronimo merely stared at him.

"Okay, okay, it must be pretty damned bright if you can spot it from two thousand miles away."

"He must come to my lodge."

"You mean the one near Tombstone, down in the Arizona Territory?" asked Holliday.

"Yes. And he must come quickly."

"Well, now, we have a little problem in that regard," said Holliday. Geronimo looked at him quizzically. "In case it has escaped your attention, I am sitting in a cell in the Leadville Jail. I can't contact him from here."

There was an instant of extreme cold and total darkness, and suddenly Holliday found himself in the Leadville telegraph office.

"You can send a message from here," said Geronimo, appearing beside him.

"We still have a problem."

The Indian stared at him, frowning. "What is it?"

"I don't have any money to pay for sending it. My wallet is back in the jail, along with my gun and my flask."

Geronimo closed his eyes and tensed, and suddenly Holliday felt somehow different. He ran his hands over his hips and torso and found that his wallet was once again in his lapel pocket and his pistol rested comfortably in its holster.

"What about my whiskey?" he asked.

"First the message."

"There's no one to give it to, and I don't know how to work the machine."

Geronimo closed his eyes briefly a second time, and when he opened them, a telegraph operator, still in his nightshirt, looking totally confused and more than a little bit frightened, sat at his desk.

"Don't be afraid, son," said Holliday. "It's all perfectly normal, except for the magic and the jailbreak and the Indian. I want to send a message."

The young man gulped and nodded.

"To Bat Masterson, in care of the *Daily Telegraph*," began Holliday.

"Where is that, sir?" asked the operator.

"New York City," replied Holliday. "Dear Bat: Got a situation here that may result in ending the barrier that exists at the Mississippi."

The operator, his eyes wide, began tapping away. "Really, sir?" he asked.

"It all depends on whether he believes me or not," replied Holliday. "Continuing: It is essential that you bring your friend Roosevelt to Tombstone as quickly as possible. I can't tell you more until you get here, but your safety has been guaranteed by a man whose abilities are not unknown, especially to you." He paused. "Okay, sign it 'Doc Holliday' and send it."

The operator finished the message and put it on the wire.

"Now, how much do I owe you?" asked Holliday, pulling out his wallet, but he found himself speaking to an empty chair.

"He is back in his bed," announced Geronimo. "When he awakes, he will remember nothing."

Holliday nodded his approval.

"Will Masterson come?" continued Geronimo.

Holliday shrugged. "I suppose so. He'll figure out that you've guaranteed his safety, and he of all people knows what you can do. After all, you're the one who turned him into an oversized bat."

"He killed one of my warriors."

"After your warrior attacked him."

"He must come," said Geronimo, ignoring what Holliday had said, "And *soon*."

"Why soon?" asked Holliday. "I mean, as long as you've decided to end the spell and let us expand to the Pacific, what difference does it make whether he gets here in a month or a year?"

"I may be dead before a year has passed," answered Geronimo.

Holliday studied him briefly. "I know I'm a dentist and not a physician, but I'd say you look pretty healthy to me."

"I will not die from disease."

Holliday arched an eyebrow and waited for Geronimo to continue. "The other medicine men, those of the other tribes, do not want to end the spell or treat with the White Eyes. When they know I am planning this, they will create a creature such as has never been seen before, and send it out to kill me and those who stand with me. That is why it must be soon. Even with my powers, I cannot evade the creature or hold it at bay for long."

"Why are you so sure they'll create such a creature at all?" asked Holliday.

Geronimo stared at him for a long moment. "Because *I* would," he said grimly.

3.

MASTERSON STROLLED INTO THE RUNNING STAG tavern on Medora's main street and walked up to the bar, which boasted an impressive set of antlers hanging just above the mirrors.

"What'll it be, sir?"

"Make it a beer."

"Coming right up." The bartender stared at him for a moment. "Ain't I seen you before?"

"I doubt it," replied Masterson. "This is my first trip to Dakota."

"You ain't seen him," said the lone customer, a gray-bearded man sitting at a table. "But you seen his picture." He turned to Masterson. "You're Bat Masterson, ain't you?"

Masterson nodded.

"I heard you gave up being a lawman and went to New York to be a writer," said the man. "What brings you to Medora?"

"I'm looking for a local resident."

"Got to be the Marquis de Mores or young Roosevelt," said the man. "Can't imagine there's anyone else out here that anyone would want to see."

"It's Roosevelt," Masterson confirmed.

"Figgers."

"Because he's American?"

"'Cause he's a lawman too, like you used to be."

Masterson frowned. "A lawman? I hadn't heard."

"The best," said the man. "Makes your pal Wyatt Earp look like a beginner."

"Tell me about it."

"I would," said the bearded man. "But my throat's gone dry, and I probably can't get all the words out."

Masterson smiled and turned to the bartender. "A pitcher of beer for the table," he said, walking over and sitting down.

"Well, that's damned generous of you, Mr. Masterson."

"Bat," said Masterson.

"Bat," repeated the man. "And I'm Jacob Finnegan." He extended a gnarled hand, and Masterson shook it. "Can't say I blame you for hightailing it back to New York. I been reading all about you in those dime novels."

"Most of it never happened," said Masterson as the bartender deposited the pitcher on the table.

"Go ahead," said Finnegan. "Ruin an old man's dreams."

"I'll do my best to," replied Masterson with a smile.

Finnegan laughed. "I *like* you, Bat Masterson! You're good with a gun, you ain't afraid to face a desperado or two, and even though you're a writer I can pretty much understand you. Your pal Roosevelt uses some of the biggest damned words anyone ever heard."

"He'll lose that habit fast enough," said Masterson. "He needed it for his last job."

"And what was that?"

"He was the youngest Minority Leader in the history of the New York legislature."

Finnegan took a swallow of his beer. "That don't sound right. He's *still* a young man, I'd say no more than twenty-five or twenty-six."

"That's about right."

Finnegan frowned, and stopped to pet a dog that had wandered in beneath the swinging doors. "Must have taken a terrible whooping at the polls to wind up out here."

Masterson shook his head. "He didn't lose. He quit."

"Hah! They're as corrupt as we always thought, right?"

"Probably," replied Masterson with a smile. "But that had nothing to do with it. His wife and his mother died something like ten hours apart, both in his house, one of disease, one in childbirth. He dearly loved both of them, and didn't want to stay there with all his memories."

"So he brung his memories out to the Badlands?" said Finnegan. "That don't make no sense."

"He's a complex man."

"He's a *determined* one, anyway," said Finnegan. "You heard about the three killers he brung back?"

Masterson shook his head. "No. Tell me about them."

"He just don't do nothing in a small way," began Finnegan. "It wasn't enough that he bought two ranches . . ." His voice trailed off as he searched his pockets, found a small piece of jerky, and tossed it to the dog.

"*Two?*" said Masterson, surprised.

"Your pal thinks *big*. Anyway, he volunteered to be the local deputy. Refused to take any money for it. Wore that damned star everywhere. We figured he just wanted it the way a woman wants a pin or a necklace, but then a trio of killers done their evil deeds and Roosevelt went after them. I don't know where he was when he heard about it, but he didn't have no gun with him, and he decided not to waste time getting one, so he just started riding in the worst blizzard you ever saw. We get bad winters up here, really terrible ones, but we never had nothing like this. 'The Winter of the Blue Snow,' the local paper called it."

"Evocative name," commented Masterson.

"Whatever 'evocative' means," replied Finnegan, reaching down to gently push the dog away. "Go on, pooch. I ain't got no more." The dog ducked around his hand and remained where he was. "Anyway," continued Finnegan, "he eventually caught up with 'em, beat the crap out of them, took away their guns, and marched 'em all the way to Dickenson. Must have been fifty miles through that blizzard. They took turns sleeping, but he didn't dare nod off. Says he read this huge novel by this Russian guy, and when that was done he read some dime novels about you and the Earps and that Holliday guy, and somehow he stayed awake for three days and nights, until he finally delivered his prisoners."

Masterson nodded his head. "Yeah, that sounds like Theodore."

"Okay, you know him," said Finnegan. Masterson looked at him curiously. "He hates to be called Teddy."

"That he does," agreed Masterson. "You got any idea where I can find him?"

"He'll either be at Elkhorn or the Maltese Cross, probably Elkhorn."

"Those are his ranches?"

"Yeah. Though if you wait long enough, he'll show up here. The Marquis de Mores has challenged him to a fight." Finnegan chuckled. "He offered to let Roosevelt choose the weapons." A pause and a grin. "I figure he'll choose words."

"It'd be best for the Marquis if he did," replied Masterson. "Theodore was a boxing champion at Harvard."

"You don't say?" said Finnegan. "Is there anything he *can't* do?"

"Not much," answered Masterson. "Before he was twenty he was already considered one of America's three or four leading ornithologists and taxidermists."

"Orni—?" said Finnegan, frowning and trying to pronounce the word. "Orni—?"

"Ornithologist," repeated Masterson. "Bird expert."

"He sure as hell shoots enough of 'em," remarked Finnegan.

"Can't stuff and mount them while they're still alive," responded Masterson with a smile.

"How'd you two meet?" asked Finnegan.

"He wrote me, asking some questions about a series of books he's writing about the West."

"He's a writer too?"

Masterson nodded. "And a damned good one. Anyway, I wrote back, we started corresponding, and we finally met at one of John L. Sullivan's prizefights." Masterson finished his beer and got to his feet. "And now, if you don't mind, please tell me how to get to Elkhorn and maybe I can make it before dark and not get totally lost."

Finnegan got up, gestured for Masterson to follow him, and walked out onto the raised wooden sidewalk. "Just head in that direction, and you'll be there in two, maybe three hours, depending on how lazy your horse is."

"Thanks," said Masterson.

"And when you see him, tell him Jacob Finnegan would be proud to hold his coat while he beats the shit out of that Frenchman."

"I'll do that," promised Masterson, shaking the old man's hand.

Then he was atop his horse, heading through the hilly, thickly forested country in the direction Finnegan had indicated. At first he was on the lookout for wolves or perhaps even a bear. Then it occurred to him that Roosevelt had been in the Medora area long enough to make it safe for travelers, and he stopped staring apprehensively at every bush and shadow.

He rode for ninety minutes, dismounted when he came to a stream and filled his canteen while his horse drank, then continued the rest of the way. He saw an expansive wooden house in the distance, and as he approached it he heard a sound that he couldn't identify. It occurred every few seconds, and finally he saw a well-built young man wearing what were clearly stylish, store-bought buckskins splitting logs with an axe.

"Greetings, Theodore!" he cried as he drew closer.

Roosevelt lay his axe down and squinted through his glasses until he finally identified his visitor.

"Bat Masterson!" he said. "What in the world are you doing out here in the Badlands?"

"Looking for you," said Masterson, climbing down off his horse and leading it the last few yards.

"It's good to see you!" said Roosevelt. "Let me just finish this last log, and we'll go inside and visit."

"Why are you even splitting logs?" asked Masterson. "Winter's over."

"Got to keep fit," answered Roosevelt as he brought the axe down on the log. "I run a few miles every morning, but it rained last night and it was a little too muddy today, so I'm doing this instead."

"Don't overdo it," said Masterson. "You're already the fittest man I know."

"The Marquis de Mores is pretty fit himself," said Roosevelt.

"Yeah, I heard about that."

"You couldn't have come all the way out from Manhattan just to watch us fight."

"No, I never even heard of the Marquis until a few hours ago. Which reminds me: Jacob Finnegan wants to be your second."

Roosevelt offered a toothy smile. "Good old Jacob! In his youth he could probably have beaten both of us."

"I doubt it," said Masterson.

"Well, if you're not here for the fight, and indeed we haven't set a date for it, what *has* brought you all this way?"

"Therein lies a story," said Masterson.

"So tell me," said Roosevelt.

"You know that the Indian medicine men have let some miners and settlers and farmers past the Mississippi, but that the United States, as a nation, has been stopped there."

"Of course I know," said Roosevelt. "Hell, every schoolboy knows it." He paused. "And I also know it can't last forever. It's our destiny to expand from one coast to the other."

Masterson stared at him. "How would you like to be the man who brings it about?"

Roosevelt returned his stare. "You're serious?"

"I'm here."

Roosevelt let his axe fall to the ground. "Come on inside and tell me about it," he said, throwing an arm around Masterson's shoulder and leading him into the sturdy wooden house, the living room of which was lined with books on all subjects, and featured a large writing desk and a comfortable chair.

"I'm here because Doc Holliday knows I know you," began Masterson.

"Doc Holliday? The shootist?" Roosevelt began reeling off a list of Holliday's gunfights and victims.

"That's the one," said Masterson. "But he and I are just middle-men. The person who is really sending for you is Geronimo."

Roosevelt's face reflected his excitement. "Geronimo? The greatest of the Apache medicine men. True name: Goyathlay. Leader of the Apaches since Victorio was killed four years ago." He spent another minute recounting Geronimo's achievements.

"Yes," said Masterson when Roosevelt paused for breath. "*That* Geronimo."

"This is *exciting*, Bat!" exclaimed Roosevelt. "Will your friend Wyatt Earp be involved in whatever this is?"

Masterson shook his head. "I doubt it."

"All right. Why does Geronimo want to see me?"

"You're not going to believe me when I tell you."

"That's always possible," answered Roosevelt. "But we won't know for sure until you do tell me."

"He's ready to lift the spell," said Masterson. "And of all the white and black men in America, you're the only one he'll deal with."

"But I've never met him!"

"*He* knows *you*."

Roosevelt frowned in puzzlement. "How?"

"A dozen men can stop the entire nation from expanding across the Mississippi, and you wonder how one of them can know anything about you?"

"Forgive me," said Roosevelt with an embarrassed smile. "I'm so excited by your news that I hadn't thought it through."

"Then you'll come?"

"To double the nation's territory? Of course!" There was a brief pause. "Hell, I'd come just to meet Doc Holliday and Geronimo. I mean, Billy the Kid, Wild Bill Hickok, Jesse James, and at least one of the Younger Brothers are dead, the Earps have gone to California and Alaska, and John Wesley Hardin has been rotting in a Texas prison for years. Of all the bigger-than-life figures of the West, Holliday and Geronimo are just about all that's left. Of course I'm coming!"

"You'll get to meet Tom Edison, too. I'm not certain what he's doing out there, but he seems to have become a friend of Holliday's."

"Thomas *Alva* Edison?" said Roosevelt, his eyes widening with excitement. "The inventor?"

Masterson nodded his head. "He's made a lot of changes to Tombstone. Whole town was lit up by electric lights at night when I was there three years ago."

"Holliday, Geronimo, *and* Edison?" said Roosevelt excitedly. "What are we waiting for?"

"You sound like a hero-worshipping kid at the ballpark," commented Masterson.

"There are very few exceptional men in this world, Bat," replied Roosevelt seriously. "I'm willing to ride halfway across the continent to meet three of them." Suddenly he began pacing back and forth. "I'll take Manitou, of course, and—"

"Manitou?" repeated Masterson curiously.

"My horse. Meanest bronco you ever saw—or he was when I first encountered him." Another grin. "He must have thrown me twenty times before we finally reached an understanding." He continued pacing. "I'll need a few blank notebooks and some pencils, and my telescope, and—" He stopped and suddenly turned to Masterson. "What kind of game do you have out there?"

"In Tombstone?" said Masterson. "An occasional snake or jackrabbit. And once in a while a hawk."

Roosevelt nodded, more to himself than to Masterson. "The Winchester will do. And I'll have to prepare a pack for a second horse."

"Just to carry a Winchester?" asked Masterson, puzzled.

"No, of course not," answered Roosevelt. "But I can't be without my books. Let me see now. For this trip I think Tolstoy, and Jane Austen, and . . ." He spent the next five minutes deciding on the books he wanted, then rummaging through the six rooms of the house until he'd found them all.

In another hour he had packed his weapons, books, clothes, everything he thought he might want or need, even a spare pair of spectacles.

"Okay, Bat, help me load Manitou and the pack horse and we can be on our way."

"It's going to be dark in half an hour," noted Masterson. "We can start tomorrow."

"Now," said Roosevelt firmly.

Masterson shrugged. "Okay, mount up."

As they were leaving Elkhorn, Masterson remarked that without encountering any serious obstacles, he thought they could reach Tombstone in ten days.

"Nonsense," said Roosevelt, clicking to Manitou. "We'll do it in seven."

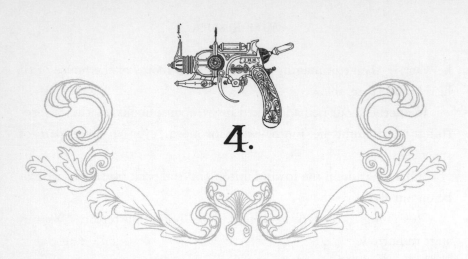

4.

THE BUNT LINE's self-propelled heavily armored brass stagecoach came to a stop on Third Street in early evening, and Holliday climbed down, then waited for the driver to unsecure his small suitcase and pass it down to him.

He turned and walked half a block to the Oriental Saloon, which had been his home away from home when he'd been living in Tombstone with Kate Elder. He was surprised to see how dilapidated it had become in just three years.

It was still open for business, though, and he entered, walked over to a table, laid his bag on it, and sat down.

"Well, I'll be damned!" said the bartender. "Look who's back!"

Suddenly all eyes turned to Holliday, who touched the brim of his hat with a forefinger. "Bring a bottle and a glass," he said.

"What are you doing back in town, Doc?" asked the bartender as he grabbed a bottle of whiskey, found a mildly clean glass, and approached the table. "The Earps are long gone, and the silver mines are pretty much played out. If it wasn't for your pal Edison, this place'd be a ghost town."

"I'm just passing through," replied Holliday noncommittally.

"You're here to kill Johnny Behan!" said the bartender suddenly.

"You mean someone hasn't done it already?" said Holliday. "What's the matter with you people?"

"He's still around," was the answer. "But we threw him out of office a year after you left town. Caught him stealing five thousand dollars of the county's money."

"Yeah, that's Behan, all right," said Holliday.

"When are you going after him?" persisted the bartender. "Tonight? Tomorrow?"

"I'm really and truly not here for him," said Holliday.

"Good!" said a man sitting a couple of tables away. "He owes me money. I'd like him to live long enough to pay me."

Holliday gave him a look that said, *You still haven't figured out who you're dealing with, have you?* He poured a drink, downed it in a single swallow, and made a face. "That's pretty awful stuff."

"It's the best we got, Doc," said the bartender.

"Somehow I'm not surprised," said Holliday, pouring another glass. He remained seated at the table until he'd killed half the bottle. Then he got to his feet, grabbed his suitcase in one hand and his bottle in the other, and walked out into the twilight.

He turned on Fremont Street, passed a pair of rooming houses, and headed toward the Grand Hotel. When he arrived he took a room, left his bottle on a table and his carpetbag on the floor, and then walked back out the front door. It had grown a little darker, and now the streets were illuminated by Edison's electric streetlamps.

He considered lighting a cigar, decided he didn't need to bring on a coughing fit, and instead began walking toward Edison's and Buntline's side-by-side buildings. He tried to spot all the protective devices as he approached Edison's front door, saw four and was sure he'd missed at least two or three others, and was about to knock when the door suddenly swung open.

"Come on in, Doc," said Edison's voice, and he entered as the door silently closed behind him. He knew his way around the house, and walked directly to Edison's office, which was at least as much laboratory and workshop as office.

Edison was seated at his stained and battered desk, scribbling in a notebook. There were notes tacked to every available surface, vials of chemicals, batteries in various stages of design and completion, and a huge electric light. When he saw Holliday, he closed the book and put it in a drawer, then got to his feet, walked around the desk, and shook Holliday's hand.

"I got your wire," he said. "Is Mr. Roosevelt with you?"

Holliday shook his head. "He's coming with Bat. Truth to tell, I don't know what the hell he looks like."

"Neither do I," admitted Edison, "but I know that he's the most accomplished young man I've ever heard of." A pause. "Can I get you a drink."

"I don't recall ever saying no to one," replied Holliday.

Edison walked to a cabinet and pulled out a bottle and two glasses. "I'll be interested to try this out," he said, handing a glass to Holliday and filling both. "Ned picked it up the last time he took the Bunt Line to St. Louis."

Holliday took a sip. "It's better than the horse piss they're serving at the Oriental, I'll give it that."

Edison smiled. "I'll tell him you said so."

"He's not around?"

"Oh, he's in town," answered Edison. "He's repairing one of the metal harlots at what used to be Kate's establishment."

"I'm surprised he's not fixing them all the time, given the use they get."

"They're not in as much demand as they were when we created them three years ago and the population was three or four times larger," said Edison. "On the other hand, they're machines, and they're three years old, and it's natural that some of them break down."

Holliday brought his bloody handkerchief to his mouth and coughed. "I know all about things breaking down," he said sardonically.

"No better?"

Holliday shook his head. "I thought I was just a month or two away from entering the sanitarium when Geronimo broke me out of jail."

"Jail?" repeated Edison, surprised.

"It's a long story," said Holliday, "but the usual one. The only good thing about it is that sometimes stupidity is genetically self-limiting. Anyway, he got me out, and that's why I'm here. In law offices and other criminal enterprises, they call it a *quid pro quo*."

"And he *really* wants to lift the spell that's kept the country confined to the other side of the Mississippi?" asked Edison.

"I don't know if he *wants* to," said Holliday. "But he's a realist. The United States gets bigger and stronger every day. I know the Indians' magic is pretty powerful, but how long can they hold us east of the river? It had to be a lot easier back in Washington's time, or even Andy Jackson's . . . but how many millions do we total today?" He took another sip of his drink. "We've got numbers, we have firepower"—he paused and smiled at Edison—"and we have *you*."

"Me?" said Edison, surprised.

"Don't be modest. You're our greatest genius. That's why they sent you out here—to find the weak spots in the medicine men's magic."

"And I haven't accomplished a thing," said Edison.

"You haven't accomplished what you wanted to accomplish," agreed Holliday. "But you've weakened them. You helped cause a rift between the two most powerful medicine men, Geronimo and Hook

Nose, and now Hook Nose is dead. I think that's another reason Geronimo's ready to deal. The other Indians blame *him* for Hook Nose's death."

"He *did* kill him," noted Edison. "We were there."

"Did they ever have a falling-out before you were sent out West?"

"How would I know?"

"Take a guess," said Holliday.

"No," admitted Edison. "Not an important one."

"That's why you've got an artificial arm. They knew early on that you were the catalyst. That's why they got Curly Bill Brocius to take that shot at you. You were just damned lucky he was liquored up and couldn't see straight."

"Let's not talk about it. It makes it very difficult not to hold a grudge against Geronimo."

"He's an honorable man," said Holliday. "And there ain't too many of them in *any* race."

"So when is young Mr. Roosevelt due here?" asked Edison, changing the subject.

Holliday shrugged. "Four, maybe five days." He smiled. "If it was me, and I had to ride horseback, it'd be a lot closer to a month."

"So what do we do when he gets here?" continued Edison. "Take him to Geronimo's camp? I mean, we can't have Geronimo walking or riding into Tombstone."

"*We* don't do anything," answered Holliday. "Geronimo never mentioned you. I imagine Roosevelt wants to meet the great Tom Edison. The only person Geronimo wants to meet is Roosevelt. I don't even know if he'll let Bat come along." A grim smile. "I don't know if Bat'll want to, either. You know what happened to him last time he rode out with me to Geronimo's camp."

"So I just sit by and do nothing?" asked Edison. "If that's the case, and the spell's going to be lifted, I suppose Ned and I might as well close up shop and go back East."

Holliday shook his head. "Oh, I think your services are going to be needed—and soon."

"But if he's lifting the spell . . ." said Edison, frowning.

"He's making peace with Roosevelt," said Holliday. "But while he speaks for the Apaches, he's not the king of all the Indians, and Roosevelt's not the president of the United States. There are lots of Indians who *don't* want to lift the spell, and that includes every medicine man and shaman on this side of the Mississippi except Geronimo."

"So you're saying that there may actually be a war coming . . ."

"Right," said Holliday. "With Geronimo and Roosevelt on one side, and every other Indian on the other."

"Where do you fit in, Doc?" asked Edison.

"Me? I'm just a dying man who's putting two interested parties together."

"Rubbish. For one thing, you're the best shootist alive."

"Well, alive and free," amended Holliday. "Don't forget John Wesley Hardin."

"Is he still incarcerated in some Texas jail?" asked Edison.

"Last I heard."

"Anyway, you're not the type to sit on the sidelines."

"I may be so sick I'll have to lie down on the sidelines," replied Holliday.

"I hope you're joking."

"I hope so too," said Holliday. "But if I were a betting man . . ."

"Enough," said Edison. "For a dying man, you're as indestructible as any man I've ever met."

"Good," said Holliday. "Then I'll be around to see what you bring to the battle."

"Me? But Geronimo doesn't even want to see me."

"He'll want to see what you can produce."

"What makes you think I'll produce anything?" asked Edison irritably.

"Because if we're to have a country that extends to the Pacific, I have a feeling Geronimo and Roosevelt are going to need all the help they can get." Holliday smiled at Edison. "And that means you."

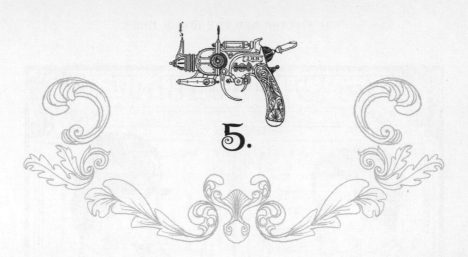

5.

HOLLIDAY WAS SITTING AT A TABLE in the Oriental when Masterson entered the saloon, followed by his companion.

"Damn, but you made good time!" said Holliday, surprised to see them. He got to his feet. "You must be Theodore Roosevelt."

Roosevelt extended a hand. "I've been anxious to meet you," he said. "I've heard and read a lot about you."

"Most of it lies, I'm sure," said Holliday, taking his hand. "I've heard a bit about you myself."

"From Democrats?" said Roosevelt with a grin. "*All* of it lies."

Roosevelt released Holliday's hand, and Holliday immediately began trying to shake some life back into it. "That's quite a grip you've got there," he said. "Shake my hand three or four more times and I'll have to learn to shoot left-handed."

Roosevelt laughed heartily. "I like you already!" he said. "But of course I knew I would."

"You have an affinity for dentists?" said Holliday sardonically.

"Not that I'm aware of. I hope you have one for politicians. Well, former politicians."

"The only good politician is a former one," said Holliday. "Or a dead one."

"I wish I could offer more than a token disagreement," said Roosevelt. He looked around the interior of the Oriental, then pulled a chair over and sat down, and Holliday and Masterson followed suit.

"Any problems along the way?" asked Holliday, offering his bottle to Roosevelt, who shook his head, and to Masterson, who took a swallow.

"Nothing to speak of," replied Masterson. "A couple of high-waymen tried to hold us up on our way through the New Mexico Territory." Suddenly he grinned. "The world is changing."

"What happened?"

"Young Mr. Roosevelt got the drop on them with his rifle—they must have figured anyone wearing spectacles is blind, because they weren't paying him any attention—so he disarmed them, offered to go a few rounds of fisticuffs with them, beat the crap out of them, then patched them up and treated them to dinner." Masterson chuckled at the memory. "Now I know how he wins the voters over. Those two volunteered to ride shotgun for us as we passed through Southern Cheyenne country, and swore their eternal friendship when we parted." He shook is head in wonderment. "It's not like riding with Wyatt, let me tell you."

Holliday laughed. He expected Roosevelt to look uncomfortable, but the Easterner simply looked pleased with the result of the story.

"Too bad Johnny Behan's not sheriff anymore. I'd love to see you run against him."

"I'm through running for office, for a little while yet," answered Roosevelt. "I'm here to see Goyathlay."

"You know his real name?" asked Holliday, surprised.

"Once I knew I was coming out here, I made sure I packed a couple of books about the Apaches. I don't know how good his English is, so I thought I'd better learn to speak his language."

"Must be recent books," remarked Holliday. "He's only been the boss since Victorio died."

"But he's been one of the leaders for twenty years now," said Roosevelt. "An admirable man, from all I've learned."

"He's responsible for the death of thousands of white men," said Masterson.

"He killed them while protecting his people," responded Roosevelt. He turned to Holliday. "You've spent time with him. What's your opinion?"

"He's an honorable man," said Holliday. "On those occasions that he's a man at all."

"I don't understand."

Holliday smiled. "You will." He paused. "You really speak Apache?"

"I'm not sure of the pronunciations," answered Roosevelt, "but I'm pretty sure I can understand it if it's spoken to me."

"Geronimo will like that," said Holliday. "He's not some ignorant savage, and he resents being treated like one."

"When do we meet him?" asked Roosevelt.

"Tomorrow we'll ride down to his lodge," answered Holliday. "I'm sure he knows you're here."

"I'll stay here," said Masterson.

Roosevelt turned to him. "Why?" he asked curiously.

"Bat had an unpleasant experience the last time he paid a visit to Geronimo," said Holliday with an amused smile.

"Stop grinning!" snapped Masterson. "There was nothing funny about it!"

"It sure as hell wasn't funny while it was happening," agreed Holliday.

"I have no idea what you're talking about," complained Roosevelt.

"Bat killed one of his warriors, and Geronimo, who speaks enough English to know what a bat is, turned him into a huge one every night from sunset to sunrise." Suddenly Holliday smiled again. "So if you've got a nickname like Bull or Hawkeye, I'd suggest you keep it to yourself."

"It wasn't funny," growled Masterson. "It was a living hell."

"Clearly it ended," said Roosevelt. "You kept me awake half of each night with your snoring."

"I did a service for Geronimo and he lifted the curse," said Holliday.

"Ah!" said Roosevelt with a smile. "A *quid pro quo*."

"Damn!" said Holliday happily. "Latin! I *knew* I was going to like you. Have a drink!"

"No offense, but I want to keep a clear head until this business is over. The results are too important."

"Fair enough," said Holliday. "You got a room yet?"

"Yes, we took out a pair of rooms at the Grand Hotel," said Roosevelt.

"Yeah, we took a quick tour of the town—well, what's left of it—before we came over here," added Masterson. "I see you've got a baseball diamond outside town."

"I thought it was just a flash in the pan when it came to Denver," said Holliday, "but then it spread to Leadville, and damned near every town between there and here." He shook his head. "Doesn't make any sense, a bunch of people paying to watch other people trying to hit a ball with a stick."

"I prefer prizefighting myself," said Roosevelt.

"Is this John L. Sullivan all he's cracked up to be?" asked Holliday. "We've heard about him all the way out here."

"He's a drunkard and a braggart, but he's as good as they say," replied Roosevelt. "I wish I was about thirty pounds heavier. I'd like to take him on myself."

"And Bat would write the story," said Holliday.

"And the obituary," added Masterson. "I've *seen* the great John L. Best athlete around, now that Hindoo's retired."

"Hindoo?" asked Holliday.

"Best racehorse in American history," said Masterson. "He'd run down the backstretch at Belmont Park and the trees would sway."

"Really?"

Masterson smiled. "Well, they would if there were any trees there."

"You really don't miss being a lawman at all, do you?" asked Holliday.

"It cost me a brother, got me shot at pretty regularly for seven years, and kept me broke all the time," answered Masterson. "What do you think?"

"Well, I'm glad you're finally happy."

"I hope I still am after tomorrow," said Masterson without smiling.

"Of course you will be," said Roosevelt. "He sent for us."

"He sent for *you*," replied Masterson. "He and I are not each other's favorite people."

"You're staying in town," Roosevelt reminded him.

"Tell him, Doc," said Masterson. "He could appear right next to you right now if he wanted to."

"From what I understand, once he and Theodore make their deal, whatever it is, we're all in a lot more danger from every Indian who *isn't* an Apache," said Holliday.

"I take very little comfort in that," said Masterson.

"Once we leave for Geronimo's lodge, go over to Tom Edison's place," suggested Holliday. "You'll be safer there than anywhere else."

"I almost forgot!" said Roosevelt so loudly that he startled a couple of men at the next table. "I want to meet the fabulous Thomas Edison before we leave town. Do you think he's available right now?"

"He'll be in his office, which doubles as his lab," affirmed Holliday.

"Then what are we wasting our time here for?" demanded Roosevelt, getting to his feet.

"Just a second," said Holliday. He pulled a pencil out of his pocket, scribbled *Doc* on the bottle, and carried it over to the bar, where he handed it to the bartender.

"I don't suppose Wyatt Earp's in town?" asked Roosevelt as they walked out into the street.

"Not for a couple of years," answered Holliday.

"How far are we from the O.K. Corral?"

"A four- or five-minute walk," said Holliday. "At least, at the speed I walk at."

"Let's stop there on the way to Edison's," said Roosevelt.

"Any particular reason?" asked Holliday.

"You've no idea how famous it is, even in New York. I'd hate to be in Tombstone even for a day and miss the chance to see it."

"Or Edison," said Holliday. "Or probably Buntline, too." He paused. "Is there anything you're not enthused about?"

"Ignorance," answered Roosevelt. "Now, which way is the Corral?"

6.

THEY TRUDGED ACROSS THE FLAT, barren, featureless desert, where even the snakes and scorpions waited until dark to come out.

"Let's stop for a rest," said Holliday, reining his horse in.

"It's got to be a hundred and twenty degrees, Doc," said Roosevelt. "The sooner we get there, the sooner we can find some shade."

"I'm a sick man, Theodore," said Holliday. "Either I climb down for a few minutes now, or I fall off in the next mile."

"All right," said Roosevelt. He pointed at a shaded outcrop a few hundred yards away. "But let's stop *there*, so we can enjoy what little shade there is."

Holliday nodded and steered his horse toward the outcrop, dismounting and immediately sitting down on the ground with his back against a tree. Roosevelt considered hobbling the horses, decided they were too hot to run off, then squatted down, stood up, and repeated the process half a dozen times.

"What the hell's wrong with you?" asked Holliday, frowning.

"Nothing," replied Roosevelt. "But I didn't get my running in this morning, and a man's got to keep fit."

"Just surviving in this heat ought to be enough," said Holliday, pulling out a flask and taking a drink.

Roosevelt shook his head. "A fit mind and a sloppy body are no better than a fit body and a sloppy mind."

Holliday stared at him for a long moment. "I'm surprised you didn't *run* here from the Badlands."

"If we weren't operating on such a tight schedule, I might have run part of it," admitted Roosevelt with a grin. "How long a rest do you think you'll need?"

Holliday shrugged. "I don't know. Until I feel stronger. Why?"

"Well, I thought if it would be more than ten or fifteen minutes, I'd pull a book out of my saddlebag and read a chapter or two."

"Damn!" said Holliday, shaking his head in wonderment. "You are the most remarkable young man I've ever met."

"Surely you're not going to tell me you never read," said Roosevelt. "Bat told me you minored in classical literature."

"I did," agreed Holliday. "But I know better than to take a book along when it's a million degrees and we're on our way to visit Geronimo in his own lodge."

"Are you expecting trouble?" asked Roosevelt curiously. "After all, he *wants* to see me."

"He's seeing you in the one place he feels protected," noted Holliday. "Remember, he told me that the other medicine men aren't ready to lift the spell yet. They don't figure to be too thrilled with this meeting."

"They don't know who I am or what I'm doing here."

"Damn it, Theodore, they're *medicine men*. They can hold an entire nation on one side of the Mississippi when it wants to expand. Believe me, they know what you're here for."

"Tell me about them," said Roosevelt, taking a sip of water from his canteen. "What *can* they do besides keeping most of us—not *all*, I must point out—east of the river?"

"You ever hear of Johnny Ringo?"

"Yes," said Roosevelt. "I think he was killed about four or five years ago in Texas."

"He was," agreed Holliday. "The first time."

Roosevelt frowned. "The *first* time?"

Holliday nodded. "A medicine man named Hook Nose brought him back from the dead, bullet holes and all, and sent him to kill Tom Edison."

"He obviously didn't succeed."

"Tom had an equalizer."

"You?" asked Roosevelt.

Holliday smiled. "He invented the equalizer. *I* fired it."

"I'm glad I hit it off with him and Ned last night," said Roosevelt. "I have a feeling we may need his help."

"That's what he's here for," said Holliday. "The government sent him West to study the medicine men and try to invent something to counter their magic."

"He's turned Tombstone into a more futuristic town than Manhattan," noted Roosevelt. "Has he had any luck with the medicine men?"

"Minimal," answered Holliday. "Little bits here and there, against Hook Nose and others. But he hasn't been able to lift the spell. Hopefully Geronimo will do it for him."

"Geronimo's the most powerful of them?"

"He'd better be, because he's going to have fifty or sixty of them opposing him." Suddenly Holliday smiled. "And you."

"And *us*," Roosevelt corrected him.

"Not me. I'm just an onlooker."

"Sure," said Roosevelt with his characteristic grin. "That's why you contacted me and why you're riding across the desert to Geronimo's lodge."

"Circumstance," said Holliday.

"We'll see," said Roosevelt.

"A month from now I'll be checking into a sanitarium in Colorado, and living out what remains of my life as comfortably as possible," said Holliday.

"I don't think so," said Roosevelt.

"Why the hell not?" demanded Holliday pugnaciously.

"Because exceptional men are few and far between. You happen to be one, John Henry Holliday. You are capable of remarkable feats, some of them distasteful, all of them exceptional—and it's my observation that Fate usually has plans for exceptional men."

Holliday pulled out a fresh handkerchief and coughed into it. It came away bloody. "Fate's played enough tricks on me already," he said, pocketing the handkerchief. "All I want it to do is leave me alone." He paused. "All I ever wanted to be was a dentist and a loving husband. I didn't plan to be a shootist, or spend most of my adult life living with a hard-drinking madam. I could tell five minutes after I met you that you *want* to be something special, that you revel in your exceptionalism." A bitter smile. "Not all of us do, Theodore. You want to be a mayor or a governor? More power to you. I just want to lie in a bed and have a little less trouble breathing."

"I hope you get your wish, Doc, truly I do," said Roosevelt.

"But?" said Holliday. "Sure sounds like there's a 'but' in there somewhere."

"But you and I are riding to meet the most powerful medicine man on the continent. If we don't make a deal, America's stuck on the other side of the Mississippi for God knows how many years and decades, or even centuries. And if we *do* make a deal, you assure me that every other medicine man will be out to kill us." An amused smile crossed his face. "I just don't see how that leads to a bed in a sanitarium. An earlier grave than you anticipate, perhaps—but not one near a sanitarium in the Rockies."

Holliday took another swallow from his flask. "I wish you didn't sound so goddamned sensible," he growled, and Roosevelt chuckled.

"Have we rested long enough?" asked the younger man.

Holliday grimaced and got to his feet. "I'm tireder now than when we sat down. Might as well try to rest on the horse."

They mounted up and began heading south again, Roosevelt identifying every bird, insect, and snake they saw by their scientific names. "When this is all over," he said, "I've love to come back and collect some specimens for the Smithsonian and the American museum."

"They're just birds and flies, and the occasional rattler," replied Holliday in bored tones. "Wouldn't be the most exciting hunt you've ever been on."

"I'm not looking for excitement," said Roosevelt. "I've hunted grizzlies for that, and someday I hope to go to Africa after really *big* game. But many of these species aren't in the museums back East, and the ones that are have been carelessly mounted."

"That's right. Bat said you were a taxidermist too."

"I dabble in it."

Holliday smiled. "No false modesty. He said you were considered one of the country's top ornithologists and taxidermists while you were still in your teens."

"He's being too generous," said Roosevelt.

"Probably," agreed Holliday, and was pleased to see a little tightening of Roosevelt's expression when he agreed with him.

"Have you ever been to the Smithsonian?" asked Roosevelt. "I'm told you didn't grow up all that far from it."

"I grew up in Georgia," replied Holliday, "and we were fighting a war with the people who ran the Smithsonian."

"Not by the time you got to college."

Holliday shrugged. "I was busy learning to be a dentist, and then I was busy coughing on all my patients, so I moved West where the air was dryer." He snorted. "You can see how much it helped."

"It helped get rid of a lot of desperados," remarked Roosevelt.

"A lot of people think *I'm* one."

"I'd heard of you and read about your exploits," said Roosevelt. "You've been arrested your fair share of times, but as far as I can tell, you've never been convicted of anything."

"True enough," agreed Holliday.

They rode for two more hours, with Roosevelt finding fascinating things all over the barren landscape, and then Holliday brought his horse to a stop.

"What is it?" asked Roosevelt.

"We're getting close," replied Holliday. "I don't see them yet, but I can't imagine he hasn't got some warriors watching us."

"He does," said Roosevelt. "I've seen them for the last mile. I thought you'd seen them too."

Holliday peered into the distance. "By that boulder off to the left," he said.

"Right. And a couple in the gully over there."

"Damn! For a man with spectacles, you've got damned good eyesight, Theodore."

"Comes from being a hunter," answered Roosevelt. "You get an instinct for things that don't seem quite right, even before you can spot what's wrong with them." He looked ahead again. "I assume they're just making sure we're not coming with what I think you call a posse."

"Yeah," said Holliday. "When we get a little closer to the lodge, they'll ride out and accompany us. They'll probably take our weapons, too. I'd advise you not to make a fuss about it."

"*Can* the greatest of the medicine men be hurt by a bullet?" asked Roosevelt curiously.

"Probably not," said Holliday. "But any member of his tribe can."

"Ah!" said Roosevelt, nodding his head. "I hadn't even considered that."

"That's because you've never been to his camp before."

"How did Bat kill a warrior if he was unarmed?"

"Man pulled a knife on him," replied Holliday. "I think he was just trying to scare him. Bat took the knife away from him and stabbed him." He looked off to his right. "Six more, and they're not making any effort to hide themselves."

A moment later they were surrounded by Apache warriors, who offered no word of greeting or sign of recognition to Holliday as they rode along. After another mile the party came to a stop.

One of the warriors rode up to Holliday and held out his hand, and Holliday carefully withdrew his pistol and handed it to him. The warrior gave it to another, and held out his hand again.

"Damn!" muttered Holliday, pulling out a Derringer he kept tucked in his pocket in his vest.

Roosevelt followed suit, handing over his rifle and his pistol. The warrior held out his hand for more.

"That's all I've got," said Roosevelt.

The warrior gestured again.

"Here," said Roosevelt, removing his coat and handing it to the warrior. "See for yourself."

The warrior examined the coat, handed it back, hopped down from his horse, and ran his hands over Roosevelt's pants, then nodded his head. He climbed back onto his horse, and the little party began moving forward again.

"How's that for irony?" said Roosevelt. "I just started carrying a six-gun today, and I've already lost it."

"They'll return it later," Holliday assured him.

Five minutes later Geronimo's lodge came into view.

"It's smaller than I imagined," remarked Roosevelt. "This can't be the headquarters of the whole Apache nation."

"It's just where he stays when he's in this area," explained Holliday. "No one knows where the bulk of his people live, which is probably why they're still a large and powerful tribe."

When they reached the first of the structures, they stopped, and Roosevelt and Holliday dismounted. One of the warriors took their reins and led their horses off.

Roosevelt frowned. "I hope they don't intend on keeping them," he said. "I don't relish a walk all the way back to Tombstone."

"I thought you'd relish a run to it," said Holliday with a smile. "Don't worry. They're just making sure we don't leave before the negotiations are over."

"Where is he?" asked Roosevelt, looking around.

"Who knows?" replied Holliday. "He could be one of the birds in that tree, or a snake, or even one of the horses. He'll be Geronimo when he's convinced himself you're the man he sent for."

A mangy dog sauntered up, wagging its tail and panting heavily.

"Geronimo?" Roosevelt asked Holliday.

Holliday shrugged. "Who knows?"

Roosevelt squatted down and petted the dog. As he did so, he saw a burly shadow fall across the dog. He looked up and found himself facing an imposing figure of a man, stern and dignified.

"You're Goyathlay," he said with absolute certainty.

"And you are Roosevelt," said Geronimo.

"I have come a long way to meet you," Roosevelt said in Apache.

"I speak your language," said Geronimo. "And we have important things to discuss."

"If this is a private conversation," said Holliday hopefully, "I can just go sit in the shade of that hut, and maybe relax with a drink from" —he padded his flask through his coat—"my special water supply."

"No," said Geronimo.

"No?" repeated Holliday, making no attempt to hide his annoyance. "I brought him. What more do you want?"

"It is important that you listen too," said Geronimo, "because when we are done, it will start a war such as you have never dreamed about."

Holliday stared at him for a moment, then pulled out his flask. "I think I'll have that drink right now," he said.

7.

"IT IS TIME," said Geronimo when he and Roosevelt were sitting cross-legged on the ground in the shade of Geronimo's hut, facing each other. Holliday, who had some trepidation about lowering himself to the ground gracefully and an absolute certainty that if he managed it he could never get up on his own power, remained on his feet a few feet away. "That is why I have sent for you."

"I appreciate that," replied Roosevelt. "I have two questions." Suddenly he grinned. "Well, two right now. A lot more later."

"You may ask."

"Why me?"

"You are a man of honor."

"Thank you," said Roosevelt. "But there are many men of honor."

"Not as many as you think," said Geronimo. "And though you are a very young man, you are the best of them."

"I'm flattered that you should think so," replied Roosevelt, "but there are many better men."

Geronimo stared at him for a long moment. "Do you truly believe that?" he said at last.

Roosevelt stared back for just as long. "No," he finally admitted. "No, I don't."

"Good. Because if you answered otherwise, I would not know that I can trust you." He paused. "You had a second question?"

Roosevelt nodded. "Why now?"

"It is time."

"It is past time, but why have you decided to lift the spell now?"

"Many reasons," said Geronimo. "The man Edison will soon know how to negate much of our magic."

"We both know you could kill him before that happens," offered Holliday from where he stood.

"He has done me a service. I will not kill him while I am obligated to him."

"You paid it off," said Holliday. "He found a way to remove the spell and the railroad from your burial ground, and you removed Billy the Kid's supernatural protection."

Geronimo shook his head. "I paid *you*, Holliday. You were the one who faced McCarty called the Kid. I did not pay Edison, and until I find a way, he is safe from me." Another pause. "But he is not safe from the other tribes."

"You said many reasons," said Roosevelt. "What are some others?"

"There are too many White Eyes," answered Geronimo. "Already many thousands of you have crossed the river. You have even built towns. We no longer have the power to stop you, only to hinder you. Eventually your nation will reach from one ocean to the other, and if we fight you every step of the way is it not beyond your people to wage a war of extermination, which we cannot win."

"I would fight against that," said Roosevelt.

"I know. That is another reason I have chosen you."

"After you, Hook Nose was the strongest of the medicine men," said Holliday, "and you killed him almost two years ago. This should be a stroll in the park."

Geronimo frowned. "I do not understand."

"With no Hook Nose, there should be no meaningful opposition," said Holliday.

Geronimo shook his head. "How little you know."

"Enlighten us," said Roosevelt.

"The medicine men of the other Indian nations have always resented my power, and now they have a reason to openly oppose me. They have no intention of lifting the spell."

"If you're the strongest . . ." began Holliday.

"I am stronger than any one of them," explained Geronimo. "I am not stronger than most of them acting in concert."

"How many others are there?"

"More than fifty."

"And how many oppose you?" continued Holliday.

"Perhaps thirty-five, perhaps forty."

"And you think with Theodore on your side, you can beat them?"

"Theodore?" asked Geronimo, frowning.

"Roosevelt," said Holliday.

"It will take more than him," said Geronimo.

"What or who else will it take?" asked Roosevelt.

"Edison and Buntline," answered the Apache.

"What will you want them to do?"

Geronimo shrugged. "It depends on what the other nations do."

Roosevelt shook his head. "We need a better strategy than to just sit here waiting for them to strike first." He turned to Holliday. "Doc, you've got to have a lot of friends who are good with guns."

Holliday smiled a bittersweet smile. "I have never had a lot of friends."

"Then we'll recruit them."

"To face the warriors of fifty-five Indian nations?" asked Holliday in amused tones.

"There have to be alternatives." He turned to Geronimo. "You didn't send for me just so I'd be an easier target for your enemies. What do you have in mind?"

"I chose right," said Geronimo, nodding his head in satisfaction. "I sent for you to make sure you had not changed since you first came to me in a vision three years ago, that you were still the man best fit to lead your nation across the river, and to make peace with *my* nation."

Roosevelt looked at him expectantly, and finally the old man continued.

"I will show you what you must eventually face, Roosevelt."

"Eventually?"

"They are still learning how to control it," said Geronimo. "Little do they know that it cannot be controlled, only aimed like a rifle or an arrow."

Roosevelt frowned. "I'm not sure I understand."

"I will show you."

Geronimo closed his eyes and uttered a chant. Roosevelt tried to follow it, but though he had studied the Apache language, most of the words were unfamiliar to him.

Then, suddenly, a naked warrior with bright red skin, perhaps two feet high, stood on the ground between them. Roosevelt leaned forward and studied him. His red face was almost that of a skeleton's, but it was somehow capable of expression, and right now it was frowning and glowering. His arms were as long as an ape's, and ended not in hands or paws, but in flames.

"What is it?"

"The man Edison would call it a test model," answered Geronimo.

"It is a creation of my rivals and your enemies. It has a name, but you cannot pronounce it. The closest approximation is War Bonnet."

"And this is what the other tribes are sending against us?" asked Roosevelt.

"That is correct."

"I could smash his head with my pistol right now," offered Holliday. "Or put a bullet through it."

"This is not War Bonnet," said Geronimo, "but merely what he will look like."

Roosevelt reached out for the image, and his hand passed right through it. "If that's the worst they can do, I don't think we've got much to worry about," he said.

"As I said, it is only a model. This is what the true War Bonnet will look like when they are done with him." Geronimo muttered another chant, and suddenly the image of War Bonnet began growing taller and broader, the flames that were his hands become longer and brighter, his skeleton's face grew more fearsome, and when he finally reached his full height the top of his head towered some twelve feet above the ground.

"Interesting," commented Roosevelt.

"He is not just a giant, but will have powers even I cannot guess at," added Geronimo.

"He's a couple of feet taller than the biggest grizzly I've ever seen."

"And mighty few grizzlies can reach out and set you on fire," added Holliday.

"Will he be able to shoot those flames like arrows?" asked Roosevelt.

"Almost certainly," answered Geronimo.

"And he'll have other powers too?"

Geronimo nodded. "Many." He paused. "I will make him vanish now."

"No," said Roosevelt, pulling a notebook out of a pocket. "I'm not much of an artist, but let me sketch him so I can show Tom what we're up against."

"Tom?" repeated the Apache.

"Edison."

"The White Eyes have too many names," declared Geronimo.

"His whole name is Thomas Alva Edison," said Holliday with a smile.

"You are sure?"

"As sure as my name's John Henry Holliday."

Geronimo snorted but made no reply.

"Okay, I'm done," said Roosevelt a moment later, putting the notebook away. Geronimo made a gesture and the image of War Bonnet vanished.

"I've got a question, if I may," said Holliday.

Geronimo turned to him. "Ask."

"You're the most powerful medicine man of them all. Why can't you just magic War Bonnet away, send him back to whatever hell they pulled him out of?"

"His magic is too strong for that—or it will be, once he truly exists," answered Geronimo. "They know better than to create a creature that I can scatter on the winds."

"Let me make sure I understand our agreement," said Roosevelt. "You lift the spell, and I agree to fight War Bonnet with help from Edison or anyone else I can enlist?" He paused, frowning. "We have an army. Why don't I just send for it?"

"Your army cannot cross the river, for I cannot lift the spell with all of the other medicine men arrayed against me," answered Geronimo. "First they must be defeated. Only then can I lift the spell."

"Not much of a bargain," commented Holliday. "Especially since you admit that sooner or later we're going to spread across the river anyway. Did I hear that right?"

"You heard it right," confirmed Geronimo.

"You didn't ask him the operative question, Doc," said Roosevelt.

"What question was that?" asked Holliday.

Roosevelt turned to Geronimo. "If the spell isn't lifted, *when* will we freely cross the river and settle the land to the Pacific Ocean?"

Geronimo opened both hands, extended his fingers, then closed them and repeated the process seven more times.

"Eighty years," said Roosevelt. "Almost everyone who is alive today, even newborn infants, will be dead by then." He grimaced. "That's why I have to do this, Doc. It is our manifest destiny to reach from one coast to the other. I can't make an entire nation wait for more than three-quarters of a century because I find the task daunting." He reached his hand out. "Goyathlay, we have a deal."

Geronimo took his hand. "It is not written that you shall succeed," he said grimly. "Only that you are the best of them."

"Doc and I have to get back to Tombstone and meet with Edison," said Roosevelt, getting to his feet. "How long will you remain here?"

"I leave tonight," answered Geronimo.

"How will I find you if I need to confer with you?"

"Holliday knows."

Geronimo didn't say another word, but somehow his warriors knew to bring Roosevelt's and Holliday's horses and weapons, and shortly thereafter they were heading back to Tombstone across the parched landscape.

A single hawk, riding the hot thermals, circled overhead. Finally it swooped down, diving directly toward Roosevelt. When it was some thirty yards away its wings turned to flames, the same flames Roosevelt had seen at the ends of War Bonnet's arms.

"Soon!" promised the hawk, and vanished just before it reached him.

8.

HOLLIDAY, ROOSEVELT, AND MASTERSON sat on cow hide furniture in Edison's living room. Edison himself emerged from a kitchen, bringing them coffee on a copper tray.

"Ned will be here in a few minutes," he announced. "He's just finishing up some work in his lab."

"I don't want to sound unduly nervous," said Roosevelt, "but I have to ask: Is it safe to sit here with my back to a window?"

Holliday chuckled at that, and even Masterson smiled.

"Have I said something funny?" asked Roosevelt, trying to hide his irritation.

"Theodore, nothing inimical can get within a quarter mile of the house without my knowing it—on land *or* in the air. Pull your gun and take a shot at the window in question."

Roosevelt frowned. "Shoot at the window?" he repeated.

"That's right."

"Stand back, Bat," said Edison. "Just in case."

Masterson got up and walked to the center of the room as Roosevelt pulled his pistol out of its holster, took aim at the window, and fired. The bullet flattened against the window and careened off very near to where Masterson had been sitting.

"Well, I'll be . . ." said Roosevelt, obviously impressed. "That's truly remarkable, Thomas."

"I developed it about two years ago," answered Edison. "The problem is, I haven't found an inexpensive way to make it. It's effective, but it's exorbitant. I use the glass only on the house. Oh, and of course on Ned's next door."

Roosevelt leaned back on his chair. "Well, that assuages one worry."

"Just one?"

"You've been out here for three years. I've never seen a manifestation of magic until today."

Edison smiled. "I view it as a different scientific system. The effects can be startling, even frightening, but it obeys laws, just as science does. The trick is to find out what those laws are and to learn how to negate or contravene them."

"Maybe we can get you together with Geronimo," suggested Roosevelt, picking up a cup and sipping his coffee. "You're both on the same side, so perhaps he can educate you in his system's laws."

"He'll never do it," said Holliday firmly.

"I agree," said Masterson, lighting up a cigar.

"But—" began Roosevelt.

"Trust me," said Holliday. "I know him better than any of you. We were his enemy until a few months ago. We're still not his friends, just a perceived inevitability. He's not going to turn over any secrets to any of us, and especially not to Tom."

Roosevelt turned to Edison. "Do you agree with that appraisal?"

Edison nodded his head. "Doc's summed it up. We're not his

friends, and we're not his allies. We're an inevitable force that he's willing to accommodate, nothing more."

A burly, balding man entered the room from the enclosed passageway that joined the two houses together.

"Hello, all," said Ned Buntline. "How did the meeting with Geronimo go?"

"The spell's still in effect," said Roosevelt.

"Figures," said Buntline. "He didn't send for you just to say, 'Here, Theodore—the continent's yours.' What does he want from you?"

"You're very perceptive," remarked Roosevelt with a smile.

"If he was going to lift it without something in return, it'd be gone already. And if he just wanted someone killed, he'd never send for you when Doc was already obligated to him for springing him out of that jail in Leadville."

"That's what I'm here to discuss," said Roosevelt. "Ever hear of someone or something called War Bonnet?"

"No," said Buntline and Edison in unison.

Roosevelt spent the next few minutes describing the huge apparition.

"What can he do?" asked Edison. "Which is to say, what are his powers?"

"I don't know," answered Roosevelt. "In fact, I don't know for a fact that he has any, other than the strength that goes with that physique."

"Oh, he's got them, all right," said Edison. "If physical strength was all they wanted to imbue it with, they could make it the king of the grizzlies, huge and invulnerable." He turned to Buntline. "Right, Ned?"

"I agree. They didn't need to make this creature just to combat *you*, Theodore. They've got the warriors from half a hundred tribes to do that."

"May I offer an idea?" said Masterson.

"Certainly."

"Could this thing have been created to face an American regiment if Geronimo finds a way to lift the spell without their consent?"

Edison and Buntline exchanged looks.

"Makes sense to me," said Buntline at last.

"I don't know," said Edison. "I think we're missing some necessary information."

"What do you mean?" asked Roosevelt.

"Theodore, I'm sure you and Bat made excellent time coming out here, and caused no undue commotions along the way, but believe me, you couldn't have kept your presence secret from all the other medicine men, even if none of them are quite as powerful as Geronimo. They could have attacked you at any time along the way. And that means you might not be the *only* reason this War Bonnet was created, or is being created, or will be created."

"Makes sense," said Holliday.

"It makes sense, but it means we're still in the dark," said Buntline, taking a proffered cigar from Masterson and lighting up. "What do the other tribes plan to do? How do they plan to negate Geronimo's magic and keep you from doing whatever it is Geronimo wants you to do?"

"He wants me to kill or neutralize this War Bonnet," said Roosevelt.

"Well, I'm sure he wants that too," said Buntline, "but he's a devious old devil, even when he's on our side. And somehow he always gets what he wants. The trick is to figure out on the front end just what that is."

"I don't know that I agree with you," said Holliday. "He's an honorable man. It's entirely possible that he wants exactly what he says he wants."

"Perhaps," said Edison, refilling his coffee cup. "But I think, in the meantime, that Theodore might consider being my house guest. At least he'll be safe here."

Roosevelt shook his head vigorously. "I thank you for the offer, but I'll stay where I am."

"Are you certain?"

"I'm certain," replied Roosevelt. "I didn't come all this way to hide in a room, even one with as nice a library as yours doubtless has. Whatever War Bonnet's capabilities, we know there's an Indian military force, so I've got to be out and around recruiting men to face it. We're not going to be fighting them in New York or the Dakota Badlands, so I have to become more acquainted with the terrain." He paused, as if considering whether or not to continue, and finally shrugged. "And there's something else."

The four others looked at him expectantly.

"I am not entirely lacking in the power of persuasion," said Roosevelt. "I thought I might visit the Southern Cheyenne and some of the others and convince them to come over to Geronimo's side."

"Are you crazy?" demanded Masterson.

"They were his allies until a month or two ago," said Roosevelt.

"Then let an Apache talk to them!"

"It's no different than speaking to a crowd of Democrats," Roosevelt assured him.

"The hell it isn't," said Masterson. "The Democrats weren't sworn to kill you."

"They were sworn to defeat me. So are the Indians."

Masterson turned to Edison. "*You* explain it to him. I give up."

"Theodore, you don't really want to ride unprotected into Indian territory," said Edison.

"I thought it was *all* Indian territory," said Roosevelt with a smile. "Isn't that what this is about?"

"You know what I mean."

"I do," answered Roosevelt. "But Bat and Doc have told me about some of the inventions you've come up with since the government sent you out here, and I thought you might like to supply me with some of them." He flashed the others a grin. "So you see, I don't plan to ride into enemy territory, or anywhere else, without protection."

Edison sighed. "Theodore, I don't even know what I'm supposed to be protecting you *from*."

"Then I'd say that finding out is our first order of business," answered Roosevelt.

"Geronimo's told you all that he's going to tell you," said Holliday. "Hell, it's probably all he knows right now."

"What do you propose, then?" demanded Roosevelt. "That we sit right here and wait for them to reach full strength and launch an attack?"

"Me?" said Holliday. "I propose to go back to Leadville, check into the sanitarium, and hope to hear before I breathe my last that Geronimo lifted the spell and we've crossed the Mississippi in huge numbers."

"I'm sorry," said Roosevelt earnestly. "This is *my* fight. And I don't propose to do it on an empty stomach. I saw a nice-looking restaurant across from the Oriental."

He got to his feet, and Masterson stood up as well. "I'll join you."

"I'll be back tomorrow," Roosevelt promised. "I want to consider various approaches to the problem, and see which seems to offer the greatest chance of success."

"How can you do it when you don't know what this War Bonnet can do, or even if he's the only magical thing they're going to throw against you?" asked Masterson as he followed Roosevelt to the door.

"It's a novel problem. It requires a novel solution."

Then they were out the door and gone.

"Doc, are you really going back to Leadville?" asked Edison.

"I was going to ask that myself," said Buntline.

"I'll stick around another day or two, sit in on a game or two at the Oriental, and then I plan to head back. I don't want to be too far from the sanitarium if something happens."

"I can appreciate that," said Edison, frowning.

"But?" said Holliday, suddenly alert. "There's an unspoken 'but' hiding in there somewhere."

"Doc, I studied this young man, this Roosevelt, when I heard he was coming out here. He's the most accomplished man America has yet produced. Along with everything else, he even wrote the definitive treatise on naval warfare. There are the seeds of greatness within him. Whatever the outcome here, America is going to need him."

Holliday stared at him in silence.

"You know what I'm going to ask you," said Edison uncomfortably.

"You're going to have to say it," replied Holliday.

"Doc, Ned and I will supply you with anything you need, but I want you to keep that young man alive."

"Whatever the cost?" said Holliday.

"Whatever the cost."

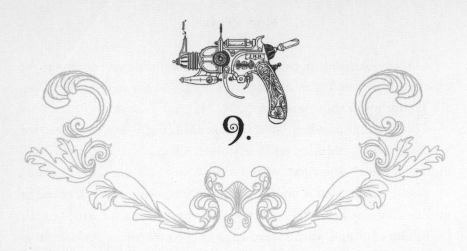

9.

OLLIDAY AWOKE TO A COUGHING FIT, thoroughly bloodied a fresh handkerchief before he was done, and painfully climbed into his clothes, then walked down the corridor to the floor's only bathroom.

As he was washing his hands, he saw a bird perched on the windowsill, staring at him.

"I hope you're enjoying yourself," he muttered.

The bird watched him silently for another few seconds, then flew off.

"OK, so you were just a bird," said Holliday. He stared into the mirror and decided that he needed a shave. He had gone to the local barber for a shave every day the last time he'd lived in Tombstone, but he'd been living with Kate Elder then, and she complained when his face had a two- or three-day growth on it. Since they'd been living apart, he'd fallen into the habit of getting a shave only when he could see the shadow of his beard on his cheeks.

He returned to his room, strapped on his holster, inserted his gun into it, put the Derringer in his vest pocket, donned his hat, and walked out of his room and down the steps to the lobby. He looked around for Roosevelt or Masterson, didn't see them, and decided to visit the barber before he faced any food.

He walked out into the street, decided that it was every bit as hot here as it had been in Leadville, with the added disadvantage that the wind constantly blew clouds of dust through the air. He began making his way down the raised wooden sidewalk, came to a corner, crossed the street, walked another half block, and finally stopped at the barber shop.

"Good morning, Doc," said the barber, dusting off a chair for him. "You're up early today."

"Morning, Sam," replied Holliday, sitting in the chair.

"Same as usual? Shave the face, don't touch the mustache?"

Holliday grunted an affirmative.

"You're going to need a haircut pretty soon," continued the barber. "This'd be a bad day for it, though. We want to get you out of here fast."

"Why?" asked Holliday.

"Johnny Behan's due to come by in about twenty minutes, and I know you and him ain't exactly what they call bosom buddies."

"I've got nothing against him these days," said Holliday. "It was Wyatt who stole his woman, not me. And I've never minded if a man was a lying, backstabbing, black-hearted bastard, as long as he didn't display those traits while holding elected office . . . and Johnny's been forcibly retired for two or three years."

"Well, I'm sure glad you ain't got anything against him," replied the barber with an amused smile as he lathered Holliday's face. "I think I'll get you out of here before he comes anyway."

"Suits me fine," said Holliday. "I hate to have to look at an ugly son of a bitch like that right before I eat."

"Doc, if you make me laugh while I'm shaving you, I'm liable to cut your nose off."

"This is the day to do it, Sam. I'm fresh out of blood."

The barber held his blade at arm's length while he chuckled, and then, when Holliday closed his eyes and leaned back, he began shaving the emaciated man, marveling that a man in such obviously poor health could grow anything, even hair.

Holliday awoke to a finger being prodded into his shoulder.

"What is it?" he asked.

"You fell asleep."

"Oh. Are you done?"

"Not quite."

"Then why—?"

"Behan's early," said the barber, pointing out the front window at the figure that was approaching the shop. He lowered his voice. "If you're going to kill him, please don't do it so that your bullet goes through him and shatters a mirror or he falls through my window."

"I'm not killing anyone," responded Holliday. He paused briefly. "Probably," he added.

The door opened and John Behan entered the shop.

"Well, well, look who's here," he said, staring at Holliday. "They let just anyone come into town these days."

"True," agreed Holliday. "Still, you were the sheriff until the people wised up to you, so I suppose you might as well hang around to remind them to be a little more careful when they go to the polls."

"Very funny," said Behan, who obviously was not amused.

"I'm known far and wide for my sense of humor," said Holliday,

"Is your friend Wyatt with you?" asked Behan.

"No. He spends all his time in bed with his wife." Holliday paused and frowned. "Come to think of it, I believe you used to know the lady."

"You're treading on dangerous ground, Holliday," said Behan, pushing his coat back and exposing his gun and holster.

"Not as dangerous as someone else in here," replied Holliday. "I've had you covered since you walked in here." The cloth over his gun hand wiggled as if for emphasis.

"That's just your finger you're pointing at me."

"If you really believe that, then you should go for your gun," said Holliday. "Sam, you're a witness that he was warned, and thought he was drawing on an unarmed man."

"I don't believe you," said Behan nervously.

"That's your right," said Holliday easily. "A man's got to disbelieve in *something*."

"You're bluffing!"

"Anything's possible."

Behan seemed to struggle briefly with himself, then spat on the floor. "Fuck it! What's one more lunger in the world? You'll be dead soon enough anyway." And with that, he opened the door and stalked off down the street.

"Thanks for not shooting him, Doc."

"Pull the cloth off," said Holliday.

The barber did so, revealing Holliday's forefinger pointing at the place where Behan had been, his pistol still securely in its holster.

The barber emitted a hearty laugh. "By God, wait'll I tell this story around town."

"I'd be very careful about that, Sam," said Holliday. "You're not as likely to scare him off as I was."

"What would you have done if he'd actually gone for his gun?"

"Killed him," said Holliday seriously.

Suddenly the barber found his client less amusing, and went to work finishing his shave.

"What do I owe you?" asked Holliday.

"A nickel."

Holliday tossed him a dime. "When Behan comes back, tell him his shave's on me, and I just wish I was holding the razor."

Then he was out onto the arid Tombstone street. He wandered past a pair of restaurants, wishing he could work up an appetite, finally realized he was headed toward the Oriental and that he was going to drink his breakfast, as usual.

As he crossed an alley, he saw a squirrel standing a few feet into it, just out of the glare of the sunlight. There weren't any squirrels in Tombstone.

"*Goddammit!*" he muttered.

He considered walking straight ahead, but the squirrel knew he'd seen it, and would just keep appearing in various guises until he stopped and found out what it wanted.

He walked into the alley, and continued walking well past the squirrel until he was totally in the shade. At least it was minimally cooler here.

The squirrel turned and walked after him, then came to a stop when it was five feet away and stared at him.

"You'd better not be a goddamned real squirrel," muttered Holliday.

As the words left his mouth, the squirrel morphed into a tall, well-muscled Apache warrior.

"What does he want this time?" said Holliday irritably.

"He says if what he thinks will happen does happen, it is essential that you remain here."

"Here in the alley, or here in Tombstone?"

"Here. Not in Leadville."

"You tell him that Mr. Roosevelt is singularly equipped to take care of himself, and is younger and healthier than I am."

The warrior closed his eyes for a moment, and Holliday got the distinct impression that he was speaking silently with Geronimo.

"He says this has nothing to do with Roosevelt."

"Oh, shit," said Holliday.

But he found he was speaking only to a rapidly retreating squirrel.

10.

HOLLIDAY WAS SITTING ALONE in the elegant bar of the Grand Hotel, drinking his lunch and playing a game of solitaire, when Masterson approached him.

"Mind if I join you?" he asked.

Holliday didn't look up from his card. "Have a seat."

"Thanks."

"Ask the bartender for a glass," said Holliday. "Unless you want to drink from the bottle."

Masterson shook his head. "Too early in the day for me, Doc."

Holliday shrugged. "Good. There'll be more for me."

They sat in silence for a few minutes, Holliday continuing his solitaire game, Masterson looking more and more uncomfortable. Finally he cleared his throat and spoke up. "Doc, I have to talk to you."

"I'm right here," said Holliday.

"I'm thinking of going back to New York."

Now Holliday looked up. "Why?"

"He doesn't need me. He's the most self-sufficient man I've ever met. He's always *doing* something. If he's not figuring out how Edison invents things, he's jogging around the city, or reading books, or sketching birds, or practicing with his pistol, or . . . hell, it makes me tired just describing it."

Holliday smiled. "Yeah, I've noticed that about him."

"He talks to me, because he's well mannered . . . but all he wants to talk about are sporting events I've seen and shootists I've known. I doubt that he thinks of me again the second I'm out of sight." He sighed deeply. "He's got you riding shotgun for him now, and I've got a job back East. I gave all this up a couple of years ago."

"Geronimo's not going to turn you into a bat again," said Holliday.

"I know," replied Masterson. "That's got nothing to do with it. I made a decision to walk out on this life, and I can feel myself getting sucked back in."

Suddenly Holliday grinned. "Now I understand."

"What's so funny?"

"You heard him talking about War Bonnet," said Holliday. "And you're afraid if you stick around a couple more days, your curiosity won't let you leave until you face him or whatever the hell it is."

"I repeat: everything I told you about Roosevelt is true."

"I know."

A guilty smile crossed Masterson's face. "But yeah, I'm dying to see War Bonnet."

"I'm kind of curious myself."

"I'm a writer now, Doc," said Masterson. "I choose my words with a little care. And I'm not willing to die to see War Bonnet."

"How much worse can he be than some of the men you faced in Dodge or back in Texas?"

"He's *magical*, Doc—and I'm still not through having nightmares about my last experience with Indian magic." An involuntary shudder ran through him. "You don't know what it was like to turn into a giant bat—a giant *hungry* bat—every night at sundown, and wake up naked on some roof or balcony every morning." He paused again, and Holliday could see the torment on his face. "I'm torn, Doc. Part of me wants to see this War Bonnet thing, maybe even face him, but part of me says to leave him to Geronimo's magic and go home while I can."

"Geronimo's magic won't work against him," said Holliday.

"What makes you think that?"

"He said so."

"Damn!" muttered Masterson. Then: "Well, hell, if Geronimo can't kill him, Theodore sure as blazes can't."

"Theodore won't be unarmed," said Holliday.

"From what he's described, bullets, even a shotgun, would just annoy War Bonnet."

"He won't face War Bonnet armed with just a pistol or a shotgun."

"What *will* he be carrying?" asked Masterson.

Holliday shrugged. "Whatever Tom and Ned can create for him. Geronimo's magic won't work, but maybe Tom's will."

"And if not?"

"Then I guess it's going to be a century or two before anyone plants the American flag on the Pacific shore."

"Well, at least he'll have you standing with him," said Masterson.

Holliday shook his head. "Geronimo tells me he's got something special planned for me."

"What is it?"

"I don't know, but he seemed to imply that it was as deadly as War Bonnet, and more to the point, that no one else could face it."

"What the hell have we gotten ourselves into, Doc?" asked Masterson, frowning.

"I'm going to die soon anyway, so it doesn't make much difference

84

to me. But I think you've got the right idea: go back East and be a sportswriter."

"Oh, shut up," said Masterson. "You don't think I can leave him to face War Bonnet alone now that I know he won't have Geronimo or you by his side, do you?"

Masterson signaled for a glass, then filled it when the bartender brought it over, took a quick swallow, and made a face. "God, that's horrible stuff! How can you drink it this early in the day?"

"My taste buds don't wake up 'til sunset," answered Holliday.

"That stuff'll kill you," said Masterson.

"It's better than what's killing me right now. Besides, I thought you were more worried about what might kill our Mr. Roosevelt."

"He's a very special young man, Doc. He'll never leave himself an escape route, because it'll never occur to him that he could fail at anything he tries to do." A wry smile. "After all, he never has yet."

"What the hell was he doing in the Badlands anyway?" asked Holliday. "What makes a man with his credentials just walk away after he's not only been elected to office but risen right to the top so fast?"

"His wife and his mother had died, and he wanted to get away from all the memories."

"What did they die of?"

"I don't know about the mother," replied Masterson, "but his wife died in childbirth." Masterson shook his head sadly. "He must have loved her very much. He won't allow anyone to talk about her or even mention her name in his presence."

"In childbirth?"

"Right."

"Lost the baby too, did he?" said Holliday, taking another drink. "Now I can understand why he left. Hell, that's three generations in one day."

"No, I gather she's still alive."

Holliday frowned. "He just walked out on her?"

Masterson shook his head. "Doc, it was a newborn baby. There was no way he could take her out to the Badlands alone. He hired a wet nurse, and people to watch her, and when she can manage it I'm sure he'll send for her." He paused thoughtfully. "Or maybe by then he'll be through playing at being a cowboy and writing this history of the West he's working on, and be ready to go back to New York. One or the other."

Holliday picked up the cards, shuffled them, and dealt himself another hand of solitaire. "Well, have a nice safe trip back East, Bat," he said, staring at the cards and starting to manipulate them around the table.

"Oh, hell, I'm not going anywhere," muttered Masterson with a sigh.

"I thought you just said—?"

"That was before you told me you won't be backing him up." Masterson cursed under his breath. "That little girl has already lost a mother. I don't aim to let her lose a father too."

Holliday looked across the table at him for a long moment.

"What are you staring at?" demanded Masterson.

"You're a good man," said Holliday. "We haven't always seen eye to eye, but you're a good man."

"Thanks," replied Masterson. "I guess."

"Of course, you understand that all I'm really good at evaluating is teeth," said Holliday with a sudden smile.

Masterson laughed at that, and was still laughing when John Behan entered the bar, accompanied by three hard-looking men, all of them armed.

"They let just anybody into the Grand these days," said Holliday, staring at them.

"The barber's been talking about what happened between us all over town," said Behan angrily.

"Nothing happened between us," replied Holliday. "If it had, they'd be planting you in Boot Hill right about now."

"You've made me a laughing stock for the last time!" yelled Behan.

"You're leaving town?" asked Holliday wryly. "Have a nice trip."

"I've had just about enough of you! You haven't got the Earps to protect you now."

"You've got it all wrong, Johnny," said Holliday. "*I* protected *them*."

"But if it'll make any difference to you," interjected Masterson, "*I'm* protecting him today."

Behan stared at him. "I know you."

"I'm flattered beyond belief," replied Masterson.

"You ran out of Tombstone with your tail between your legs once before," said Behan. "We can make you do it again."

Masterson tensed, and his hand edged down below the table top toward his gun.

"Johnny, go home and sleep it off before you do something even stupider than usual," said Holliday.

"I'm not drunk!" bellowed Behan. "I'm mad!"

"Thanks."

"For what?"

"For saying that," answered Holliday. "Personally I could never tell the difference."

"You'll never change!" snapped Behan.

"Don't say that too loud," said Holliday. "You'll ruin Charlie Ho's day down at the laundry."

"I've had it with you and what you think is funny," said Behan. "I want an apology for what happened in the barber shop, and while I'm thinking of it, I want another one for your behavior right here and now."

"That's a small enough thing to want," replied Holliday. "Me, I'd like a million dollars, one of those robot chippies that used to work at Kate's place, and thirty years of good health."

"Are you going to apologize or not?" demanded Behan.

"Not, I think."

Behan stepped off to a side and nodded to the three men. "He's all yours."

The three of them tensed and faced the table.

"I'll take the three on the left," said Holliday in conversational tones. "You take Behan."

"No," replied Masterson. "I've already spotted two I don't like much."

"I'll bet they never thought when they woke up today that they'd be facing Doc Holliday and Bat Masterson," said Holliday. "If they had any brains, they'd just shoot Johnny Behan for getting them into this fix and then turn around and walk out. I'll swear it was self-defense if you will."

"Oh, I don't know," said Masterson. "I think it might be more fun to kill them. I haven't appeared in one of those dime novels for almost a year."

"That's because everyone you've faced has been dead for over a year. Come to think of it, I suppose you could use the practice."

As they spoke, the three men were getting visibly nervous. Finally one of them turned to Behan.

"You just said you wanted us to put a scare into someone," he said accusingly. "You never said we'd be facing Doc Holliday."

"And Bat Masterson," said Masterson. "Don't forget Bat Masterson."

"Just shoot them, for Christ's sake!" screamed Behan.

"An extra hundred apiece," said another.

"Go for it, Johnny," said Holliday easily. "They're not going to live long enough to collect it."

"Fuck it!" said the first of the men. He turned to Behan. "Fuck it and fuck you!"

He held his arms out so they could see he wasn't reaching for his gun, and walked out into the lobby. The other two men followed him.

"Nice try, Johnny," said Holliday. Suddenly his smile vanished. "Next time I'll kill you, and that's a promise."

Behan glared at him for a moment, then turned and walked out of the bar.

"Keep an eye on them, Bat," said Holliday as the four men walked out into the street. "They don't look like they care whether they draw on our fronts or our backs."

Two of the men and Behan immediately crossed the dusty street, but the third lingered outside the hotel. Finally he began walking by the bar's window, then turned and drew his pistol—but before he could fire a shot, and before Holliday or Masterson had fired their own weapons, a lean, muscular body hurled itself upon the gunman, knocking him down. He got to his feet just in time to be on the receiving end of a left hook that put him back down on the wooden sidewalk, this time for the count.

"Well, I'll be!" exclaimed Roosevelt as Holliday and Masterson rushed out of the hotel. "I knew this blaggard was going to backshoot somebody, but I had no idea it was you two."

"What the hell were you doing here?" asked Holliday.

"I've been jogging at noontime," answered Roosevelt. "The morning bird-watching is too good to skip."

"I see you're growing a mustache," noted Holliday.

"Might as well," replied Roosevelt. "I've got no one to kiss out here."

Holliday looked across the street and saw Behan glaring at him from perhaps fifty yards away. The other two gunmen were nowhere to be seen.

"So, shall we carry this fellow off to the jailhouse?" asked Roosevelt.

Holliday shook his head. "No."

"He just tried to kill you, Doc!"

"He has friends, and even an employer of sorts," answered Holliday. "Someone would make his bail before nightfall."

"Do you just propose to leave him lying here until he wakes up?" asked Roosevelt disapprovingly.

"No," said Holliday, kneeling down next to the man. "I think we'll fine him."

"Fine him?" repeated Roosevelt.

Holliday took the man's gun from where it had fallen and tucked it in his belt, then pulled out the man's wallet and relieved it of all its cash.

"Okay," said Holliday, standing up again. "Justice is served."

Roosevelt flashed him a grin that would someday become famous. "I guess it has been, at that," he said.

11.

"OKAY," SAID BUNTLINE. "So you say he's how tall?"

He was standing in Edison's office, facing Roosevelt, Holliday, and Masterson, who were seated on various chairs and couches. Edison sat at his desk, taking notes.

"How tall is the ceiling?" asked Holliday.

"I'd say eight feet."

"Then he's taller than twelve feet. A few more feet."

"And what is he built like?" continued Buntline. "I don't mean the flames. I mean, is he lean? Burly? Something else?"

"He's pretty well-muscled," replied Roosevelt. "Rather like a heavyweight boxer, but without carrying any excess weight."

"All right," said Buntline, seating himself on a wooden chair at the corner of the desk and writing some figures on a piece of paper. Finally he looked up. "From your descriptions, I make him twelve feet high, possibly as tall as fourteen feet."

Roosevelt nodded. "That seems about right."

"And given the build you tell me he's got, he would go from seven hundred fifty to nine hundred pounds."

"That much?" asked Masterson, wide-eyed.

"That's right," confirmed Buntline.

"That just doesn't sound right."

"Bat, how tall are you?"

"Five feet eight," came the answer.

"And what do you weigh?"

"Maybe one hundred fifty pounds."

"And what does a heavyweight boxer who stands six feet tall weigh?" asked Buntline with a smile.

"It varies," said Masterson uncomfortably.

"But he *could* weigh two hundred pounds without anyone calling him fat?"

"Yes, he could," conceded Masterson.

"That's a difference of fifty pounds in just four inches," said Buntline. "Do you really think adding six hundred or seven hundred pounds while adding six to eight feet is so far-fetched?"

"No," admitted Masterson. "No, I guess it's not. In fact, when you put it that way, an extra six hundred pounds would probably have him looking skinny as a rail."

"Which brings up another question," continued Buntline. "How does he get from here to there?"

"From here to there?" repeated Roosevelt, frowning.

"If he appears in, say, a Southern Cheyenne village two hundred miles away," said Buntline, lighting up a cigar and using an ashtray of his super-hardened brass, "and he doesn't magic himself from there to here, how does he get here? I guarantee no thousand-pound horse is going to carry him for more than half a mile or so."

"I suppose he travels by magic," said Roosevelt. "And why not?"

he added. "Geronimo conjured up an image of him, which was clearly magic . . . and his physical attributes, from his size to his flaming hands, would seem to be magic too."

"I wish I knew just how hot those flames are," said Buntline. "And if he can fire them like bullets, or at least flaming arrows, or if he had to reach out and grab you with them."

"Either way they're gonna be hot," offered Holliday dryly.

"It makes a difference, Doc," replied Buntline. "I can make some super-hardened armor for Theodore, and even for his horse—but don't forget that I shape it in a special oven at very high temperatures, and if War Bonnet can match those temperatures, he can totally enclose Theodore in melted brass."

"Not quite the suit of armor I've always imagined," remarked Roosevelt wryly.

"So what else can you do for them?" asked Masterson.

"It's difficult, because we're really working blind here," answered Buntline. "I could create a hood for Theodore's horse, for example, one that would allow Theodore to close the cups over the horse's eyes on a second's notice . . . but I have no idea if the sight of a twelve- or fourteen-foot-tall man would upset the horse at all, whereas blinding him by closing the cups might panic him. By the same token, I don't doubt that we could craft ear plugs, but not being able to see or hear might panic the animal more than seeing and hearing something it hadn't experienced before."

"Maybe it's time to ask the genius what to do," said Holliday, taking a drink from his flask and passing it to Masterson, who took a swallow, wiped his mouth on a shirtsleeve, and handed it back.

"You mean the *other* genius," replied Edison with a smile. "Never forget that while my inventions may work in theory, it's Ned and his manufacturing business that makes them work in practice."

"Okay, so what does the other genius think?"

"I think we're working in the dark here," replied Edison. "The unhappy truth is that someone's going to have to see this War Bonnet in person before we can create a weapon that will work against him, and even that probably won't be enough."

"Why the hell not?" persisted Holliday.

"Pretend he's standing right over there, by the door, and that the ceiling is high enough to accommodate him," said Edison, getting up, walking to the door, and turning to face them. "He's here to kill you. Ned's already talked about some of the problems of defending yourself, but let's concentrate not on that but on killing, or at least neutralizing, War Bonnet. Okay, Doc, you draw your gun and fire six quick shots. Either they bounce off him, or he absorbs them with no ill effects. *Now* what do you do?"

"Run like hell," said Masterson, only half-kidding.

"Well, right at the moment, so would I," said Edison, returning his smile. "And that's why we need to know more about him."

"For example?" asked Roosevelt.

"If Doc shoots you in a vital spot, you'll die—and if you shoot him, *he'll* die. That means you each have the same physical weaknesses. Is that true of War Bonnet? Which is to say, it seems obvious that those fiery hands of his are meant to burn you, either at close quarters, as when he grabs you, or at a distance, if he has some mechanism whereby he can aim and release that fire. So the obvious question is: Is himself susceptible to fire, or at least to heat? If he is, I can create a carbon arc projector that I guarantee will throw more heat at him than he can throw at you . . . but will that harm, or even bother him? I don't know." Edison returned to his chair while considering his next line of approach. "All right, let's say that he's immune to fire and heat. It's a reasonable assumption, given that his arms and hands are made of flame. Will water put the fire out, or at least negate it to some degree?"

"It seems reasonable," agreed Masterson.

"I see Theodore is shaking his head," noted Edison with a smile. "Would you care to tell Bat why?"

"I'd have to position myself next to a large source of water. This is not a small warrior, this War Bonnet, and those aren't small flames. And we don't know how hot the flames are. Could they turn the water to steam even before it hits them? Remember: he's a magical creature, so he doesn't necessarily obey all the laws of Tom's science."

"Absolutely right," agreed Edison. He smiled again. "I would expect no less of a Harvard man."

"Let's concentrate on keeping the Harvard man alive," said Holliday. "At least long enough for someone from Yale to come along and kill him."

Roosevelt uttered a hearty laugh. "Says the man who did not have the benefit of a New England education."

"Getting back to War Bonnet," said Edison, "so far we've spoken about only heat, flame, and water. How about one of Doc's or Bat's bullets? I assume they won't bother him because of his magical origin, but until we know that for sure, we have to consider the possibility that the direct means of confronting and combating him may be the best. And there are factors that *seem* extraneous but may not be. For example, how's his endurance? Most huge men, well-muscled or otherwise, tire more easily than small, lithe men. What if you face him out in the desert, shoot his horse out from under him, and ride off?"

"He won't be riding a horse, Tom," said Buntline.

"Are you quite sure, Ned?" retorted Edison. "If they can create War Bonnet, why can't they create a horse that stands sixty hands at the shoulder and weighs three tons?"

"Damn!" muttered Buntline. "I never thought of that."

"Anyway, gentlemen, I could give you all the dozens of possibilities that have occurred to me, but the end result would be the same: it's all guesswork, and it's not even educated guesswork since, based on his very origin, we have to assume that War Bonnet doesn't necessarily obey the laws of science as we know them. The problem," he added with a wry smile, "is that he may very well obey *all* of them. We just can't know until he shows himself, by which time it may be too late."

"If one of us does make contact . . ." began Roosevelt.

"Then based on your firsthand observations, I would hope Ned and I can create a weapon that can be effective. At least we won't be working in the dark."

"You might be anyway," said Holliday.

"Oh?" said Edison, turning to him.

"There's a difference between seeing and shooting him, throwing him in a lake, and giving him a hotfoot." He looked around the room and saw nothing but puzzled expressions. "What I'm saying is that if all we do is *see* him, you won't have learned anything except that he's as big as Geronimo says, and if we try to harm him without knowing what works, we can't report back to you. Either it works and he's dead, or it doesn't work and *we're* dead."

"You're not thinking it through, Doc," said Edison.

Holliday arched an eyebrow. "Oh?"

"I'd never ask you to face this monster without taking a lot of precautions."

"You're not telling us to turn tail and run," said Holliday, trying to comprehend what Edison was suggesting.

"Of course not."

"Then I'm stumped."

Edison turned to Roosevelt. "Theodore?"

Roosevelt frowned for a moment, then snapped his fingers and let out a whoop. "We go to the source!"

"The medicine men?" asked Masterson, confused.

"No," said Roosevelt. "To Geronimo. He's the one who told us War Bonnet exists. He's the one who knows what he'll look like. He's the most powerful medicine man of all. If anyone knows what War Bonnet can and can't do, it'll be Geronimo."

"Then why didn't he tell us when we were at his lodge?" asked Holliday.

"Maybe he thinks I'm bright enough to figure War Bonnet out myself. Remember, I'm the one American he trusts. Or maybe he wants to see if I'm bright enough to come back and question him." He paused. "Or maybe War Bonnet is a work in progress, and the longer he waits, the more he'll know—or maybe he really doesn't know. At any rate, that's where I'm going as soon as we leave here."

"No you're not," said Holliday.

"Oh?" said Roosevelt pugnaciously. "And why not?"

"He's not there. He left a few hours after we saw him. Remember, he's a target too, so he's going to keep on the move."

Roosevelt frowned. "Then where will we find him?"

Holliday looked at the window ledge, where a wren was perched.

"Oh, I think a little bird will tell us," he said with a confident smile.

12.

WHEN HOLLIDAY, ROOSEVELT, AND MASTERSON left Edison's house, the wren swooped down toward them, then paused, fluttering in place about ten feet above the ground, and flew off very slowly to the east.

"He wants you to follow him," said Holliday.

"Are you seriously suggesting that's Geronimo?" said Roosevelt, frowning.

"Geronimo or one of his warriors."

"That's difficult to believe."

"Is believing in War Bonnet any easier?" asked Holliday.

"Why doesn't he just appear as himself?" asked Roosevelt.

"You've made your peace with him," answered Holliday. "The rest of the town—of the country, for that matter—is still at war with him."

Roosevelt stared at the bird for a moment. "All right," he said. "Let's see if you're right."

"Of course I am," said Holliday. "I'm going to the Oriental. You can find me there." He turned to Masterson. "What about you?"

"What the hell. There's no law says I have to gamble once I get there." Suddenly he smiled. "Besides, there's always a chance Johnny Behan will be there. I don't like him any better than you do."

"That's a powerful lot of dislike to reside in just two men," said Holliday, heading off toward the Oriental, and Masterson fell into step beside him.

Roosevelt followed the bird, which kept distancing from him and then coming back. He walked out of town, and in another hundred yards came to an abandoned barn and corral. The wood was starting to crumble, and a number of the cross posts in the corral were broken. The bird flew around to the far side of the barn, and when Roosevelt reached the spot where he couldn't be seen by any resident of the town, he found himself face-to-face with Geronimo.

"That's quite a trick," said Roosevelt. "Can you do it whenever you want?"

"Yes," answered the Apache.

"Just birds, or can you change into other things as well?"

"I can change into other things."

"Then why not turn yourself into a mighty warrior, three times as big as War Bonnet, and just step on him when he shows up?"

Geronimo seemed amused by the question. "War Bonnet is the product of the combined magical might of many medicine men. With Hook Nose dead, I can match any three or even four of them, but not many more than that."

"Then, not to put too fine a point on it, we're as good as dead," said Roosevelt.

"You show no sign of fear."

"I'm not afraid to die," was the answer. "But I still have a lot of things I want to do first."

"Then we must defeat him and them."

"You just told me that you couldn't," said Roosevelt.

"But I did not say *you* couldn't," answered Geronimo.

Roosevelt frowned. "I possess no magic."

"You possess an indomitable will."

"That's not much to put up against a thousand pounds of magical warrior," replied Roosevelt. "You saw me talking to Edison and Buntline. They're capable of things that seem like magic, but they need more information. We're hoping you can supply it."

"War Bonnet is not a finished creation," answered Geronimo. "I showed you what I can."

"Is he impervious to bullets?"

"He can be."

"Can a large supply of water douse those flaming hands?" continued Roosevelt.

"Under some circumstances."

"You're not helping much."

"I told you: he is not yet finished."

"Will he be able to feel pain?"

"Possibly."

"Damn it!" snapped Roosevelt. "I need to know *something* about him!"

"When he is ready to be sent against us, I will know more," replied Geronimo.

"That may be too late." Roosevelt paused, trying to come up with some answerable questions. "Once he looks the way you showed me, can he change his shape? Can he sneak up to me as a beetle or a butterfly and then turn into a giant warrior?"

"*That* he will not be able to do," Geronimo assured him. "Once he is completed and sent forth, no one medicine man can change him. It must be done with the consent of all, and they will disperse the moment he is activated."

"Why?"

"If you were at war, would you want all your generals in one location?" asked Geronimo with the hint of a smile.

"So once they send him after us, he's stuck with whatever abilities and defenses they've given him?"

"With some of them."

"But you just said—"

"I said he cannot change his shape, and he cannot. But that does not mean he cannot change other things."

"Give me an example," said Roosevelt.

"He may have abilities that may remain dormant until he needs them. The simplest example would be food. Even a magical creature must have energy for his body, but he may not feel hunger for days on end, until he finally comes upon a supply of food—and then he may eat enough to make up for all the meals he missed with no ill effects."

"I see."

"Or he may never eat at all."

"But you just said—"

"He may be a vegetable that looks like a man. He may eat sunshine. He may drink by walking barefoot across a stream."

Roosevelt muttered an obscenity.

"I know you want specific answers, but you must remember that he is the creation of more than fifty medicine men, and each will have his own ideas, and each will have some input, some trait to add or change or eliminate."

"All right," said Roosevelt after a moment's consideration. "I have another question."

Geronimo stared at him. "Ask."

"Is this creature being created just to kill you and me, or to conquer the whole damned continent?"

A smile of approval crossed Geronimo's face, as if to say, *It's about time you thought to ask that.* "We are his first challenge, not his last. He is being created solely to battle you and myself, but if he wins, be assured that they will find more for him to do."

"Wrong," said Roosevelt firmly.

"Wrong?" repeated Geronimo, frowning.

"We're going to be his first *and* his last challenge, because we're going to put an end to him."

"The spirit is strong within you. I approve."

"Well, I wish I'd found out a little more about him, but at least you gave me a few facts."

Geronimo looked surprised. "I did?"

Roosevelt nodded.

"What?" asked the Apache.

"They're creating him to kill you and me. So his strengths will be those strengths that work against us, and his weaknesses—and everything has weaknesses—will be those we're not likely to take advantage of."

Geronimo frowned. "And you find that useful?"

"It could be."

"How?"

"Our friend Holliday is just about the best shootist still alive and unjailed. You don't use a pistol, and I freely admit that I'm not very good with one. The medicine men must know that, so it's possible that War Bonnet will be susceptible to Doc's six-gun." Geronimo gave a noncommittal grunt, and Roosevelt continued.

"Or perhaps if I were to train a couple of large dogs to attack, it might be that War Bonnet has no defense against them."

"Other than his size and strength, you mean?" said Geronimo, looking unconvinced.

"At least these are possibilities. And there are others. For example, if there's any quicksand around here, and I can lure him into it because he's chasing me . . ."

"What do you think will happen?" asked Geronimo.

"He'll sink into it," answered Roosevelt, surprised at the question.

"And then what?"

Roosevelt frowned. "I don't understand."

"It will not suck him all the way through to the other side of the world. There is a floor to every quicksand pit, and if he does not have to breathe—and he may not; that is certainly a trait *I* would give him—he will come to the floor, and walk through the quicksand to the edge of it and then climb out."

"All right," said Roosevelt. "I haven't seen any quicksand around Tombstone anyway. But the principle is still valid: *everything* has weaknesses. I just have to figure out what War Bonnet's are—and if I can figure them out soon enough, then Tom and Ned might be able to help me devise a weapon that will work against him."

"It is important that you find a way," said Geronimo. "Because if our treaty does not come to pass, there will be lakes of blood spilled when your armies finally cross the river and confront *our* armies. As thirsty as the earth is, even it cannot drink all the blood that will be shed on both sides."

"I know," said Roosevelt. "I won't let you down."

"It is not *me* you will let down," answered Geronimo. "I am an old man. It is your unborn children and grandchildren you will betray if our agreement is broken by War Bonnet or any other."

"It won't be," said Roosevelt. He turned and waved a hand in the direction of the distant Mississippi. "We will cross that river, in peace and friendship, in both our lifetimes."

"That depends on the coming days," said Geronimo.

103

Roosevelt turned back to argue, but all he saw was a small bird climbing higher and higher in the sky, and then heading south toward Geronimo's Arizona lodge.

13.

HOLLIDAY WALKED DOWN THE STREET, shading his eyes against the setting sun and wondering once again why he wore a derby instead of a broad-brimmed hat. It was more stylish than a Stetson, but totally useless in these bright desert surroundings. He doffed the derby to a pair of women who were walking on the raised wooden sidewalk in the opposite direction. One smiled at him, the other pretended he wasn't there. He felt pretty good about that; he'd settle for half the people not hating him.

He passed a tobacco store, looked longingly at a box of cigars, decided as always that he coughed more than enough without any help from tobacco, and kept walking.

He realized that he hadn't eaten all day, so he stopped in at the Lazy Bull, ordered a rare steak, thumbed through a dime novel that had him teaming up with Jesse James (who he had never met), put it aside long enough to eat about half the steak, left a quarter on the table, then added a dime for the tip (he was feeling generous), and continued making his way to the Oriental.

When he got there he went over to what had become his usual table, and didn't even have to ask for a bottle. The bartender brought him a glass and what was left of the previous night's bottle, with the word "Doc" still visible where he'd scrawled it with a pencil. He poured himself a drink, considered playing solitaire, decided against it, and simply sat and stared at the patrons, seeing how many of them he could recognize from previous encounters or Wanted posters.

Then a dapper little man entered, looked around, saw Holliday, and promptly approached his table.

"Hi, Doc," said Henry Wiggins. "I heard you were back in town, but we just haven't connected."

"Hello, Henry," said Holliday. "I thought I'd see you over at Tom's or Ned's place, or aren't you working for them any longer?"

"Oh, I'm still with them. I gave up traveling around selling their inventions. They're doing so well that now I run a team of half a dozen salesmen from St. Louis to California."

"Sell enough metal chippies and you might put real women right out of the oldest profession," remarked Holliday.

"They're awfully expensive," replied Wiggins. "These days mostly I sell protection."

"Protection?" repeated Holliday, frowning. "You mean like armed guards?"

Wiggins smiled and shook his head. "Like Tom and Ned have installed around their houses. You know, machines that let them know who's approaching, what they look like, if they're armed. Just about every bank has ordered at least one. So have a bunch of stores, and even some rich ranchers."

"I hope you're getting rich yourself," said Holliday.

"I was, but then Matilda left me, and I don't want the kids to grow up poor, so I give most of it to her."

"*Left* you?" repeated Holliday. "I've known you for three or four years, and I don't recall her ever being *with* you."

"That never bothered her much," said Wiggins. "It was when . . . ah . . . well, when . . ."

"When she found out you were testing the merchandise?" suggested Holliday.

Wiggins nodded. "Damn it, it gets lonely being on the road for months on end."

"Not like being home alone with a pack of kids for months on end, right," said Holliday wryly.

"Whose side are you on, Doc?" said Wiggins irritably.

"Mine."

"Ah, what the hell, why am I telling you my problems?"

"Here," said Holliday, shoving the bottle toward him. "Have a drink or two and they won't seem so major."

"Thanks," said Wiggins. "I think I will." He raised the bottle to his lips and took a long swallow, then made a face. "Man, that stuff'll burn a hole in your throat!"

"I've tasted better," agreed Holliday. "But never in the Oriental."

"How have you been, Doc?" said Wiggins, pushing the bottle back to Holliday's side of the table. "I don't mean any insult, but I've seen you looking better. You seem kind of pale."

"I just had dinner," said Holliday. "Food doesn't agree with me these days."

"You're kidding, right?"

Holliday merely stared at him.

"Okay, you're not kidding. Is there anything I can do?"

"Don't offer me a cigar or a sandwich and we'll be fine," said Holliday, and this time Wiggins chuckled.

"So what are you doing back in Tombstone?" he asked. "Last I heard, you were planning to live out your life in the mountains up in Colorado."

"I plan to go back there in a couple of days," answered Holliday. "Though for the life of me I don't know why."

"I thought there was this sanitarium that could cure you . . ."

"*Nothing* can cure me. But they can make dying minimally less objectionable." Holliday shook his head in wonderment. "I'll never know why they put a facility for consumptives up in the goddamned mountains, where the birds find it easier to walk and even the spiders have trouble breathing."

"So stay here," said Wiggins.

"You see any sanitariums around here?" asked Holliday with a sardonic smile. "All Tombstone's got are abandoned silver mines and unabandoned cemeteries."

"Okay, I'll ask again. Given all that you said, why *are* you here?"

"I don't think you'd believe me if I told you," replied Holliday.

"You'll never know until you try."

Holliday sighed. "I'm helping a young man from back East. Possibly."

"Possibly?" repeated Wiggins.

"I could be helping an old Indian from out West," said Holliday. "Or it could be that nothing will help either of them."

"I don't understand."

"It gets complicated. If everything works, the young man will become a hero, or maybe even a king, and if it doesn't, we'll bury what's left of him, which probably won't come to ten pounds, somewhere in the Arizona Territory."

"You're not being very informative, Doc."

"You noticed."

"So who is this young man?"

"You ever hear of Theodore Roosevelt?" asked Holliday.

Wiggins shook his head. "No, I can't say that I have."

"Well, if he survives the next few weeks, you will."

"How about the old Indian you mentioned."

"You've heard of *him*," replied Holliday with a smile.

"I haven't heard of a lot of them, not really," answered Wiggins. "Victorio, Sitting Bull, Crazy Horse, Geronimo, Hook Nose, maybe half a dozen others."

"Makes no difference," said Holliday. "It'll work or it won't, and either way I plan to go back to Colorado and die in peace, or at least less discomfort."

"How soon are you leaving?"

Holliday shrugged. "A couple of days. Maybe sooner if I win big tonight, maybe an extra day or two if I don't."

"You still living with Kate?"

A rueful smile crossed Holliday's face. "We've parted company." A pause. "For the fourth time." Another pause, and another smile. "Possibly the fifth."

"I don't know why the two of you don't get married."

"You mean, like you?" said Holliday with an amused chuckle.

"I'm a bad example."

"It's all right, Henry. I'm a worse one."

"Didn't you tell me once that she broke you out of jail?"

"True," said Holliday. "But two weeks later she took a shot at me. She was a good whore, and a better madam, and she'd make a great bodyguard . . . but I think she'd have as many shortcomings as a wife as I'd have as a husband."

"Okay," said Wiggins with a sigh. "It's none of my business anyway."

"Have another drink," said Holliday, pushing the bottle to him again.

"Anyway, I'm glad I got a chance to see you before you leave again," said Wiggins, taking a small swallow, making a face, and handing the bottle back. "You've always treated me well—and if it wasn't for you I'd never have met Ned and Tom."

"Yeah, you'd probably be a happily married man working in a civilized town," said Holliday. "I'll take full credit for that."

"Damn it, Doc, you have a way of turning everything anyone says," complained Wiggins.

"The benefits of a classical education and a pending death," replied Holliday. He looked at the swinging doors at the front of the saloon. "Speak of the devil and in he strides, spectacles and all."

"I've never seen him before," said Wiggins, turning to see who had entered. "Is this the young man you mentioned?"

Holliday nodded, then waved to catch Roosevelt's attention. "Over here!"

"Look at those buckskins and that fringe," said Wiggins with a smile. "It must have cost him a month's pay. No question that he's from back East. I've been reading dime novels for years, and that's what they think we wear."

Roosevelt approached the table.

"Theodore, I'd like you to meet a friend of mine."

Wiggins got to his feet and extended his hand. "Henry Wiggins."

"Theodore Roosevelt," replied Roosevelt. He turned to Holliday, "Mind if I sit down?"

"Of course not," said Holliday, and Roosevelt and Wiggins both seated themselves. "How'd it go?"

"He was about as useful as Tom and Ned," answered Roosevelt grimly. "It's all guesswork until it happens, at which point it may very well be too late."

"You think he's holding anything back?"

Roosevelt shook his head. "Hell, he *sent* for me. Why would he do that and then conceal information or lie to me?"

"I can't help but notice you're being vague," said Wiggins. "I can leave if you wish."

"No, stay here, Henry," said Roosevelt. "I'm all through being vague. The subject is closed, and we can talk about anything you wish."

"Doc tells me you're from back East," said Wiggins. "How far east?"

"About as far as possible," replied Roosevelt with a smile. "New York City."

"It is as big as they say?"

"In terms of area, no. You could fit a few dozen New York Cities into the Territory here and never notice any land was missing. But in terms of population, it's crowded east to west, north to south, and top to bottom."

Wiggins frowned. "Top to bottom?" he repeated.

"The island of Manhattan is only maybe twelve or thirteen miles long and a couple of miles across," said Roosevelt. "So when they ran out of room on the ground, they started building *up*. They've got buildings that are seven and eight stories high."

"And people *live* in them?" asked Wiggins.

Roosevelt nodded his head.

"What do *you* do there? Work in some store?"

"Right at the moment, I don't do anything there. I live on a ranch in the Dakota Badlands."

"I thought—"

"I *did* live in New York State until a few months ago," said Roosevelt. "I had a job with the government."

Holliday chuckled. "I love the way you describe it." He turned to

Wiggins. "He was one of the three or four men who ran the damned state."

"It doesn't matter," said Roosevelt with a shrug. "It's history."

"Survive the next month or two and I have a feeling you'll make your share of history," said Holliday. Suddenly he was seized by a coughing fit. "Of course," he continued, taking a bloody handkerchief from his mouth, "I won't be around to see it or read about it."

"Maybe you'd better consider going back to Denver," suggested Roosevelt.

"Leadville," Holliday corrected him. "And I plan to do just that in a day or two."

"Good," said Roosevelt, nodding his approval.

"I hate to leave you without any help."

"I've got Tom and Ned," answered Roosevelt.

"I meant frontline help."

"I've got Bat."

Holliday shook his head. "What Geronimo did to him the last time he was out here in Tombstone isn't exactly a secret. You can bet some other medicine man will remember it."

"It's not Bat's battle anyway," said Roosevelt.

Holliday was about to reply when there was a commotion at the bar. Finally a tall, deeply tanned man walked over to the table and stood in front of Roosevelt.

"You can settle a bet for us, Four-Eyes," he said. "I say you're a dandy from back East, and my friends say that no, you just stole that outfit from some other dandy."

Roosevelt got to his feet. "I have a name," he said. "And it's Theodore, not Four-Eyes."

"It's Four-Eyes to me, you Eastern creampuff," said the man.

Roosevelt took off his glasses, folded them, and handed them to

Wiggins. Then he swung a roundhouse right that knocked the man sprawling. "How may eyes do you see now?"

The man went for his gun, but Holliday was faster, and was pointing his own pistol between the man's eyes before he could pull his gun out of his holster.

"Take it out, real gently," said Holliday, "and hand it to me. You can have it back after the bloodletting's over."

The man glared at Holliday, slowly removed his gun, and handed it to Holliday, butt first.

"Good luck," said Holliday. "And may God have mercy on your soul."

The man got to his feet and charged at the smaller Roosevelt, who ducked under his outstretched arms and delivered two quick blows to the stomach. The man growled a curse, spun around, and raced at Roosevelt again. This time he got a broken nose for his efforts.

The one-sided fight went on for another five minutes. Roosevelt offered to end it three different times, but the man, his face a bloody mess, refused. Finally he uttered one final bellow and made one final attempt to connect to Roosevelt, who blocked one punch, ducked another, and delivered a haymaker to the man's jaw. He dropped like a stone.

"Anyone want to claim this trash?" asked Holliday.

There was no response, and Roosevelt dropped to one knee and began examining the damage he'd done to his opponent's face.

"Henry, get me a wet rag from the bar, will you, please?" said Roosevelt.

"He'd have been happy to let you lie on the floor 'til Doomsday," remarked Holliday.

"I'm responsible for my actions, not his," said Roosevelt. Wiggins returned with the towel, and Roosevelt began cleaning away some of the blood.

The man awoke, and Roosevelt spoke to him soothingly, instructing him to lie still until he finished getting rid of the blood. Finally he helped the man to his feet.

"I'm willing to admit when I been beat," said the man. "You got one helluva punch, Dandy."

"Thank you," said Roosevelt. "How are you? Nothing broken?"

"Maybe my nose. Nothing important."

"What's your name?"

"Luke," said the man. "Luke Sloan."

"And I'm Theodore. Let me buy you a drink."

Sloan looked at him as if he were crazy. "You sure?"

"I'm sure," said Roosevelt. "We had a disagreement. It's over." He took his glasses back from Wiggins. "I hope you don't mind if I wear my glasses."

"If they make you fight like that, maybe I'll buy a pair myself," said Sloan. Roosevelt threw back his head and laughed, Sloan joined him, and soon everyone at the bar was laughing as the tension faded away.

"I don't know what you're doing out here, Dandy—I mean, Theodore," said Sloan, "but me and my horse are at your service if you're looking for help. Maybe I ain't quite as rough as I thought," he said, "but against most people I can hold my own and then some."

"You're rough enough for me, Luke," said Roosevelt. "I just might have some use for a rough rider like you."

"I'll be around," said Sloan. "I better get over to the doc's—not *your* Doc—and get some ice for my nose before it swells up so much I can't breathe."

"I'll be in touch," replied Roosevelt, as Sloan walked out the door and he returned to his table.

"I will never understand you," said Holliday.

"Leave him on the floor and he'd be an enemy for life," replied Roosevelt. "Now he wants to ride with me." He paused and suddenly grinned. "Rough rider. I like the way it sounds."

14.

OLLIDAY CLIMBED THE STAIRS to his second-floor room at the Grand, unlocked the door, tossed his hat on the desk in the corner, unbuckled and untied his holster, hung it over the back of the desk chair, and was preparing to sit down on the bed when he saw the mouse in the corner of the room.

"You are not supposed to be here," he muttered, "but at least when I present your bullet-riddled body to the management you ought to be worth a discount."

He reached for his gun, but before his hand closed on it, the mouse was gone, and standing in its place was Geronimo.

"Don't you ever get tired of sneaking up on people this way?" complained Holliday. "Or is this your only party trick?"

"If they saw me, they would kill me," answered Geronimo. "You know that."

"Yeah, probably they would," agreed Holliday with a weary sigh. "Well, what is it? I was about to go to sleep."

"I spoke to Roosevelt."

"I hope that's not what this is about," said Holliday. "He told me about it."

"He is a brave man."

"And a soundly sleeping one," said Holliday. "Get to the point."

"He plans to face War Bonnet."

"I know. You told us that. You even gave us a hint of what he'd look like."

"He is not ready," continued Geronimo.

"Of course he's not ready," said Holliday irritably. "How do you get ready to face a magical giant?"

"By learning more about him."

"Fine. Let him go learn."

"He cannot. They will hide War Bonnet from him until they are ready to kill him."

"Okay, then," said Holliday. "*You're* the medicine man. You go learn and tell him."

"They have defenses against me."

"I'm sorry Roosevelt's not ready and you're no help," said Holliday, "but what do you expect *me* to do about it?"

"Face War Bonnet."

"*Me?*" said Holliday incredulously.

"Learn what you can, and if you survive, bring us the information."

"Shit!" muttered Holliday. "I'm sobering up."

Geronimo stood and stared at him silently.

"I thought this was your and Roosevelt's fight," continued Holliday.

"It is."

"Then what is this all about?"

"War Bonnet has been created to kill Roosevelt and me," said Geronimo.

"I know."

"Roosevelt and me," repeated Geronimo. "Not you."

Holliday frowned. "Are you saying I can kill him? Or it, or whatever the hell it is?"

Geronimo shook his head. "No, Holliday, You probably cannot kill him."

"Well, you'll forgive me if I don't like playing the sacrificial lamb. If you want to find out how fast he can tear someone apart, send Masterson or someone else."

"You do not understand," said Geronimo.

"Enlighten me."

"War Bonnet was created to kill Roosevelt and me. That is his sole purpose. His every thought is to kill us. His every defense is to protect himself against us. His every skill is a skill that is required for killing us." Geronimo paused and continued staring at Holliday. "He was not created to kill *you*."

"Well, now, I find that very interesting and almost worth being sober for," said Holliday. "Are you saying that anyone but you or Roosevelt can kill him?"

Geronimo shook his head. "No. He is a monster, created and powered by magic."

"Then what the fuck are you talking about?" demanded Holliday irritably.

"You have faced many men who were stronger that you, many who were better with their weapons, many who had no fear of you. Every man you ever faced was stronger and healthier than you. And yet you have always emerged alive and triumphant." He paused. "You do not have to kill War Bonnet. It is entirely possible that you cannot. But it is equally possible that he cannot or will not kill you, and when you return, you can report on everything you saw, everything you experienced."

"He's twenty feet high and made of fire," said Holliday. "What do you mean, he can't kill me?"

"I said he *might* be unable to kill you," replied Geronimo. "Possibly he is constructed only to kill myself and Roosevelt. Possibly he recognizes no other enemy."

"And possibly he likes killing, no matter who," said Holliday.

"That is true," agreed Geronimo.

"Then why in the world should I risk my life, and probably piss it away, just to get you some information?"

"Your remaining life is of very short duration," began Geronimo.

"That's not a very telling argument," answered Holliday.

"If you die, you will suffer no more than you will suffer at your lodge in the mountains of Colorado," continued Geronimo. "And if you live, I can foresee you having two very fortunate nights at the place you call the Oriental."

"I'll win big?" said Holliday. "How much?"

Geronimo merely shrugged.

"Well, what the hell, however much or little, it beats losing. And I don't suppose getting torn apart or set on fire is any worse than spending a final month or two gasping for air and not quite getting it." Holliday grimaced, then sighed. "Okay, I'm your huckleberry."

"It is agreed, then."

"Uh . . . before you go, where do I find War Bonnet?"

"He will not exist, not in a form that is meaningful to you, for three more days," answered Geronimo. "When that time comes, I will instruct you where to find him."

"You might also instruct me about what hurts him, or keeps him at bay."

"If I knew that, I would not be sending you."

"How comforting," said Holliday, but even as the words left his mouth he realized he was speaking to an empty room.

15.

OLLIDAY APPROACHED EDISON'S HOUSE. Long before he reached the door, it swung open and Edison's voice welcomed him in. He entered, walked into the living room, and waited for Edison to come out of his lab and greet him.

"How are you, Doc?"

"I've been better," replied Holliday. A wry smile. "Of course, that was a long time ago."

"What can I do for you?" asked Edison.

"Plenty. But before we start talking, call Ned in here. No sense repeating it all to him."

Edison frowned, but went back to his lab and summoned Buntline on the primitive communication system he'd installed between the two houses. Buntline entered the living room a moment later, chewing on a sandwich and carrying a beer.

"Hi, Doc," he said. "Can I get you anything?"

"Plenty," said Holliday. "But not to eat."

"Have a seat, Ned," said Edison. "I think Doc's got something important to tell us."

"Important to me, anyway," said Holliday.

Both men sat at opposite ends of a couch and stared at him expectantly.

"I've just had a visit from Geronimo," began Holliday.

"What did he want?"

"He wants me to face War Bonnet."

"*What?*" shouted Buntline. "He'd better make up his damned mind about who this creature is being created to kill."

"Nothing's changed," said Holliday. "War Bonnet has been or is being created for the sole purpose of killing Roosevelt and Geronimo."

"Then I don't understand," growled Buntline.

"I think I'm beginning to," said Edison, leaning forward.

"Good!" said Buntline. "Then one of you two can explain it to me."

"Let me take a guess," said Edison.

"Go right ahead," replied Holliday.

"He wants you to face War Bonnet because War Bonnet was not created with you in mind. At the most extreme, and this probably isn't the case, he is immune only to Theodore's bullets and blows, and Geronimo's spells, and at the same time, he is deadly only in combat against Theodore or Geronimo." He paused and looked at Holliday. "Am I close?"

"You're close. He doesn't guarantee that *anyone* is safe facing War Bonnet, but he's sure that I'll be safer than him or Roosevelt."

"It's possible," agreed Edison.

"I still cut and I still bleed," said Holliday. "How the hell safe can I be?"

"Is Geronimo protecting you with some kind of spell?" asked Buntline.

"He didn't say so," responded Holliday. "Besides, I have to think if there's one thing his spells are useless against, it's War Bonnet."

"So . . . you're off to face War Bonnet, and you want . . . what?" asked Buntline. "Weapons? Protection?"

"Maybe a train back East," replied Holliday with a wry smile.

"I'm being serious, Doc," said Buntline. "Have you made up your mind to face him?"

"Geronimo's made up *his* mind," said Holliday. "I suppose it comes to the same thing."

"Where is he?"

"Geronimo?"

Buntline shook his head. "No, War Bonnet?"

"Who the hell knows? I assume Geronimo will be more than happy to direct me." He sighed deeply. "I'd like to survive it. I'm not afraid to die—in fact, I've been busy doing it for years—but I hate to do it at the hand of a monster that isn't even interested in me."

"We'll do what we can to protect you," said Edison. "Is there anything new you can tell us, anything you can add to what we already know?"

"Or think we know," added Buntline, finally finishing his sandwich.

"Not much," said Holliday. "It's all guesswork. All Geronimo knows is that War Bonnet can kill him and Roosevelt for sure, but he can only kill the rest of the world maybe."

"Well, let's put our heads together, figure out what *won't* work, and concentrate on what's left," said Edison.

Holliday frowned. "I don't follow you."

"War Bonnet was made to face Geronimo and Theodore, right?" said Edison. "So, if he's the threat Geronimo thinks he is, and he's a magical being, he must be immune to anything those two can throw at him."

"Of course, being immune to magic is academic," said Buntline. "But it makes sense that he's immune to that rifle Theodore favors."

"In fact, War Bonnet could be immune to *all* bullets and shells," said Edison. "I know Theodore doesn't have much confidence in his six-gun, he's said as much to me, but the medicine men don't know that, and could assume he'll come with pistols blazing."

"Which brings up an interesting question," said Buntline. "Is he immune to *all* bullets, or just those fired by Roosevelt?"

"It's a possibility," replied Edison. "But not one Doc will want to bet his life on."

"So what weapons can we provide that neither Theodore nor Geronimo will ever use?" said Buntline.

"Well, there's acid, of course," said Edison. "But what if he swipes at it with his hand? If it's made of flame, it may not have any substance at all. Acid might go through it like water. If there *is* some substance, he still may not feel any pain, and could spill it all over Doc."

"We can attach it to an arrow and have Doc fire it from a safe distance," replied Buntline.

Holliday shook his head. "Won't work. I haven't had the strength to pull a bow back far enough to shoot an arrow home since I was a teenager."

The two older men fell silent for a moment, and then Buntline looked up. "I've got it!" he exclaimed.

"What?" asked Holliday.

"Nitroglycerin!" said Buntline, excited. "We'll blow that son of a bitch all the way back to wherever he came from." Edison seemed to be considering it, and Buntline continued: "Tom, is there a way to coat Doc's bullets with it so they explode when they hit War Bonnet?"

Edison shook his head. "Coat his bullets and they'll explode inside his gun when he pulls the trigger."

"Damn!" said Buntline. "I thought I had something there."

"Maybe you do," replied Edison. "But it requires Doc to control where they meet." He turned to Holliday. "If you can choose the site, we can salt it with nitro containers so you can shoot them from a safe distance, hopefully when War Bonnet is standing right next to them."

"I've seen nitro kill men who took a bad step while they were carrying it to the mines outside Leadville," replied Holliday. "How the hell do I get it to wherever I'm going, riding a horse over rough terrain?"

"I can give you the constituent parts, and you will mix it carefully—*very* carefully—once you get to where you're going," answered Edison.

"I don't know," said Holliday dubiously. "If this War Bonnet is magical . . ."

"Didn't Geronimo say he was created to face only Roosevelt and Geronimo?" said Buntline. "It's possible that he's immune to anything they can use against him, but that you can use the very same things successfully."

"All right," conceded Holliday. "I don't know why I'm worried about dying fast. But just in case this doesn't work, I'd like some alternatives."

"How much time have we got?" asked Edison.

"Until Geronimo tells me that War Bonnet is here."

"We'll spend the rest of the day and night coming up with possible weapons," continued Edison, "but it's also essential that we give you some defenses."

"I suppose I could accept that."

"I can make you some incredibly strong armor, something that'll resist anything even a thirty-foot-tall giant has to offer," said Buntline. "But I doubt that you'd be able to lift it, let alone walk a step in it."

"You'd be surprised how much I can't lift," said Holliday dryly.

"I just thought of another potential weakness we'll have to address," said Buntline.

"Oh?"

Buntline nodded. "I assume you're not going to meet him at the O.K. Corral."

"A fair assumption," said Holliday, wondering what Buntline was getting at.

"So you'll meet him out in the desert."

"I'd assume so."

"So you ride twenty miles out of town to meet him, and he finds that either for reasons having to do with the conditions of his creation, or the defenses we've supplied you with, he can't hurt you. He hits you with all his might, and you don't feel it. He stabs you with a knife, and the blade never breaks the skin."

"I like it already," said Holliday.

"You won't," Buntline assured him.

"Okay, why not?"

"Because he kills your horse, empties your canteen, and goes back to wherever he came from. Doc, you can't walk a mile on a cool day with all the water in the world. How are you going to walk twenty miles back to town across a hot desert with nothing to drink?"

"Well, I liked it until then," replied Holliday.

"So," concluded Buntline, "it's not enough that we arm and protect you. We're going to have to protect your horse."

"Maybe he's not bright enough to think of that," said Holliday.

"Maybe he isn't," agreed Buntline. "But do you want to bet your life on it?"

"I don't want to seem ungrateful," said Holliday, "but nobody knows anything! Geronimo doesn't know, Roosevelt doesn't know, and you don't know—and I've been elected to face this thing and see how fast he can kill his enemies. I'm headed off to the Oriental for a drink."

"I can understand your frustration," said Edison.

"I doubt it," replied Holliday irritably as he got up and walked to the door. "*You* don't have to see how fast War Bonnet can kill you so Roosevelt and Geronimo can prepare for him."

"All right," said Edison, electing not to argue with him. "If we come up with something tonight, I'll send word to the Oriental, and if you're not there, we'll leave a message at the Grand's desk. Otherwise, come by tomorrow at noon and we'll go over what we've come up with."

"And if Geronimo calls me sooner?" said Holliday.

"Then stop by on your way out of town and we'll give you what we have."

Holliday seemed about to say something, thought better of it, and walked out into the street. He saw a jackrabbit lingering near the corner and stared at it.

"If I thought you were anything but what you look like, I'd blow your damned head off," he said, and turned and walked to the Oriental.

He'd calmed down by the time he arrived, short of breath and coughing more blood. Henry Wiggins was there and waved him over to his table.

"Hi, Doc," he said. "You're here early, aren't you?"

"Don't *you* start on me, Henry," growled Holliday.

"Me?" asked Wiggins, surprised. "What did I say?"

Holliday sighed deeply. "Nothing, Henry. It's just been that kind of a day." He signaled for his bottle. "Tomorrow will probably be even worse."

The bartender showed up with the bottle and a glass, and Holliday promptly filled it to the top.

"By the way, I like your friend Roosevelt," offered Wiggins.

"Most people do," said Holliday. "That's his job."

"His job?" repeated Wiggins.

"Making people like him. He's a politician."

"He's a lot more than that," said Wiggins.

"Oh?"

"I had lunch with him at the Grand. He's a bird expert—"

"Ornithologist," Holliday corrected him.

"And a taxidermist, and an author, and a boxer, and no end of things. Did you know that he's writing a series of books on the taming of the West? I imagine you'll be one of the stars."

"Or one of the villains."

"Don't be silly, Doc. He's your friend."

"He's everyone's friend. That's what politicians do and are."

"Then he's not destined to be much of a politician," said Wiggins. "I think there are a lot of things that young man wouldn't do to get elected, and lying is one of them."

Holliday suddenly stared at the ceiling. "Let's see if he lives long enough to run for office again."

"Is someone after him?" asked Wiggins.

"You never know."

"What are you staring at, Doc?"

"There's a bat up there."

"So what? There are bats in all the rafters in town."

"Yeah," said Holliday, "but this one's staring at me, and it's broad daylight."

"That *is* unusual, isn't it?" said Wiggins.

Holliday stood up. "Henry, I have to leave. The bottle's yours."

"Are you okay, Doc?" asked Wiggins.

"So far," replied Holliday, and then added: "But it's early yet."

He knew he wouldn't be approached in the street, so he walked around the building and went into the alley behind it. The bat fluttered out through a door a moment later, and a few seconds after that Holliday was staring into Geronimo's eyes.

"He walks, he breathes," said Geronimo.

"When does he get here?"

"He comes from the land of the Tsistsistas."

Holliday frowned. "The Tsistsistas?" he repeated.

"You call them the Cheyenne."

"It makes sense," said Holliday. "After all, you killed Hook Nose. When does he get here?"

"It takes him no time to get from there to here."

"He's here now?"

"He is between Tombstone and my southern lodge, waiting for Roosevelt or myself to ride out and challenge him."

"So instead you're sending the sacrificial lamb," said Holliday, unable to keep the annoyance out of his voice.

"Remember: there is a reward."

"I hope I can collect it in hell," said Holliday.

16.

HOLLIDAY HATED HORSES. He thought he'd hated them all his life, back to when he was growing up in Georgia, and horses meant cavalry, and cavalry meant more Union soldiers. He wasn't sure about that, but he knew he'd hated them ever since he'd come out West and had to start riding them.

He knew Masterson loved horse racing, and went into rhapsodies over Hindoo and Aristides and some of the other equine champions, but he had no use for them, and only a grudging use for saddle horses. In his mind, horses were good for one thing: pulling wagons, surries, coaches, anything with four wheels.

So of course he was mounted on a bay gelding, heading out across the desert, an ugly, barren land that everyone he knew from Wyatt Earp to Theodore Roosevelt found beautiful.

"I hope to hell you've pointed me in the right direction," he muttered, but there was no answer.

He pulled his canteen off the saddle horn where it had been hanging, opened it, and took a swig of whiskey. Not bad, he decided;

maybe the barley that went into this had been fertilized by Hindoo. Probably not by John L. Sullivan, though he was such a drunk that you could never be entirely sure.

"Getting dark," he said. "Am I going to be able to see him?"

There was no answer.

"Thanks a lot," said Holliday.

He wished that he weren't riding alone, that he had someone he could count on riding shotgun for him. Wyatt would have been good at it.

Of course, the best man for the job would have been Johnny Ringo. Ringo was dead, to be sure, but that hadn't stopped the medicine men from reviving him and sending him out to kill Holliday and Edison almost three years ago. He was a drunkard with a foul temper, but even as a zombie he'd been one hell of a killer—and more to the point, Holliday had actually enjoyed his company. They were the only two college-educated shootists in the West, and there was no one else in his chosen profession that he could discuss philosophy and the classics with. They'd hit it off, and it wasn't bitterness or hatred that led them to their final confrontation. It was Fate. Not only had the other side enlisted his services, but both men craved competition at the highest level, and that meant that under any circumstances they would eventually have faced each other in the street. Of course, he had an edge, the Buntline Special that Tom and Ned had created for him—but then Ringo had an edge too; after all, he was *already* dead.

He wished he'd stopped by Edison's and Buntline's connected houses and picked up something, *anything*, with which to face War Bonnet. But Geronimo had been adamant: this was where he would be at such-and-so a moment, and if Holliday wasn't there to meet him, he'd go into town, ripping it apart in his efforts to find Roosevelt and killing dozens of innocent people in the process.

Now, Holliday wasn't convinced that there were a dozen men in Tombstone who were innocent of anything, and he didn't really give a damn if War Bonnet wiped them all out—well, except for Tom, Ned, and Roosevelt, and maybe that fawning Wiggins—but he'd consented to go, not out of any noble or heroic notions, but simply because he wanted to collect Geronimo's reward if he actually survived, and because a quick death didn't seem any worse to him than the slow, debilitating, painful one he was facing.

He estimated that he was five miles out of town, and three miles from anything or anyone remotely alive. He keep looking for hawks, eagles, wrens, prairie dogs, rabbits, *anything* that might be Geronimo or one of his braves keeping watch on him, but he saw absolutely nothing.

"It's mighty empty and more than a little foreboding out here," he muttered to his horse. "I'd sing if I knew how to, and if I didn't have to take any deep breaths."

The horse grunted, as if pleased to know that his rider was neither asleep nor dead.

Holliday kept scanning the horizon, looking for a sign of War Bonnet or anything else, but it remained barren and empty, and he realized that he probably wouldn't see or hear a magical creature's approach anyway.

He pulled the Derringer out of his lapel pocket, checked it for the third time since he'd ridden out from town, and replaced it. He drew his six-gun to make sure there were no obstructions—there had never been any, but he was a careful man—and slid it back into his holster. He knew that young guns practiced their draws all the time, as if fast were more important than accurate, or as if either meant more than cold, emotionless efficiency. He'd been outdrawn many times, and yet except for a minor wound at the O.K. Corral, he'd never been hit in any of his gunfights.

"I hope you're listening," he said aloud, "because I'm going to give it just ten more minutes, and then I'm turning around and heading back to town. He's got enough advantages already; there's no sense facing him in the dark."

There was no answer.

He looked down at the back of his horse's neck, which was obscured by a long black mane.

"I don't suppose it's *you*, is it?" he said.

The horse continued walking, and didn't reply.

And then, suddenly, the horse stopped, and Holliday could feel it tense beneath him, because standing there some fifty yards away from him was War Bonnet. Not Geronimo's wavy, semitranslucent apparition, but a real—well, surreal—flesh-and-blood creature, his hands afire, the blaze in his eyes matching them.

"You're bigger than he said," said Holliday, some of the tension actually leaving him now that he was finally confronting the huge Indian.

"What does Goyathlay know?" said War Bonnet contemptuously in a harsh, exceptionally deep voice. "When I finish with him and the one who hides his eyes behind glass, they will be less than the dust on the ground."

"That's what we have to talk about," said Holliday, trying to steady his mount.

"We know you, Holliday," said War Bonnet. "You are a dying drunkard. We have nothing to say to you."

"We?" repeated Holliday, frowning. "All I see is one big bastard who's going to jar the ground when he falls."

"We made this warrior," was the reply. "We can address you through him. He obeys our will."

"And just who the hell are you?"

"We are the medicine men of all the assembled tribes except the Apache," replied War Bonnet expressionlessly. "We are Dull Knife of the Cheyenne, Spotted Elk of the Lakota, Cougar Slayer of the Arapaho, Tall Wolf of—"

"You're not going to bore me until sunrise with this, are you?" interrupted Holliday.

"No," came the reply, and now War Bonnet's face was animated again. "I am going to kill you."

"I and not we?" asked Holliday. "Make up your mind, or don't you have one?"

War Bonnet advanced, and Holliday drew his gun and fired three times, placing a bullet in each of the monstrous Indian's eyes and one in his forehead. They didn't bounce off, but instead seemed to be absorbed into his massive head, doing no damage. War Bonnet roared his rage and continued approaching.

"Thanks for all your fucking help," muttered Holliday under his breath as he prepared to be torn limb from limb by the approaching behemoth.

"Your skin will shrivel and your bones will melt, Holliday," roared War Bonnet, reaching out to him. "You will live only a few seconds, but they will be the most agonizing seconds any man has ever suffered."

Holliday fired three more shots into War Bonnet's chest, then reached for the pistol in his lapel as the monster reached out a blazing hand for him.

Holliday tensed, and prepared to suffer exactly as War Bonnet had predicted, but instead the insubstantial blazing fingers passed right through him.

"Shit!" said Holliday. "They're not even warm!"

War Bonnet cursed, beat his chest like a bull gorilla, and tried once again to grab Holliday. He terrified the horse, who started bucking and squealing, forcing Holliday to hold on to the saddle horn with both hands, but the monster was completely unable to make physical contact with him.

Finally he backed off, glaring at Holliday, who used the opportunity to dismount before he was thrown off.

"Well, Fred, Joe, Tom and Johnny, and whoever else is in there, what now?" he said, starting to reload his gun as the horse calmed down.

War Bonnet wasn't done yet. He lifted his massive foot high and brought it down on Holliday's head—and this time, instead of passing through him, the foot bounced off, and Holliday could tell from his face that he was in pain.

"I take it all back," he whispered. "You were right."

War Bonnet spent the next five minutes alternately trying to burn, grab, hit, and kick Holliday, but to no avail. Then he spotted a massive rock, weighing perhaps a thousand pounds, on the ground a few yards away. He walked over to it, lifted it with ease, held it aloft, and approached Holliday, who eyed him very nervously, since unlike War Bonnet himself, the rock was not magical and was solid and real.

But as War Bonnet drew closer, he began straining, the veins stood out on his neck, and his arms started trembling. Finally he could walk no farther but stopped and dropped the rock onto the ground, where it landed with an audible thud.

"Are you getting tired of this yet?" asked Holliday.

War Bonnet glared at him, and lifted the rock again. Once more it was apparent that he could barely hold it aloft, and Holliday fired two quick shots into him to see if his weakness had spread to his invulnerability, but they had no more effect than before. Then the huge Indian turned his back to Holliday, and Holliday could see that he was no longer straining. With a scream of rage, War Bonnet hurled the massive rock some fifty yards away.

"Do not smile at me, Holliday!" roared War Bonnet, turning back to him.

"Oh, call me Doc, now that we're not going to be killing each other," said Holliday, still smiling.

"Your days are numbered," vowed War Bonnet.

"I've heard *that* before," said Holliday. "Usually it's come from men who could at least draw blood."

"It is true that I cannot kill you," said War Bonnet in his deep, thunderous voice. "I have been created for one purpose, and one purpose only: to kill the invader Roosevelt and the turncoat Goyathlay."

"I wish you the same luck with them that you had with me," said Holliday.

"It is true that *I* cannot kill you," repeated War Bonnet. "But there is one who can, and he shall be my surrogate."

"You know words like 'surrogate'?" said Holliday. "I'm impressed. Now why don't you shamble off to whatever hell you came from and forget about all this?"

"How little you know," said War Bonnet. "You, Roosevelt, and Goyathlay are all doomed, corpses who do not yet know you are dead."

"Are you guys inside this clown going to send another ugly creature here to scare me to death?" asked Holliday.

Suddenly War Bonnet vanished. Holliday looked around, but knew that something that big couldn't hide on this barren, featureless landscape. He waited a moment, then walked to the side of his horse, pulled down his canteen, and had two quick swallows of whiskey.

And as quickly as he vanished, War Bonnet returned, standing exactly where he had been.

"Nice trick," said Holliday. "Did you run home to get some advice?"

"No, walking corpse. I went to the land you call Texas."

"Waste of time," said Holliday. "They don't scare any easier than I do."

"There is a jail there. After I reached an agreement with an inmate, I tore his cell apart and freed him."

Holliday stared at him, waiting for him to finish his story.

"There is a man who is even a greater killer than you," continued War Bonnet.

Holliday finally saw where the tale was going, and nodded his head. "You broke John Wesley Hardin out of jail."

"In exchange for his promise to hunt you down and kill you."

"You might be disappointed."

"You think you and the thing that was once Johnny Ringo were the greatest killers of all, but John Wesley Hardin has killed more than both of you put together."

"I'll make you a promise," said Holliday.

"Your promise to leave and not involve yourself is too late," said War Bonnet.

Holliday shook his head. "That wasn't what I had in mind."

"What is your promise?" demanded War Bonnet.

"I promise that after I kill Hardin and Roosevelt kills you, we'll bury you side by side."

"This is Hardin—the greatest killer ever to walk across this land," said War Bonnet. "And you are a dying man who cannot walk fifty paces without gasping for breath."

"Nevertheless."

"You are a fool, Holliday. If you run now, perhaps you will die before he finds you, for you will surely die the day he *does* find you."

"Remember what I said," replied Holliday. "Side by side."

War Bonnet glared at him furiously, but said nothing.

"It won't be so bad," continued Holliday. "You're not a Christian, so you won't care that we don't put a cross on your grave. And once

Geronimo finds all the medicine men who are pulling your puppet strings, we'll bury them opposite Hardin on the other side of you."

War Bonnet was silent for a few seconds. Then he began to hum, a very low, very soft sound that became louder and louder until Holliday clapped his hands over his ears. The sound morphed into a scream, louder and louder still, until Holliday was sure it could be heard all the way back to his ancestral home in Georgia.

And then, suddenly, both the scream and War Bonnet himself vanished.

Holliday waited five minutes to make sure he wasn't coming back, then climbed onto his horse, noticed that the animal was thoroughly lathered with sweat and still tense and nervous, and began riding slowly back to Tombstone.

"John Wesley Hardin," he muttered. "Why couldn't it have been something easier, like all fifty medicine men at once?"

He continued riding, and every half mile or so he'd take another sip from his canteen, close it, look off into the distance in the direction he thought Texas lay, and say, grimacing, "John Wesley Hardin. Shit!"

He was still repeating it when he finally rode back into town.

17.

IT WAS TEN O'CLOCK AT NIGHT when Holliday entered Tombstone. He considered waking Edison and Buntline, decided not to, and continued riding. He returned his horse to the stable where he'd rented it, walked to the Grand, asked for Roosevelt at the front desk and was told he'd gone to bed, and stopped by the bar for a drink.

"I'm surprised to see you here this early, Doc," said the bartender. "Usually you shut down the Oriental and then find another game or two before you come back here."

"I'm just giving the cards one night to recover," said Holliday.

"I'm sure some of the other gamblers appreciate it," said the bartender with a smile.

"They'd better," said Holliday. "I'll be back tomorrow with a vengeance." He was silent for a moment. "Tell me, did John Wesley Hardin ever visit Tombstone—before he was jailed, I mean?"

"I don't think Tombstone even existed when they put him away, Doc," said the bartender. "He's been gone a long while."

"Just curious," said Holliday.

"You ever meet him?"

Holliday shook his head. "No, never had that pleasure."

"I gather it wasn't all that much of a pleasure for something like forty-five men," said the bartender with a grin.

"Forty-two," Holliday corrected him. "At least, that's what they were able to prove in court."

"Word has it that he's become a lawyer."

"That's what I hear," said Holliday. "No reason why not. There's not much else to do in jail."

"It means if he ever gets out, he can prosecute and defend himself," said the bartender, laughing at his own comment.

"Anything's possible," agreed Holliday.

"Not getting out," said the bartender. "If he lives three hundred more years, he'll still be serving time."

"Let's hope you're right," said Holliday without smiling.

He finished his drink, got to his feet, stopped by the desk long enough to leave a note for Roosevelt to meet him at Edison's house at noon the next day, and went up to his room, where he had another coughing fit. When it had passed, he looked out the window to see if any of the birds or bats looked like an Apache in disguise, decided they looked like birds and bats, and went to sleep.

There was blood all over his pillow when he awoke, which was becoming a regular occurrence these days. Sometime during the night, while he was sleeping, he'd had another coughing seizure, but not bad enough to bring him to instant wakefulness, and he'd coughed up blood on the pillow and bed linens.

He got up, climbed into his clothes, and left a quarter on the pillow to pay for it, for the blood had seeped through and he knew they wouldn't use it again. Then he descended the stairs to the main floor. He pulled his watch out, checked the time, decided he could either have breakfast or get a shave, decided that he couldn't take the sight or smell of food this early in the day, and opted for the shave.

"Morning, Doc," said the barber with a big smile.

"What's causing that shit-eating grin?" asked Holliday as he seated himself in the chair.

"Johnny Behan," answered the barber. "You put a real scare into him, so he showed up at nine this morning for a shave, because he knows you sleep until early afternoon." A pause. "Matter of fact, you're a little early today."

"I thought maybe you'd like a tooth pulled," answered Holliday, leaning back and closing his eyes.

"I might, if I had any left," said the barber. "These things in my mouth were all the tusks of an elephant or hippo or something half a world away."

"Or a cow from the next town," replied Holliday.

"Makes no difference to me, as long as I can bite into a steak over at Sarah's Restaurant. You been there since you got back to town?"

"Not yet."

"You ought to go," urged the barber. "Not only does she make one hell of a steak, but she's got photos of you and the Earps and the O.K. Corral plastered all over the wall. I'll bet she'd give you a couple of free meals if she could advertise that you've eaten there."

"I'll look into it," promised Holliday, though he knew he wouldn't.

"Okay," said the barber, spreading the lather and producing a razor. "Don't laugh or stick your tongue out."

"I'll try not to," said Holliday.

Five minutes later he was clean-shaven except for his mustache. He paid the barber, told him to tell Behan that now that he knew Behan's schedule he was thinking of showing up at nine o'clock in the morning for his shave, though of course he had no more intention of getting up early than of eating at Sarah's, and then he was out the door and on his way to Edison's house.

He arrived a couple of minutes later, walked up to the door, and waited for it to recognize him and swing open. Then he walked into the living room, where Edison, Buntline, and Roosevelt were all waiting for him.

"I see you survived," said Edison. "Of course, we knew you had, because of the message you left for Theodore. Can I get you something to eat or drink?"

"Maybe later," said Holliday. "We have things to talk about first." He looked around the room.

"Is something wrong?"

Holliday shook his head. "No, nothing. But Geronimo should be part of this. I was hoping he was busy being a bird or a cat, hanging around just outside the window."

Buntline got up and walked to the window, then shook his head. "Nope, there's nothing out there."

"What the hell, he was probably watching every minute of it last night."

"So tell us about it," said Buntline. "Did you learn anything?"

Holliday nodded. "A bit." He turned to Roosevelt. "I learned that he was created to kill Theodore Roosevelts. His eyes seek out Roosevelts, his hands are shaped to choke Roosevelts, his teeth are uniquely suited for biting off Rooseveltian ears, his—"

"Spare us your flights of fancy," interrupted Roosevelt. "What, exactly, happened?"

"He tried to kill me, and he couldn't, and I tried to kill him, and I couldn't," answered Holliday. "His skin is impervious to my bullets."

"Surely you're not impervious to his blows," said Roosevelt.

"Well, you know, that's the funny part," said Holliday. "It seems that I *am*, and so are Tom and Ned and anyone who isn't named Roosevelt or Geronimo."

"With size and muscles like that, he couldn't hurt you?" said an incredulous Roosevelt.

"He picked up a boulder," replied Holliday. "Damned thing must have weighed twice what a horse and wagon together would weigh. Picked it up like a feather—until he tried to throw it at me. Then it seemed so heavy that it was about to crush him, so he turned away, and was able to throw it farther than from here to the street. He can do anything with that size and strength, as long as it doesn't involve killing anyone besides you and Geronimo."

"What about these flaming hands of his?" asked Buntline. "Did he try to grab you with them?"

Holliday nodded. "Those flames are hot when he's thirty feet away, or twenty feet, or five feet—but the second he tries to touch me, they're as cool as the air and pass right through me."

"Interesting," said Edison.

Holliday turned to Roosevelt. "But they won't pass through *you*. They'll melt your bones inside your skin."

"I've been studying the medicine men's magic for almost four years now," said Edison, "and this is the first time I've heard of it being so selective, where it will work against just two people and no one else. I wonder if it's not a bluff, if he's incapable of doing anything except threatening them?"

"It's no bluff," said Holliday. "I told you: he picked up a boulder ten strong men couldn't lift, and threw it maybe a hundred feet."

"When I go up against him, I'd like you to come along," said Roosevelt. "Maybe you can spot something, something that makes sense or shows a weakness, that's different from last night."

"If I live long enough."

"The consumption getting worse again?" asked Buntline.

"No worse than usual," said Holliday. "But I've got another

problem since last night. When he couldn't harm me, he decided to find someone who could."

"I don't understand," said Buntline.

"He broke John Wesley Hardin out of jail."

"Even if that's true, why would he come after you?"

Holliday smiled. "It's a *quid pro quo*. Theodore can explain the term to you."

"I know the term," said Buntline irritably.

"Do you think he really set him free, or was it just bluster?" asked Roosevelt.

"He didn't strike me as the type who needs to bluster," said Holliday. "After all, why does he care if I come along with you? I can't hurt him, he can't hurt me." He frowned. "I suppose I shouldn't have taunted them."

"*Them?*" said Edison.

"Four, five, I don't know how many medicine men. They control him, and they spoke to me through him. It had to be their idea to free Hardin. War Bonnet doesn't think. He just kills, or tries to."

"Can Geronimo use that knowledge?" asked Buntline.

Roosevelt shook his head. "He knows who created War Bonnet, so it stands to reason he knows who controls him."

Buntline sighed deeply. "You know what puzzles me more than anything else? He confronted Doc just a few miles out of town. Why the hell didn't he just come the rest of the way and try to kill Theodore?"

"I think I can answer that," said Edison. "Doc's made it clear that the medicine men haven't just totally turned him loose, that they're controlling him. That's got to take a *lot* of energy, be it psychic or physical or whatever. I have a feeling that bringing him into existence for more than a few minutes drains them, and then he vanishes back to whatever limbo they store him in."

"It's a possibility," agreed Buntline. "So what's our next step?" He turned to Roosevelt. "Even if he's fifteen feet high, even if he's got a blow like a horse's kick, I can create armor that'll protect you from that." He frowned. "But if he can also use magic, and those flaming hands of his make me think he can . . ." He sighed. "I just don't know. I can protect you against fire, of course . . . but eventually I can protect you against so many possibilities that you won't be able to move or breathe." He turned to Edison. "Tom?"

"It's so hard to tell without actually seeing him first," said Edison, frowning. "For example, I can design a weapon that will hurl an electric charge at him. We can rig a trap where he has to stand on a conductor to confront Theodore, and I can shoot enough voltage into that conductor to light the whole city—but will it work? I think it comes down to this: Is he alive as we understand life? I can design a weapon to use against any living thing—but what living thing has hands of flame, and is impervious to bullets?"

"So you have to see him first?" said Roosevelt.

"It would certainly help," replied Edison.

"Then you shall!" exclaimed Roosevelt, getting to his feet.

"What are you talking about?" demanded Holliday. "You lure him here, maybe he can't kill Tom and Ned, but he can destroy all their equipment and three years' worth of notes and documents."

"Not *here*," said Roosevelt excitedly. "*There!*"

"I'm afraid I don't follow you, Theodore," said Edison.

"There's one aspect to this whole business I haven't been comfortable about," said Roosevelt, starting to pace the floor.

"Only one?" asked Holliday with a sardonic smile.

"I don't like being on the defensive," said Roosevelt. "We know who the enemy is. Why sit back and wait for him to pick his time and place?"

"Doc was powerless against him," noted Buntline, "and I assure you that Tom and I will be even less formidable under similar circumstances."

"They won't be similar," said Roosevelt, still pacing. "You're not going to fight War Bonnet. We already know that's impossible. You just want to see him in action. Well, the one thing that can guarantee that action is my presence."

"Let me get this straight," said Edison, frowning. "You want the three of us—you, me, and Ned—to ride out into the desert and wait for him to attack you?"

Roosevelt grinned. "I'm not suicidal. No, if these medicine men spoke to Doc in concert, they probably got together to create War Bonnet and are still in the same place. Geronimo must know where."

"Even if he does," said Edison, "that's still a New Yorker and two noncombatants against this monster."

"Oh, we'll have more than that," Roosevelt assured him.

"Who?"

"I've already got one Rough Rider—Luke Sloan," was the answer. "Give me a week and I'll have a damned formidable team of them."

"Rough Rider?" repeated Buntline, frowning. "What the hell is a Rough Rider?"

"It's a man with special skills who pledges his loyalty to me," said Roosevelt. He turned to Holliday. "We can start by sending for your friend I've heard a lot about—Texas Pete . . ."

"Jack," Holliday corrected him. "Texas Jack Vermillion."

"Would he come?" asked Edison.

"He came on Wyatt's Vendetta Ride," answered Holliday. "Wild horses couldn't keep him from something like this."

"I'll start recruiting as soon as we're done here," said Roosevelt enthusiastically. "I'll wager I'll have a handpicked dozen within three days."

"And you'll be the Roughest Rider of all?" suggested Holliday.

"Why not?" responded Roosevelt with a grin.

18.

ROOSEVELT AND HOLLIDAY were sitting at a table in the Oriental. Holliday had his omnipresent bottle in front of him, while Roosevelt sipped a tin mug of tea.

"Now, you have to understand, these are not the most elegant and polished men you're ever going to come across," Holliday was saying.

"I can't use elegant men," said Roosevelt. "I want Rough Riders."

"You've fallen in love with that term," remarked Holliday with an amused smile.

"It describes what I want. Anyway, I need to meet these men. I can't imagine we have more than a couple of days before War Bonnet walks into town, bold as brass, looking for me. If we were back East, I'd enlist the great John L. and some of his rivals—and there are some football players I'd add."

Holliday shook his head. "You mean baseball."

"No, football."

"Never heard of it."

"You will," Roosevelt assured him. "Anyway, we're *not* back East, so I need the best Tombstone and the surrounding area's got to offer."

"Some have only a nodding acquaintance with the law," said Holliday. "And some have an out-and-out contempt for it."

"Are they brave?"

"Without exception."

"And competent with their fists and their weapons?"

"They are."

"Have they the courage to ride against overwhelming odds, look Death in the eye, and laugh at him?"

Holliday smiled. "Some will laugh. Some'll curse. And most of 'em will shoot first and leave the laughing and cursing for later." He took a drink from his glass. "Anyway, I've passed the word, and told Henry Wiggins to do the same."

"He doesn't strike me as a Rough Rider," noted Roosevelt.

Holliday chuckled. "He's just a well-meaning little salesman who I introduced to Ned and Tom. But he's—what would you call him?—a hero-worshipper, with a misplaced sense of what constitutes a hero."

"Well," said Roosevelt, "if he chooses the wrong men, we'll know soon enough."

"There are still a few left over from the Vendetta Ride," said Holliday. "I'll vouch for any of them."

Roosevelt frowned. "You mentioned the Vendetta Ride before, but . . ."

"It got quite a lot of publicity when it was occurring and right after," said Holliday with a smile. "It's the reason I had to leave Tombstone, in fact all of the Arizona Territory, for a while."

"Tell me about it," said Roosevelt.

"Well, you've heard about the shootout between the Earps and the Clantons."

"The Gunfight at the O.K. Corral," said Roosevelt, nodding his head. "It's famous even in New York."

Holliday grimaced. "I guess that's the way it's going to be known from now until doomsday, but it didn't take place in the Corral, but in the alley that backed up to the Corral. Anyway, it was me and Wyatt and his brothers on one side, and a couple of Clantons, a couple of McLaurys, and a kid named Claiborne on the other. When the shooting was over, both McLaurys and Billy Clanton were dead, and Virg and Morg— Wyatt's brothers—were wounded. I even caught one myself, on my belt. Didn't break the skin, but it hurt like a sonuvabitch for a few days."

"I know the story," said Roosevelt. "Or, more likely, a fictionalized version of it. What does this have to do with a Vendetta?"

"A Vendetta Ride," Holliday corrected him.

"Okay, a Vendetta Ride?"

"There were still a lot of Cowboys left after the gunfight."

"Well, of course," said Roosevelt. "The West is full of them."

Holliday shook his head. "Means a different thing. Back East, a cowboy is anyone out here who rides a horse and carries a gun. But in Tombstone Territory, it was a proper noun. You spelled it with a capital C, and it was an organized gang of horse and cattle thieves. Anyway, the Cowboys didn't like that we'd killed some of their people, so one night a few weeks later they backshot Morgan while he was playing pool right across the street from here and killed him." Holliday grimaced again. "I loved that young man like he was my own brother. A few weeks later they ambushed Virgil and crippled him up pretty badly, badly enough that Wyatt shipped him out of here."

"Is he still alive?" asked Roosevelt.

Holliday nodded. "But he's got an arm he'll never use again. Anyway, we knew Johnny Behan, who was still sheriff, was never going to do anything about it, so we formed a punishment party, and no matter what the courts said, it was legal, because Wyatt was still a marshal and he deputized all the rest of us."

"How many were you?"

"Maybe half a dozen, maybe a little more," answered Holliday. "There was Wyatt, and me, and Texas Jack Vermillion, and, let me see, Turkey Creek Johnson, Hairlip Charlie Smith, Sherman McMaster, Tip Tipton, one or two more."

"And the outcome?"

"You didn't see any Cowboys on the way into Tombstone," replied Holliday, "and you ain't going to see any while you're here."

"Good!"

"You got something against the Cowboys, Theodore?" asked Holliday. "You didn't even know what they were two minutes ago."

"I mean good, that's the kind of men I want for my Rough Riders," responded Roosevelt. "This isn't a mission for milquetoasts."

"Maybe you'd like to explain just what the hell this mission is about?" said Holliday. "I've seen War Bonnet, been close enough to touch him or at least spit on him—and the fact that he couldn't harm me doesn't make any difference if he can get his hands on you."

"What am I suppose to do?" growled Roosevelt. "Just sit here and wait for him? You don't get results by waiting for good things to happen, Doc."

"You live a lot longer if you don't go out hunting for bad things that were created for the sole purpose of pulping your body and biting your head off," answered Holliday. "You can't stand against him, Theodore. Take my word for it."

"I know."

Holliday frowned in confusion. "Then if you know, what the hell are you doing? I'm the one who's supposed to not care whether he lives or dies."

"You gave me a clue when you were describing your encounter with him."

"If I told you how to hurt him, what did I miss when I confronted him?"

"Nothing," said Roosevelt. "But you confronted him on neutral ground."

"And you think it's safer to face him on his home turf?" said Holliday. "What the hell's in that tea you're drinking?"

Roosevelt smiled. "Not *his* home turf, Doc. *Theirs*."

Holliday looked completely confused. "Whose?" he all but shouted.

"The medicine men who are controlling him," said Roosevelt. "If I can't harm him, then maybe my Rough Riders and I can kill the men who give him his orders."

Holliday shook his head. "You don't even know where they are. Or if they're in one place."

"I think Geronimo can tell me," said Roosevelt. "After all, he's the single most powerful of them. And he has no desire to die, or so he says, so why wouldn't he tell me?"

"And if they're spread out in forty or fifty villages?"

"Then we'll hunt them down and kill them one at a time."

"Before War Bonnet can kill you?" said Holliday dubiously.

"If they're in fifty villages, then he's only got one chance in fifty of guessing right," replied Roosevelt. "You're a gambler, Doc. Wouldn't you bet those odds?"

"And if they're in one place?"

"Then we'll have to kill them all before he can kill me."

"I don't know . . ." began Holliday.

"The alternative is to sit here until he walks through those swinging doors looking for me," said Roosevelt.

"He wouldn't fit."

"All the more reason to *do* something before he tears the place apart trying to get to me."

"Well, when do we leave?" asked Holliday.

"*We?*" said Roosevelt, arching an eyebrow.

"You're going to be recruiting all the worst gamblers," replied Holliday with a smile. "No sense hanging around here with nothing but men who know how to count."

Roosevelt threw back his head and laughed. "Damn, I knew I liked you, Doc Holliday!"

"It's my shy and gentle manner, no doubt," said Holliday, taking yet another drink.

"Well, I suppose we'd better devise some tests."

"Tests?"

"For our potential Rough Riders," explained Roosevelt. "How well can they shoot? Can they ride a horse that's bucking in panic? If it comes to close fighting, how are they with fists and knives?"

"First, they're your Rough Riders, not ours," complained Holliday. "And second, what you're describing is a rodeo, except for the fist-fighting part." He paused and stared at Roosevelt. "Theodore, there's an easier way to look at it."

"Oh?"

Holliday nodded his head. "Just consider this: any man who walks in here wearing a gun is undefeated."

Roosevelt's eyes widened. "I never thought of that."

"This isn't like one of Bat's boxing matches back East," said Holliday. "We play for keeps out here. When you lose, you're dead. There are no rematches."

"You're right, of course," said Roosevelt. "But even if they're all undefeated, they aren't all of equal value."

"No, they're not. But if they rode on the Vendetta Ride, it means Wyatt and I vouch for them."

"If they survived that and they're willing to ride against the medicine men with me, that should be all the qualifications they need," agreed Roosevelt.

Holliday looked up at the swinging doors. "Here's one. Care to meet him?"

"Of course!"

Holliday signaled to the short, burly man who had just entered. He turned and began approaching the table, and Roosevelt saw there was something wrong with his upper lip.

"Charlie, I want you to meet a friend of mine, Theodore Roosevelt," said Holliday without getting up. "Theodore, say hello to Hairlip Charlie Smith."

Smith offered his hand to Roosevelt, who rose to his feet. "It ain't a real hairlip," he explained. "I got shot in the lip in a gunfight back in Abilene ten, twelve years ago."

"Have a seat, Charlie," said Roosevelt. "Doc's been telling me about you."

"Nothing good, I imagine," said Smith with a smile. "Doc's just pissed because that teenaged chippie went off with me instead of him last time he lived here." He turned to Doc. "We both know Kate would have killed you if you'd taken her home with you."

"There are a lot of rooms in town," replied Holliday easily. "And hard as it may be for you to believe, I was saying favorable things about you."

Smith chuckled. "Maybe so, but I ain't loaning you no money."

"Mr. Smith . . ." began Roosevelt.

"Charlie," Smith corrected him. "Or Hairlip, if you want."

"Charlie, I am about to embark on an exciting enterprise, and I'd like your help. Doc's told me about your heroism during Wyatt Earp's Vendetta Ride. I have something similar on tap."

"What's the job pay?" asked Smith.

"Not a single penny," said Roosevelt. "What we're going to do, we're doing because it's the right thing."

"I dunno," said Smith. "Whenever someone talks about doing the right thing, some other folks usually wind up getting themselves shot all to pieces."

"What if I told you that Geronimo has decided to lift the spell that's kept the United States bottled up east of the Mississippi?"

Smith frowned. "You want to kill him for *that*? I thought that's what everyone back East wanted."

"I want it too," said Roosevelt. "We all do." He paused. "Well, *almost* all of us. But there's a group of medicine men who don't want Geronimo to make peace with us, who are determined to kill him."

"And you're after *them*?" asked Smith.

"That I am," Roosevelt assured him.

"So it's whoever you can put together riding off to kill some medicine men?"

"Almost," said Roosevelt.

"Almost kill them?"

"That's almost all we're riding off to kill."

Roosevelt spent the next few minutes explaining about War Bonnet, having Holliday describe him and their meeting, and suggesting that if he and his Rough Riders didn't go hunting for War Bonnet and the medicine men, that War Bonnet would probably tear Tombstone apart looking for him.

"So that's the situation," said Roosevelt in conclusion. "Are you man enough to come with us?"

"Of course," said Smith. "So will damned near every other man you ask."

"They grow them brave out here," said Roosevelt.

"Brave's got nothing to do with it," said Smith with a smile. "Doc's already explained that War Bonnet can't hurt nobody but you and Geronimo, so the rest of us are safe."

"Then you'll come?"

"Hell, yes! Once in my life I ought to do something because it's the right thing."

"I'm glad to have you on our team!" said Roosevelt, reaching out and shaking his hand again.

"Hard to resist," replied Smith. "I don't know what the hell a Rough Rider is, but I sure like the notion of calling myself one."

19.

HOLLIDAY, LUKE SLOAN, AND HAIRLIP SMITH spent the day passing the word—as Roosevelt explained, they probably didn't have much more than a day to select and assemble the Rough Riders—and they began showing up at the designated spot, which was Baltimore Jack Miller's abandoned ranch a mile north of town.

The first to make an appearance was Jack "Turkey Creek" Johnson, a burly man with pale-blue eyes, a nose that had clearly been broken a few times, a thick but well-trimmed beard, a colorful shirt, and stove-pipe chaps over his jeans.

He rode up to the decrepit ranch house with its broken windows and missing door, tied his horse to a very shaky railing, and walked up to Holliday.

"Howdy, Doc," he said. "I hear tell you're looking for men."

"Not me," said Holliday. He pointed to Roosevelt, who stood on the porch. "Him."

Johnson walked over and extended his hand. "Turkey Creek Johnson at your service," he said. "Any friend of Wyatt's is a friend of mine."

"I appreciate that," said Roosevelt. "But it's a bit removed from the source. I'm a friend of Doc's."

"And Doc's the best friend Wyatt ever had, and that's good enough for me," said Johnson.

"May I ask what precipitated this friendship for Wyatt?" said Roosevelt.

Johnson merely frowned in puzzlement until Holliday spoke up. "He means, what caused it, Turkey?"

"Johnny Behan locked my brother away on a trumped-up charge, and Wyatt got him out." Suddenly Johnson smiled. "I was on the Vendetta Ride with him and Doc."

"So I assume you know how to use that?" said Roosevelt, pointing at his six-gun.

"You just tell me who you want shot, and if it ain't Doc, the deed is as good as done," replied Johnson.

"Doc?" asked Roosevelt.

"He's as good as he says," replied Holliday. "With a pistol, anyway. It gets a little stranger with a rifle."

"That's 'cause I lost my specs a couple of years ago, and we ain't got no lens grinders out here since the Apaches killed old Hermanson as he was taking his wagon from one town to another," said Johnson. "But trust me: I can hit anything I can see."

"How far do you have to be before you can't see it?"

"I don't know," admitted Johnson. "A ways."

"Let's find out," said Roosevelt. "Luke, take that bucket"—he indicated an old bucket at the corner of the porch—"and set it out a couple hundred feet away."

Luke Sloan lifted the bucket and began walking.

"You sure you want me to do this?" asked Johnson. "I mean, if I put a hole in it, you can't use it no more."

"We're not using it now," Roosevelt assured him.

Johnson shrugged. "You're the boss." He paused. "By the way, I didn't catch your name."

"I didn't throw it," said Roosevelt with a smile. "But it's Theodore Roosevelt."

"Okay, Teddy—glad to be working with you."

"You'll be gladder if you call me Theodore."

"Whatever you say."

"That's far enough, Luke!" called Roosevelt. "Set it down."

Sloan put the bucket on the ground. "Don't shoot yet!" he hollered, trotting back.

"Is something wrong?" asked Roosevelt.

"Everyone knows Turkey Creek is blind as a bat," said Sloan. "I don't want to be standing anywhere near what he thinks he's aiming at."

"I don't suppose you'd like to hit leather right now?" said Johnson angrily as Sloan reached the porch.

"Hell, even a bat can see from ten or twelve feet away," said Sloan.

"To hell with Sloan," said Holliday. "Just kill the bucket."

Johnson pulled his pistol, held it in front of him with both hands, took aim, and pulled the trigger. The bullet plowed into the dirt about three inches in front of the bucket."

"You missed," said Hairlip Charlie Smith.

"The hell I did," said Johnson. He turned to Roosevelt. "The bucket's a man, right?"

Roosevelt nodded. "That's right."

"Anyone can shoot him in the head or the chest," said Johnson. "I just shot him in the balls!"

Everyone laughed at that, even Roosevelt.

"So am I on your team?"

Roosevelt shook his hand. "Turkey Creek Johnson, welcome to the Rough Riders."

"Who are we going up against?" asked Johnson.

"Certain select medicine men."

"Geronimo? I been waiting for a chance to go hunting for that Apache bastard."

"No," said Roosevelt. "He's on our side."

Johnson frowned. "If a bunch of white men are siding with a bunch of Apaches, who the hell's the enemy—a bunch of Chinamen?"

"I'll explain it once we've assembled all the Rough Riders," answered Roosevelt. "No sense saying it half a dozen times."

"Wouldn't bother me none," said Johnson. "It's either that, or listening to Luke tell me how no woman has ever said no to him, or having Hairlip Charlie tell me how he caught a bullet in his lip without flinching, or maybe Doc give me odds on how many scorpions live between here and that bucket, and if I have to listen to a bunch of bullshit, at least I ain't heard yours yet."

"I'm almost flattered," said Roosevelt. "But I think we'll wait anyway."

"Just as well," said Holliday. "Here comes another."

"He doesn't look like a typical cowboy," remarked Roosevelt.

"A fair assumption," agreed Holliday.

The man riding toward them wore a top hat, smoked a pipe, and carried a bright-yellow umbrella to protect himself from the sun. He didn't wear a holster or a six-shooter, but Roosevelt could see tell-tale bulges in every one of his coat pockets.

"Good day, one and all," said the newcomer in a thick British accent. "Word has come to my ears that you're recruiting men of action."

"And are you one?" asked Roosevelt.

"My *bona fides*," said the man, pulling a rolled-up poster out of his otherwise-empty rifle sheath and handing it to Roosevelt.

"Stay three rounds with English Morton Mickelson and win fifty dollars!" read Roosevelt. "You're a boxer?"

"The best."

"Then if I may ask a question, what are you doing here?"

"My manager took my money and ran off with it," said Mickelson. He flashed a satisfied smile. "I found him. I didn't want to take a chance of breaking a finger on his jaw,"—he pulled out a pistol and twirled it around his finger, then replaced it—"so I put a bullet in his head and two more in his heart, always assuming he had one. That was, let me see, eleven days ago. I thought it was a nice time to take a vacation—I'd been fighting in Wichita—so I thought I'd see the Arizona Territory before the Apaches drive everyone else out of it."

"Are you any good with that gun?" asked Roosevelt.

"Absolutely deadly, up to five or six feet, after which it becomes problematical."

"How about your fists?"

"I stand behind my offer. I'll pay fifty dollars to any man here who can last three rounds with me. Doc Holliday excepted, of course; he could knock me out just by breathing on me after he's got a morning's worth of booze in him."

Everyone laughed, even Holliday.

Suddenly Roosevelt took his glasses off, placed them in a jacket pocket, then removed his jacket and hung it over a chair. "Well," he said, "since you can't shoot, I suppose we'd better find out just how well you can defend yourself in close quarters." He unbuttoned the cuffs on his sleeves and rolled them up.

"Are you quite certain you can see me without those cheaters?" asked Mickelson.

"If you're close enough to hit, you're close enough to see," said Roosevelt, walking down the three wooden steps from the porch to the ground.

"Good answer," said Mickelson. He closed his umbrella, hung it on his saddle horn, then put his top hat over it. He took off his coat and tossed it over the porch railing, where the hidden pistols clattered as they bumped against wood.

"Two-minute rounds, Mr. Mickelson?" said Roosevelt.

"That suits me fine, Mr. . . . I don't know your name."

"Roosevelt. But call me Theodore."

"Fine. And you may call me Morty."

"Odd name," remarked Roosevelt.

"But fitting, as you're about to find out."

"Doc," said Roosevelt, "pull out your watch, and yell 'Time' when you're ready. We'll fight two-minute rounds with one minute in between."

"He's got you by thirty pounds, Theodore," said Holliday, grabbing his watch chain and pulling out the pocket watch that was attached to the end of it.

"I'll be gentle with him, Doc," said Mickelson.

"Exactly what I was going to say," replied Roosevelt with a grin.

Holliday stared at his watch for a few seconds, then yelled, "Time!"

Mickelson rushed right at Roosevelt and swung a mighty round-house that would have decapitated him if it had landed—but Roosevelt ducked beneath it, stepped forward, threw a quick right-left combination to the Englishman's belly, then stepped to the side.

"Well, I'll be damned!" said Mickelson with a guilty grin. "You do know what the hell you're doing. I won't make that mistake again, Theodore."

He leaned forward, holding his fists up in front of him. Roosevelt darted in, went for his face once, then for his belly, and finally for his face again, but Mickelson caught all the blows on his forearms.

"Not bad," said Roosevelt with a grin.

"I'm a lot more than not bad, Yank," said Mickelson. "Get ready."

That was all the warning Roosevelt needed. He began bobbing and weaving, never presenting a stationary target. Mickelson landed a heavy blow on Roosevelt's right shoulder that momentarily numbed his entire arm, but he managed to sneak a left through, bloodying the Englishman's nose.

"Time!" said Holliday.

"Where the hell's my corner?" demanded Mickelson.

"We seem to have forgotten about corners and such," said Roosevelt. "Keep your fifty dollars, Morty. You've shown me you can box, and that's what I wanted to know."

"Well, when it comes right down to it, you ain't so bad yourself, Yank," said Mickelson, taking his hand. "You ever think about going pro?"

"I'm already in a tougher profession," replied Roosevelt.

"Shootist?"

Roosevelt grinned. "Politician."

Mickelson threw back his head and laughed. Then he looked around the porch. "Anyone got a towel? If I don't wipe this blood off pretty soon, people are going to think I've got a bright red mustache."

Luke went into the house, found a rag, emerged, and tossed it to the Englishman.

"Thanks, Tall Man," said Mickelson. He turned to Roosevelt. "So am I a member of your gang?"

"In good standing," said Roosevelt.

"This calls for a celebratory drink, and forgive me if I don't think our dental expert looks like he feels much like sharing." So saying, Mickelson walked to his horse and pulled a flask out of his saddlebag, took a swig, and replaced the flask in the bag.

The next to show up was Sherman McMaster, another member of

the Vendetta Ride, and Dan "Tip" Tipton, who'd been a sailor, a miner, a gambler, and was just about the only one present who'd never either been a lawman or the face on a Wanted poster.

The last to arrive was a Mexican bandit—a *former* bandit, as he kept pointing out—named Louis Martinez, but whom Holliday and the others knew as "Loose" Martinez.

"Is this everyone you passed the word to, Doc?" asked Roosevelt when they were all assembled.

"All except Charlie Bassett," replied Holliday. "Too bad he didn't show up. Six-gun, rifle, or knife, you couldn't ask for a gutsier fighter."

"He sends his regrets," said Tipton. "I forgot to mention it 'til I just heard his name. He's riding a winning streak at the Blue Peacock, and he's not about to leave the table."

"Can't blame him for that," said Holliday. "Well, if we don't leave until morning, maybe the cards'll cool off." He grimaced. "Not that I'd wish that on anyone."

"If we're all here," said Turkey Creek Johnson, "maybe you'd like to finally tell us what the hell this is all about."

"Yes, there's no sense putting it off any longer," agreed Roosevelt. "If this Bassett fellow shows up, one of you can tell him." Roosevelt rolled down his sleeves, buttoned the cuffs, put his coat back on, and faced the assembled group of men, his hands on his hips, his jaw jutting forward. "Gentlemen," he began, "we are going to play a part in the greatest American enterprise since the Revolution."

"Just the nine of us?" said Hairlip Smith.

"And Charlie Bassett, if he makes it," said Roosevelt.

"Oh, excuse me," said Smith sarcastically. "That makes all the difference."

"Sometimes one man is all the difference you need. Ask Mr. Lincoln what kind of difference Ulysses S. Grant made."

"It's a little late to ask him anything," said Johnson.

"All right," said Roosevelt. "Let me get to the gist of it. As you know, the United States has been unable to expand beyond the Mississippi River due to the magical power—there is no other term for it—of the Indian medicine men. They've let some of us through, because we represent little or no threat to them. They've allowed some cattle ranches, because they don't eat cattle, and they've allowed mining towns, because they don't care for what we pull out of the mines. But they have made sure that we have not and cannot overrun their land or bring our government to the West." He paused, looking from one man to another. "That, gentlemen, is about to change."

"They're lifting the spell?" said Sloan. "How many hundreds of millions is *that* going to cost?"

"Nothing," replied Roosevelt. "One visionary medicine man has decided that even magic can't keep the United States confined forever, and that he'd rather lift the spell and make peace now than have us destroy the spell when we grow strong enough and annihilate every Indian on the continent."

"I haven't heard anything about this," said Martinez.

"Neither have I," chimed Johnson. "How come only you seem to know about it?"

"I'm the one he sent for to negotiate with."

"And who is this medicine man?" continued Johnson.

"Geronimo."

"Geronimo?" demanded Smith. "He's the worst of them all!"

"He's the strongest of them all," replied Roosevelt. "And he's the one who's decided that it's time to make peace and lift the spell."

"Why *you*?" said Tipton. "Last I heard, Jim Garfield was the president."

"It's Chester Arthur," Roosevelt corrected him. "And as to why he chose me, you'd have to ask Geronimo. I just know that he sent for me, and I came."

"And you don't trust him, and that's why we're all gathered here today?" suggested Sloan.

Roosevelt shook his head. "He's on our side. The other medicine men know it, and *that's* the problem."

"Just have Geronimo wipe 'em out," said Sloan.

"If it were that simple, I wouldn't have gathered you here," said Roosevelt. "The medicine men have created a monster, a huge, magical warrior named War Bonnet. He was created for one purpose and one purpose only: to kill Geronimo and myself. I have yet to see him, but Doc has faced him. Doc, you want to describe him?"

"He's about two and a half times a normal man's height," said Holliday. "Built like an athlete. Muscles everywhere. Except his hands and forearms, which are, as best as I can explain it, living flames. Not much of a mouth or nose, which leads me to think he doesn't breathe, or at least not as much as real men." He paused long enough for the men to get at least a vague mental picture of the creature. "And he's got another feature you should know about. I pumped half a dozen bullets into him at point-blank range. I still don't know if they went into him or bounced off, but I know they didn't hurt him or slow him down."

"Bullshit," said Hairlip Smith. "If he's half what you say he is, how could you live through it?"

Roosevelt forced a grin to his face. "Tell him, Doc."

"He was built for one purpose," said Holliday. "Theodore already told you what it is: to kill him and Geronimo. *That is the only thing he can do.* He grabbed at me with those flaming hands; they passed right through me without burning me. He picked up a rock that must have weighed a thousand pounds. He had no problem holding it up over his head . . . *until* he tried to carry it over and crush me with it. The closer he got, the more effort he had to put into carrying it, and finally he couldn't . . . but when he turned his back and threw it away, I could see that it was light as a feather to him."

"So he can't hurt us and we can't hurt him," said the Englishman. "Therefore, I have to ask: What possible purpose can be served by our confronting him?"

"You're not here to confront War Bonnet," said Roosevelt. "I just want you to know what he is, and just as importantly, what he isn't. There are only two people he can kill, or even harm. The problem is, if he kills either of us, the spell at the Mississippi will never be lifted, at least not in our lifetime. So we are going to seek out the medicine men who create and control the monster, and we are going to kill them,"

"Does War Bonnet vanish just because we kill his . . . ah, his *parents*?" asked Mickelson.

"I don't know," admitted Roosevelt. "But at least he'll be without orders, without direction. I'd like to think he'll vanish, but even if he doesn't, this should buy us enough time to figure out how to destroy him." He looked at the assembled men. "If any of you want to withdraw from this enterprise, now is the time."

Nobody moved and nobody spoke.

"Good!" said Roosevelt. "We meet in front of the Grand Hotel at sunrise tomorrow morning." He bared his teeth in his familiar grin once more. "And then the Rough Riders will prove that a small but motivated group of men can make a difference!"

20.

OLLIDAY SAT AT A TABLE in the Grand's restaurant, facing Roosevelt, who was clearly enjoying his meal.

Finally the gambler could stand it no longer. "You *ever* going to talk to me, Theodore?"

"I thought we'd been talking all day," answered Roosevelt, sprinkling some salt on his lamb chops. "By the way, you really should dig in," he continued, indicating Holliday's untouched plate. "These are excellent."

"Damn it, Theodore!"

"You don't like lamb? Then maybe I'll have one of yours when I'm done with mine."

"Keep this up and you won't have to wait for War Bonnet," said Holliday irritably. "I just may kill you myself."

Roosevelt chuckled heartily. "Yeah, I've heard about your skills as a dentist, Doc."

"*Theodore!*" growled Holliday.

"Doc, haven't you figured out that I'm not about to discuss anything concerning tomorrow while we're in public. We'll finish our meal, grab some of that scrumptious pecan pie for dessert, and then we'll go up to my room, where there won't be anyone around to overhear."

"What difference does it make who listens and who doesn't?" demanded Holliday. "You're leaving town at sunrise anyway."

Roosevelt looked to his left, then his right. Finally he learned forward and said, very softly, "Can you keep a secret?"

"Of course."

Suddenly Holliday was facing the familiar Roosevelt grin again. "So can I."

"Wyatt had his faults," muttered Holliday, "but you make him look pretty goddamned good as a partner."

"Doc, you're a bright man," said Roosevelt. "If you'll just put that brain to use, you'll know exactly what's going to happen when we go up to my room."

Holliday stared at him, frowning in puzzlement, for almost a minute. Then, suddenly, he smiled and relaxed. "All right, Theodore. I apologize. I've had a lot on my mind."

"Apology accepted," said Roosevelt. "Now, are you going to eat your lamb chops or not?"

Holliday pushed his plate across the table, and poured himself a drink.

"I would never tell a man who seems totally unaffected by liquor to give it up," said Roosevelt, "but you've *got* to eat more, Doc. What are you—five foot ten or eleven? You can't weigh a hundred thirty pounds."

"A hundred twenty-two, last time I looked," said Holliday. "I guess I'll have to drink more to make up the weight."

"Just out of curiosity, have you *ever* been drunk?"

Holliday nodded. "Oh, yes," he said, nodding his head. "Worst time was about two years ago. I got so drunk I couldn't count, I thought I couldn't lose, and I blew every penny I'd saved for the sanitarium in one night at the tables."

"I'm sorry," said Roosevelt.

"You should be happy."

"That you went broke?" asked Roosevelt, frowning.

"That I needed money," said Holliday. "That's why I turned bounty hunter and killed Henry McCarty."

"Never heard of him."

Holliday smiled. "Yes, you did. Out here most people called him Billy the Kid."

"I thought Pat Garrett killed him."

"That's what most people think," replied Holliday. "We made a deal. I got the money, he got the fame—and the book sales. I think in the long run he'll make out better than I did. Part of my reward money's gone already, and Garrett's book keeps on selling."

"I had no idea," said Roosevelt.

"Well, now that you know, put that idea out of your head, or at least to the back of it where you keep other stuff you're never going to tell anyone." Holliday downed his drink. "It was an interesting couple of days. I killed the Kid, and Geronimo killed Hook Nose. I think he'd just had enough. Hook Nose and Geronimo were the two most powerful medicine men, and they did everything in concert. I think if Hook Nose hadn't gone against him, Geronimo would never have sent for you or been willing to deal."

"Interesting," said Roosevelt.

"History," replied Holliday with a shrug.

Roosevelt finished his lamb chops, went to work on one of Holliday's, and finally ordered dessert.

"You sure you won't have some?"

Holliday shook his head, and suddenly smiled. "I probably haven't got the strength any more to tote around a hundred twenty-five pounds. I'd better keep away from sweets."

Roosevelt laughed, dug into his pie, and a few minutes later the pair of them ascending the stairs to Roosevelt's room.

"I see the maid closed the window," noted Holliday as they entered and Roosevelt closed the door behind them. "Better open it."

Roosevelt nodded, crossed the room, and opened the window, then sat down on his desk chair while Holliday seated himself on the edge of the bed.

"I kept wondering," said Holliday, "just how the hell you expected to lead your men—"

"My Rough Riders," Roosevelt corrected him.

"Your Rough Riders," amended Holliday, "when you didn't have any idea of who you were up against or where you could find them. But you've sent for Geronimo, and he's going to show up and tell you."

"I hope so," said Roosevelt. Another grin. "If he doesn't, I'm going to feel mighty silly tomorrow morning."

"Just out of curiosity, how *did* you send for him? It's not as if he's got a mailbox."

"I know he'd be curious about why I was recruiting the Rough Riders," said Roosevelt. "I don't know if he was the jackrabbit or a snake or one of the birds, and I figure he didn't want to show himself in front of what on the surface seems like a gang of gunfighters, but every time I saw an animal watching me I told it to come to my room tonight, that I was going after War Bonnet in the morning."

"He can be forgiven for thinking you've assembled a gang of gunfighters," said Holliday with a sardonic smile. "Now let's hope that one of those animals was actually him."

"You think not?"

"No, I'm sure he's keeping a close eye on you," answered Holliday. "That's why I think he'll probably stop you from going in the morning. You're the white man he chose to make peace with."

"There's not going to be any peace until we take care of this War Bonnet and see to it that the medicine men don't create another one."

"Damn it, Theodore, I've *seen* him! You're not going to beat him, not on your own, not with your Rough Riders, not even with Tom Edison inventing a new weapon a day."

"I have to try, Doc."

"Why?" demanded Holliday.

"Do you think he'll stop if he kills me and Geronimo? If you were a nation, and you created a weapon that killed your two most powerful enemies, would you willingly disassemble it? Or would you say, 'We stopped them at the Mississippi and protected our land without anything remotely resembling War Bonnet. Now, how much of their land can we take back *with* him?'"

"Shit!" muttered Holliday irritably. "Don't you get tired of always being right?"

"I assume that's a compliment."

"It's a complaint. If you were wrong on occasion, I'd be in Leadville, preparing for a comfortable if brief old age."

"You're an interesting man, John Henry Holliday," said Roosevelt with a smile. "Your compliments sound like insults, and your insults sound like compliments."

They sat in silence for a few minutes, and then a bird fluttered down out of the sky and perched on the window sill.

"If that's you, come on in," said Roosevelt. "And if not, then I hope you have the instinct to fly away fast, because my friend Doctor Holliday is not in the best of moods."

Before the words were out of his mouth, the bird had hopped down onto the floor, and an instant later had become Geronimo.

"Welcome to my humble abode," said Roosevelt.

Geronimo and Holliday gave him identical looks that each said: *Cut the crap.*

"You have assembled a group of men," said Geronimo. "You plan to lead them against War Bonnet. I tell you now that they cannot kill War Bonnet any more than Holliday could."

"I know," said Roosevelt.

Geronimo looked at him questioningly.

"But I have to assume," continued Roosevelt, "that he cannot kill them any more than he could kill Holliday. If you can tell us where to find the medicine men, my men and I will see to it that they never create another War Bonnet."

"You have not thought this through, Roosevelt," said Geronimo. "War Bonnet cannot kill *them*, but he can kill *you*. In fact, he was created to kill you, and to kill me, and for no other purpose than that."

"I know."

"In fact, the only reason he is not here now is that he is still not fully complete. They can only bring him to life and direct him for a few minutes at a time." Geronimo's expression hardened. "But he will grow stronger every day. You must send your men to fight the medicine men, but stay well behind them where you will be safe."

Roosevelt shook his head. "I belong at the head of my men. I can't send them where I fear to go."

"But—"

"I'm no safer here. Doc was just a few hours out of town when he confronted War Bonnet. What's to stop him from coming to Tombstone and tearing apart every building in town until he finds me? If I'm going to die, it'll be fighting against my enemies, not hiding from them."

Geronimo laid a hand on Roosevelt's shoulder. "I knew you were a brave man. I only wish you were a little less brave." He sighed. "But then you would not be the man whose soul I found in the spirit world. When do you plan to leave?"

"My Rough Riders will be here at sunrise," answered Roosevelt.

Geronimo turned to Holliday. "You will be riding with them?"

"Hell, no," said Holliday. "I've already seen War Bonnet. I can't accomplish anything by seeing him again. As for the medicine men, if they lived at the edge of town I'd lead the charge, but I'm not much good on horseback, and I know there's no Indian lodge besides yours within a two-day ride, so by the time we got to where we're going, I'd probably be too weak to pull my gun out of my holster." He grimaced. "Besides, I've got my own problems. War Bonnet broke John Wesley Hardin out of a Texas jail, in exchange for his promise to kill me. I've never met him, but I know all about him. This is no Frank McLaury or Billy Clanton we're talking about, or even a Billy the Kid. This is the greatest killer in the West, a man with more than forty notches on his gun—and he's coming straight for me, so I've got to be ready for him. Unless it was all a lie."

Geronimo closed his eyes for a moment, then opened them. "It was not a lie. The man Hardin is no longer in jail."

"You can see him?" asked Holliday.

Geronimo nodded an affirmative.

"How soon will he get here?"

Geronimo shrugged. "It depends on Hardin. He has already killed two men."

"That's Hardin, all right," said Holliday. Suddenly he paused, staring off into the distance. "I wonder how fast he really is."

"I'll be damned!" exclaimed Roosevelt. "I do believe you're actually looking forward to this."

"As my friend Johnny Ringo was fond of saying, whatever your area of skill, you seek competition at the highest level."

"Your friend? You killed him!"

"He was my friend anyway," said Holliday. "Truth to tell, I had a sneaking fondness for the Kid, too." He smiled. "It's a lonely trade, especially at the top, and you find you have things in common with the best of your rivals. Hardin and I have one thing in common that no other shootists have."

"What's that?" asked Roosevelt curiously.

"We're both over thirty."

"From what I hear, that's unique for a shootist, all right." Roosevelt turned to Geronimo. "What medicine men are we looking for, and are they in one lodge or spread out all over the West?"

"All the medicine men created War Bonnet, but only four currently control him, and they are banded together in a lodge two days north of Tombstone."

"Who are they, and how will we recognize them?"

"They are Spotted Elk, Dull Knife, Tall Wolf and Cougar Slayer, and this is not a permanent lodge. It was built when they built War Bonnet, and there are no women or children there, only warriors."

"How many?"

Geronimo held up ten fingers, closed them into fists, then repeated the process four more times.

"Fifty," said Roosevelt. "And we're nine or ten. Do they have rifles?"

"Yes."

"And where will War Bonnet be?"

Geronimo shrugged. "I do not know. He may attack before you reach the lodge, or while you are there, or not at all. He obeys their orders."

Holliday could tell from Roosevelt's face that he was already digesting and processing the minimal information Geronimo had given him and was working out a strategy.

"And how will we find this lodge?"

"I will lead you," answered Geronimo.

"As a bird?"

"You will know me when you see me," said Geronimo. "But I tell you now, I will guide you to the lodge, but I will not enter it. You and I, we are the only two men in the world who are defenseless against War Bonnet."

"Is he also defenseless against us?" asked Roosevelt.

Geronimo's eyes widened. "I do not know."

"I guess we'll find out, won't we?" said Roosevelt, suddenly anxious for morning to come.

But he found he was speaking only to Holliday, as a small bird flew out the window and was soon riding the warm thermals to the south.

21.

ROOSEVELT HAD RISEN, SHAVED, BATHED, eaten a hearty breakfast, and was sitting astride Manitou before English Morton Mickelson, the first of his Rough Riders, showed up.

"Good morning, Morty," said Roosevelt.

"Oh God!" moaned Mickelson, shading his eyes, something his top hat didn't do. "You're not cheerful in the morning, are you?"

"Why not? It's a beautiful day."

"No day is beautiful that begins with the sun rising."

"You could use some coffee."

Mickelson made a face. "Didn't anyone ever tell you? Brits drink tea."

"All right, have some tea. We've got a little time before everyone's assembled."

"I hate tea."

"I think this is a little early for whiskey, even for Doc," said Roosevelt, amused. "You'll just have to suffer."

"Speaking of Doc, where is he?" asked Mickelson. "That's one man

I'd swear never saw the sun in the eastern half of the sky except when he's on his way home from a hard night of gambling."

"He won't be coming with us."

Mickelson frowned. "Bad decision."

"It was his, not mine," answered Roosevelt. "But I agree with him. You've seen him. We could be in for a hard two-day ride. It could damned near kill him."

"But if it didn't, you'd be happy to have his gun on your side. He's the best I ever saw, except maybe for Johnny Ringo."

"He killed Johnny Ringo."

"The second time around," noted Mickelson. "Who the hell knows what a dead man's responses are like? I'd have been more impressed if he'd been the first one to kill him."

"You don't seem to find it at all unusual that Ringo required killing twice," said Roosevelt.

Mickelson shrugged. "Couldn't happen in England. But what the hell—this is the New World, and clearly you haven't exorcised all your ghosts and demons yet."

Luke Sloan and Hairlip Smith rode up.

"'Morning, Dandy," said Sloan.

"It's Theodore," replied Roosevelt.

"I never asked yesterday, but what does this job pay?" said Sloan.

"Not a single penny."

Sloan smiled. "Then it's Dandy."

"Pay *me* and I'll be happy to call you Theodore," said Smith. "Hell, pay me and I'll call you President Arthur if it makes you happy."

"You're freedom fighters, not mercenaries," said Roosevelt.

"We could be both," offered Smith.

Roosevelt laughed. "No money."

"Oh, hell, I guess I'll call you Theodore anyway."

Loose Martinez was the next to arrive, followed by Turkey Creek Johnson and Sherman McMaster. McMaster informed Roosevelt that Charlie Bassett's winning streak hadn't ended and he sent his apologies, but *nothing* was going to get him to walk away from the table.

The last to show up was Tip Tipton, who galloped down Third Street, raising quite a cloud of dust behind him. He turned and reached the hotel a few seconds later.

"Are we ready to go?" he asked.

"Yes, we're all assembled now," said Roosevelt. "You seem anxious to get started."

"That I am," replied Tipton. "I didn't see any sense waking up the desk clerk at my hotel, so I jumped down from my balcony." He frowned furiously. "That goddamned bastard actually took a shot at me!"

"Just for running out on your hotel bill?" laughed Mickelson. "The nerve of some people."

"My view exactly," said Tipton. He turned to Roosevelt. "Even if he's after me, and I didn't hear no more shots, he'd be half a mile down Third Street and running on foot, and he's packing one helluva belly, so I don't figure he's going to bother us in the next couple of minutes, but it might be a good idea to be on our way."

"Just where *are* we going, Theodore?" asked Johnson.

"I'll know in a minute," replied Roosevelt, looking down the street. He couldn't see what he was looking for, but then a small, golden bird swooped down from the roof of the Grand and headed toward the north end of town.

"Well?" asked Mickelson.

"I'm going to feel like an idiot saying this," answered Roosevelt, "but follow that bird."

"One of Geronimo's pets?" asked Sloan as they began riding north.

"Or Geronimo himself," said Roosevelt. "He'll get us most of the way, but we'll do the last part on our own."

"Why?" asked Sloan.

"Because he has no defenses against War Bonnet."

"Neither have you, you know," said Michelson.

"Wrong," said Roosevelt, flashing him a grin. "I have my Rough Riders."

"Against a creature that's bigger than an oak tree and stronger than an elephant and can't be hurt," said Mickelson with a laugh. "That must bring you real comfort."

"Have you ever seen an elephant?" asked Roosevelt curiously. "I don't mean in a zoo, but in the wild."

"I hate to break it to a proud American," said Mickelson, "but we have mighty few elephants strolling down Piccadilly or bathing in the Thames."

"I mean, have you ever hunted them in Africa."

"Good God, no. Why would I?"

Roosevelt shrugged. "No reason. It's just that Britain's thousands of miles closer to Africa than we are."

"By that same token, you're closer to South America than we Brits are. Have you ever gone hunting for jaguar?"

"Not yet," said Roosevelt. "But one day I will." He looked ahead to make sure the bird was still in sight. "But for the moment, let's concentrate on hunting for the medicine men who stand in the way of America's progress."

"This probably ain't a bad time to ask," said Sloan. "Just what do we propose to do when we get there?"

"The four medicine men we find where we're going—there may be more, but we know we're after Dull Knife, Spotted Elk, Cougar Slayer and Tall Wolf—are the men who are currently in control of War

Bonnet, so to disable him we're probably going to have to kill them. I'd love to talk them into deactivating him, but if they were the talking kind, they wouldn't have created him in the first place."

"Might as well wipe out the whole lodge," said Hairlip Smith.

"Not if it's avoidable. This isn't a war; we will be living side-by-side with the various Indian tribes once Geronimo has ended the spell."

"You can say it isn't a war, but will *they* agree?"

"Let's hope so," said Roosevelt. "I want as little bloodshed as possible."

"And as fast as possible, if this critter is anywhere near the lodge," added McMaster.

"I don't know about this," said Martinez, who had been silent since they began riding.

"About what?" asked Roosevelt.

"The white men want to cross the Mississippi. The Indians say no, and now you're riding off to kill the ones who are stopping you." He paused, frowning. "Let's say we succeed. You kill the medicine men and War Bonnet and anyone else who stands in your way, Geronimo lifts the spell, and the United States expands to the Pacific."

Roosevelt stared at him, wondering what the point was.

"So you reach the Pacific," continued Martinez. "And then you turn your gaze south, and there is Mexico. Do you also kill any Mexican who says, 'No, this is my land, you may not come here?'"

Roosevelt frowned. "As far as I know, the United States has never had any territorial ambitions in regard to Mexico."

"I believe you are telling the truth," said Martinez, "but how far *do* you know? Many of you are my friends, and I do not wish any of you ill, but I have decided I cannot ride with you."

"I understand your concerns," said Roosevelt, "and I can only assure you that I believe them to be groundless."

"Let us hope so," said Martinez. "I would not like to take up arms against you." He jerked on the reins, and his horse reared and spun around. "*Adios!*" he cried as he rode back to the south.

"Our noble few just got nobler and fewer," remarked Mickelson wryly.

"He has a legitimate concern," said Roosevelt. "If we live through this, I'll do everything within my power to see to it that his fears remain only fears, that the United States has no territorial interest in Mexico."

"In the meantime, we're one less gun," said Hairlip Smith, "and a damned good gun at that."

"Well, we're certainly not turning back," said Roosevelt. "The rest of you will just have to shoot a little faster and a little more accurately." Suddenly he smiled. "When you come right down to it, what's one gun more or less when we're facing a bunch of warriors and four powerful magicians?"

"You ever study maths at Harvard?" asked Mickelson.

The Rough Riders all laughed at that, and continued on their way to their confrontation with War Bonnet and the mages who controlled him.

22.

"**S**O HOW FAR ARE WE TRAVELING, DANDY?" asked Sloan as the sun reached its zenith and started moving slowly to the west.

"We'll know when we get there," replied Roosevelt.

"Could be worse," said Hairlip Smith. "Could be heading south. I always figured that's pretty much what hell feels like, except for the occasional stream."

"And the occasional widow-woman," added Turkey Creek Johnson. "It's an unforgiving land. Lot of men die before their time."

"Of course, our friend Doc has added to that total," said Smith.

"I wonder how many men he's really killed?" mused Tip Tipton.

"Probably more than he's been credited with," offered Johnson.

"Or less," said Smith. "I know he got into a couple a fights down in Mexico. They say he killed eight Mexicans at a poker table."

"Ah, come on now," said Johnson. "You ever see nine men play poker all at once?"

"Maybe they had friends," said Smith.

"What do *you* think, Theodore?" asked Johnson.

"I think he's a good man with a gun or a deck of cards," replied Roosevelt. "Probably a good dentist, too."

"No, I meant how many men do you think he's killed?"

Roosevelt shrugged. "Is that important?"

"Maybe," said Hairlip Smith. "Ain't you curious to know if you're riding with the greatest shootist there ever was?"

"That'd be Johnny Ringo," said Sloan.

"Bullshit!" snapped Smith. "Johnny Ringo was killed in a gunfight." He spat on the dusty, featureless ground. "Hell, he was killed in *two* gunfights."

"Can't be Billy the Kid. After all, Doc killed him."

"Ringo and the Kid were never the greatest anyway," said Morty Mickelson. "And neither is Doc Holliday, for that matter. Just because John Wesley Hardin's been locked away for seven or eight years doesn't make him any the less a killer."

"How many men do you think Hardin killed?"

"Nobody knows," answered Mickelson. "But they proved something like forty-two in his trial. You'd have a hard time proving Doc killed much more than ten or twelve once the witnesses grow old and die.

"If they met in the street, I'd take Doc anyway," said Sloan.

"Maybe five years ago," replied Johnson. "But he's a sick man. He walks with a cane more often than not, and he's always coughing up blood. I just don't figure he can be as fast, or have as true an aim, as he used to."

"Well, hell, Hardin hasn't hit leather in years," shot back Sloan. "What kind of shape can *he* be in?"

"He's out of practice, not out of health," said Mickelson.

Suddenly Roosevelt pulled Manitou to a halt and scanned the horizon.

"What is it, Theodore? You spotted some Indians already?"

"No," said Roosevelt. "I've lost him."

"Lost who?"

"The bird I was—" began Roosevelt. Then: "Ah! There he is!"

"Is that Geronimo?"

"I don't know if it's Geronimo himself," said Roosevelt, "but I know whoever or whatever it is, Geronimo's responsible for it."

"Why doesn't he just come along as Geronimo?" asked Mickelson.

"Because War Bonnet was created expressly to kill Geronimo."

"And you," said Sherman McMaster. "He was created to kill Geronimo and *you*."

"Right," chimed in Johnson. "I never figured Geronimo as a coward."

"He's not," said Roosevelt.

"He's also not riding beside us in human form," said Johnson.

"He's a medicine man," replied Roosevelt. "His skills lie elsewhere."

"I notice not being a blooded soldier or Indian fighter ain't stopped you from coming along."

Roosevelt grinned. "Let me see a show of hands. How many of you would be here if I'd stayed behind?" No hands were raised. "There's your answer," he concluded.

"Well, at least stay behind *us*, Dandy," said Sloan. "This critter is looking for you, not us."

"More to the point," added Mickelson, "if what Doc says is right, he can't hurt any of us except you anyway."

"I don't know about that," answered Roosevelt.

"But you told us Doc faced him and War Bonnet couldn't do a damned thing to him," said Johnson.

"People tend to learn from their mistakes," replied Roosevelt.

"Medicine men are people. There's no reason to think they won't learn from his encounter with Doc."

"Either way, you're the one he wants," said Sloan. "If we can stop him, we will, but if not—"

"If not, then it won't matter whether I'm leading or trailing the rest of you," said Roosevelt. "And let me explain once again: whether they've improved him or not, War Bonnet is not your target. Doc couldn't hurt him, and I have to assume you can't either. You're after the medicine men. They made him; they've got to be protecting him. We kill them, and I'll wager he's vulnerable to bullets."

"Good term: 'I'll wager,'" said Mickelson. "Problem is, what you're wagering is your life."

"I can go hunting for the men who control him, or I can sit in my room in Tombstone and wait for him to kill me," said Roosevelt. "It's an easy call."

"Well, then," continued Mickelson, "it's time to start getting practical. Let's say there are a hundred Indians where we're going. How do we know which four we want to kill?"

"There are maybe a dozen, and I'll point out the four medicine men when we get there— another reason why I shouldn't be bringing up the rear."

"You've never seen them," said Hairlip Smith, "so how the hell will you know which ones they are?"

"More to the point," added Mickelson, "if this War Bonnet is half what you say he is, what makes you think he's going to let you get anywhere near the lodge? Why won't he come out to meet you and kill you half a mile or a mile out of the lodge?"

Roosevelt smiled. "Because no matter what you think, I'm not suicidal."

"I'm sure that's a comfort," continued Mickelson, "but would you like to tell us why we should believe that when you ride two days out of your way to confront a monster that was created for the sole purpose of killing you?"

"He was created to kill Geronimo too," Roosevelt corrected him.

"Big fucking deal," said Sloan. "How about answering Morty's question?"

"Because once we're in sight of the lodge, we're going to split up. I'm going to sit on my horse and, in essence, dare War Bonnet to come out after me."

"Bright," said Smith, spitting on the ground. "Real bright."

"And the rest of you are going to ride hell-for-leather toward the lodge, and I'm betting that if it's a choice between my dying and their dying or neither of us dying, the medicine men will opt to live, by which I mean they'll call him back."

Sherman McMaster, who'd been listening intently without speaking, frowned and shook his head. "That doesn't make any sense. Doc's already proved he can't hurt anyone but you and Geronimo."

"We don't know that's still true," said Roosevelt. "And even if it is, it makes no difference. Only a crazy man would get within reach of a monster like that, especially once you see that your bullets don't harm him at all. I think they'll call him back with the intent of scaring you off." Suddenly he grinned. "*Now* do you know how you're going to identify the medicine men?"

"Well, I'll be damned!" said McMaster.

"Probably," agreed Mickelson. "Well, gents, now you see the value of a Harvard education."

The bird, which had been hovering a few hundred yards ahead of them, flew back, chirping and squawking.

"All right, Rough Riders," said Roosevelt. "I think he's trying to tell us that we're wasting time, that the enemy lies ahead of us. Shall we proceed?"

"'Shall we proceed'?" repeated Sloan with a grimace. "Come on, Dandy, you're out West now. Say it like a cowboy."

"Men," said Roosevelt, spurring Manitou forward, "let's ride!"

23.

THE HORSES RAN OUT OF ENTHUSIASM in a few miles, and they were soon walking in single file across the flat, barren, featureless ground, with Roosevelt and Manitou in the lead. Night fell, and Sloan, who knew the desert like the back of his hand, directed him to the only water hole within fifteen miles.

They slept on the ground, brushing off the occasional insect, killing the occasional scorpion, and were up at daylight. They had a quick breakfast, refilled their canteens, and began riding again, following the bird as it led them toward their destination.

Finally Roosevelt reined Manitou to a halt and, shading his eyes, looked off into the distance.

"Lose the bird again?" asked Tipton.

"He's around," said Roosevelt. "Probably just finds it too damned hot to keep fluttering his wings. I can't say that I blame him."

"He should have turned himself into a rattler, or maybe a scorpion," said Tipton. "They seem to love this goddamned heat."

"They do," agreed Roosevelt. "But they couldn't keep ahead of us to lead us to the lodge."

"I hope to hell that's what he *is* doing," said Sloan, as his horse walked up beside Manitou.

"What do you mean?" asked Roosevelt.

"Well, he *is* Geronimo, and we're a bunch of white men."

"He didn't have me come all the way out here just to kill me," said Roosevelt. "If he wanted me dead, he could have killed me a couple of times since I arrived."

"Maybe he wants his pals to take our scalps."

"No Western Indian takes scalps," said Roosevelt. "And the one or two tribes that did it—none of them do it anymore—learned it from the French."

"There's that book-learning again," laughed Mickelson.

"Ain't that our bird, Theodore?" asked Turkey Creek Johnson, pointing off into the distance.

"Yes, that's him," replied Roosevelt, urging Manitou forward again.

They continued for two more hours, and the land became a bit more interesting, dotted with small hills and some sparse bushes.

Suddenly Roosevelt pulled Manitou to a stop.

"Get ready," he announced. "We're very close."

"What makes you think so?" asked Hairlip Smith.

"Do you see that tree straight ahead, the one with the flowers?"

"Yeah."

"It's not real."

Smith frowned. "What the hell are you talking about, Theodore? That's a tree, right there, big as life."

Roosevelt shook his head and smiled. "That's Geronimo's way of saying we've arrived, and he's not sticking around as a bird or anything else that War Bonnet might be able to recognize and kill."

"How do you figure that?" asked Sloan.

"That's a white dogwood tree," answered Roosevelt. "There isn't one within almost a thousand miles. They can't bloom or even survive in this desert."

And as the words left his mouth, the tree vanished.

Suddenly guns were drawn and cocked, rifles pulled out, ammunition checked.

"The lodge has got to be behind one of those hills," said Roosevelt. "Once we can see it, they can see us. I'm surprised they haven't reacted already, but maybe Geronimo had shielded us from whatever magic they use to see approaching enemies." He paused, staring at the hills. "The lodge can't be very large, not with only ten or twelve warriors living there. Once we're within sight of it, spread out and charge, guns blazing. We want War Bonnet to react, and hopefully he'll go to protect the very men we're after. I know he's going to be pretty awesome to look at, but keep in mind that he can't hurt anyone but Geronimo and me. Some of your horses may get spooked by his flaming hands, so if there are any Indians riding out to fight you, try not to shoot their horses; you may need them to get home."

"That sounds fine, *if* all your ideas work," said Johnson. "But what do we do if this giant *thing* comes straight at you, if we don't know who to kill or who's giving it orders?"

"Then I'll be just as dead as if he'd torn the Grand Hotel apart and found me there, and you're still charged with the task of killing the medicine men before he can kill Geronimo. In fact, the main thing is to keep Geronimo alive, because he can always deal with another Easterner. If he dies, it's another century or two before we expand to the Pacific."

"I ain't afraid of no Indians, and I ain't particularly afraid to die," said Sloan, "but do we *care* if the United States never gets past the Mississippi?"

"This is a hell of a time to think of that," said Turkey Creek Johnson. "Well, *I* care. I grew up in the United States, I fought for the North in the War between the States, and I figure I'm still an American."

"Son of a bitch!" laughed Tipton. "I was a Johnny Reb. I wonder if we ever faced each other?"

"Couldn't have," said Johnson with a smile. "You're still alive."

Tipton turned to Sloan. "That war's over and done with, and I'm as much of an American as Turkey Creek. You bet your ass I care."

"I never fought in your sillyarse war," said Mickelson, "but I'm all for extending the country to the coast." He made a face. "I *hate* horses. Let's open this land up to trains."

Sloan shrugged. "Okay," he said defensively. "I was just asking."

"All right," said Roosevelt, "let's go. And keep your eyes open. They don't have to attack us with a fifteen-foot warrior. They can post a sharpshooter behind any of these hills, or even dug into the ground."

"Hell, he'll probably be a lot cooler in the ground than we are up here on horses," said McMaster.

"Well, let's put them medicine men in the ground and see what they think," said Smith.

They continued riding for another twenty minutes and then, suddenly, as they passed a small hill, the lodge came into view, half a mile off to the left.

"Don't charge yet," cautioned Roosevelt. "I know they've just been walking, but our horses are pretty spent from this heat. I don't want them tiring out or taking any bad steps before we're ready to charge in earnest."

"So where's War Bonnet?" asked McMaster. "He ought to stand out like a sore thumb."

"I don't know," admitted Roosevelt, frowning. "Since he's a magical creation, it's possible that he comes into being when they want him to, and the rest of the time he goes back into whatever limbo they pulled him out of."

"Shit," said Mickelson. "I don't know if I want you to be right or wrong." He smiled. "If you're right, we just might kill the medicine men before they call him up. And if you're wrong, at least he'll show up so we know *who* we're supposed to kill."

"It's all academic," said Roosevelt, frowning.

"What are you talking about?"

"There he is."

Roosevelt pointed to his left, where War Bonnet was either getting to his feet from a position behind a hill, or rising up from the bowels of the Earth. He surveyed the riders, and then flashed them a maleficent smile. He extended a burning arm toward Roosevelt and pointed at him with a burning finger.

"I want *you*!" he thundered, taking a step toward the party of riders.

"Now!" said Roosevelt, and his companions spurred their horses and raced to the lodge, yelling and screaming, guns blazing.

War Bonnet froze, his gaze turning from Roosevelt to the Rough Riders, back to Roosevelt, then to the men again. He seemed rooted to the spot for almost a dozen seconds. Then, with a savage scream, he began racing toward the lodge, covering the ground not only with his giant stride, but with huge, powerful, gravity-defying leaps.

"*Slow down*," Roosevelt whispered far too softly for his men—or his enemies—to hear. "*If you beat him to the lodge, you'll never know which ones you want.*"

It was almost as if Mickelson, who was in the lead, heard him, for he carefully, subtly slowed his horse down, and the others immediately realized what he was doing and why, and followed suit.

"You give new meaning to the word 'monster,'" mused Roosevelt.

"These men know you can't hurt them, but Doc had no idea when he faced you. I take my hat off to him. That is one brave man."

Half a dozen warriors suddenly ran forward from the lodge, firing rifles. But while the Rough Riders shot back their primary attention was on War Bonnet, and when he came to a halt and positioned himself in front of a hut, they knew they'd found their target.

Mickelson and Sloan brought their horses to a halt twenty feet away and fired at point-blank range. The bullets had no effect on War Bonnet, who roared like a jungle animal, stepped forward, and reached out for their horses. His flaming hands went right through them, doing them no physical harm, but the terrified animals began screaming and bucking, and it was all Mickelson and Sloan could do to stay atop them.

McMaster saw that shooting at War Bonnet was useless, and aimed his rifle at the wall of the hut. The bullet went through it, and he heard two screams—one from inside the hut, and one from War Bonnet, who grabbed his shoulder as if he himself had been shot. The others saw what was happening, and turned their fire on the hut, but War Bonnet positioned himself in front of it and absorbed most of the bullets himself.

More and more warriors raced to the hut and began firing, and finally the Rough Riders, badly outnumbered stationery targets, had to retreat, but not before Tipton took a bullet in the thigh and McMaster was shot in the shoulder.

"Oh, shit!" yelled Mickelson. "The medicine men are safe. We've got to get back to Theodore before the monster does!"

And sure enough, War Bonnet had begun striding across the ground toward Roosevelt, who sat atop Manitou, rifle in hand, watching him approach.

"Remember what Doc told Theodore!" cried Mickelson as he reached Roosevelt's side and dismounted. "He can't hurt anyone but

Theodore and Geronimo. He can't even try—and he didn't try back at the lodge. All he did was try to scare the horses."

The six of them—Mickelson, Sloan, Smith, Johnson, Tipton and McMaster—dismounted and formed a tight circle around Roosevelt. War Bonnet arrived, smiled a triumphant smile, and reached out for Roosevelt, but Sloan raised his arms and somehow War Bonnet wouldn't or couldn't brush them aside.

"Doc was right!" said Mickelson, excited. "Kneel down, Theodore!"

It went against the grain, but Roosevelt saw the wisdom of Mickelson's suggestion, and he knelt, offering an even smaller target.

War Bonnet screamed, raked his painless flames across the men, and tried twice more to reach Roosevelt, only to be thwarted again.

"We could be here all day, and I'll bet we get hungrier and sleepier before he does," said Roosevelt. "Luke, you're standing behind me, farthest from War Bonnet. Why don't you back away, get to your horse, and ride back toward the medicine men's hut. My guess is that War Bonnet will race after you."

"Then what?" asked Mickelson.

"Then we declare it a draw and ride back to Tombstone. Luke will turn and follow us as soon as he sees we've mounted."

"Why won't he chase us all the way to Tombstone?" asked Johnson. "What's to stop him?"

"I think he gets his strength from the medicine men," said Roosevelt. "And they're just men, not gods. Otherwise, why would he vanish after Doc faced him? He was only a few miles out of Tombstone, and not much farther from Geronimo's lodge. Why not go the rest of the way? But Doc made him work, and the medicine men are new to this. They've never created anything remotely like War Bonnet before. As they get more used to him, he'll grow bigger and stronger and he may not vanish at all, but for the moment, I don't think he'll follow us right after a battle."

"And if you're wrong?" asked Smith, uselessly pumping a pair of bullets into War Bonnet's belly.

"Then we won't be any worse off than we are now," answered Roosevelt. "And there's always a chance that he's even stronger here than when he gets farther away from the medicine men."

"I'm tired of talking," said Sloan, backing away and heading to his horse. He had just begun galloping toward the lodge when War Bonnet suddenly turned and raced back to protect his creators.

"Now!" cried Roosevelt, and the six remaining men mounted their horses and began galloping back toward Tombstone.

Sloan caught up with them a few minutes later, and though they kept watchful eyes on every possible ambush site, there was no sign of War Bonnet.

"Well," said Mickelson at last, "I think we hit one of the bastards."

"I agree," said Johnson. "The first couple of bullets into the hut did it. Nothing else got a response like that from War Bonnet."

"I doubt that we killed him, though," said Tipton. "Ten seconds later War Bonnet was acting just the same as before."

"So what's next, Theodore?" asked Mickelson. "You're going to need a cavalry to get to the medicine men, and all the cavalries I'm aware of are on the other side of the Mississippi."

"I agree," said Roosevelt. "Killing the medicine men seemed the likeliest answer, but not only are they well protected here, now that they know they're a target, I can see them moving a few hundred miles north and west."

"Can they still control War Bonnet from that far?"

Roosevelt nodded. "And if they can't, they'll get help. Remember: there are a lot of medicine men, and only Geronimo wants to lift the spell."

"Can they really control him?" persisted Mickelson.

"They can stop an entire nation from expanding beyond the Mississippi," answered Roosevelt. "I think you can be sure they can control one magical monster."

"Yeah, makes sense," said Sloan. "Still, you can't just wait around hoping that he can't find you."

"I had hoped I could neutralize him by killing his creators," said Roosevelt, "but in retrospect, it was doomed from the start. We know there were four medicine men there, but even if we'd killed them, there are dozens more all over the West, and doubtless some of them would have taken over control of him."

"I think if I were you, I'd go back East," said McMaster, tying a fresh handkerchief over his wound.

"I'm not a quitter."

"No one thinks you are, Theodore," continued McMaster, "but you've just explained why you can't neutralize the damn creature, so what's left?"

"I can kill it," said Roosevelt, his jaw jutting forward pugnaciously.

24.

"HE'S NOT FOLLOWING US," remarked Luke Sloan, looking back for the twentieth time.

They were half an hour from the lodge, and there had been no sign of War Bonnet.

"It's early yet," said Roosevelt.

"Got to be midafternoon," noted Hairlip Smith.

Roosevelt shook his head. "Early in War Bonnet's existence. When I first met Geronimo a few days ago, he didn't even exist. When Doc encountered him out beyond Tombstone, he was gone in seven or eight minutes. Today he didn't last for much more than ten or twelve minutes."

"What are you getting at, Theodore?" asked Morty Mickelson.

"They're still working on him, making him stronger—and I have a feeling it's taking a lot out of Dull Knife, Spotted Elk, and the others; that War Bonnet feeds on their psychic powers, maybe even their physical strength. It would make sense for him to catch up with us, trail us, wait for the moment when I'm not surrounded, and strike, and we know he can go much farther afield, because Doc encountered him a day and a half from here . . . but instead he's gone again. There might be some other reason, but that's what I think is happening."

"So you figure he's going to get stronger, and stick around longer?" asked Turkey Creek Johnson.

Roosevelt nodded his head. "I've seen what he can do now, and just as importantly, I've seen what he *can't* do. I'll talk to Thomas Edison and Ned Buntline, and we'll see what kind of weapon they can devise."

"So you never thought you could kill him this time?" demanded Johnson. "But you didn't tell us that when you got us to ride with you."

"I didn't think I could hurt the puppet," said Roosevelt. "My hope was that we could kill the puppeteers and cut the strings."

"Nice turn of phrase," said Mickelson. "Maybe you ought to give this up and become a writer."

"I *am* a writer."

"Then why aren't you at home writing?"

"I don't believe in limiting myself."

"I don't know, Theodore," said Mickelson. "There's a mighty big difference between not limiting yourself and going up against War Bonnet again."

"I've seen him, I know what he can and can't do," said Roosevelt. "Next time I'll be fully prepared."

"I got a question," said McMaster.

"Yes?" said Roosevelt.

"War Bonnet was built to kill you and Geronimo, right? And the reason for it is that his builders don't want the spell lifted that keeps the country on the other side of the Mississippi, right?"

"Right."

"So here's my question," continued McMaster. "If he kills you, there's every likelihood that Geronimo will find someone else to deal with. Maybe President Arthur, maybe U. S. Grant, but *someone*. So killing you is only a stopgap measure. So why doesn't he go after Geronimo first? After all, if he does, you have no one to deal with but the guys who spent part of today trying to kill you."

"Damned good question," said Roosevelt. "I want to say that Geronimo's a lot harder to kill, but that doesn't hold water, since War Bonnet was created solely to kill both of us. So I think the likely answer is that while Geronimo may be easy for him to *kill*, he's damned difficult for him to *spot*. I always look like a man, but Geronimo can turn himself into a jackrabbit, a bird, a toad, damned near anything. War Bonnet didn't have to jump today, and I'm sure if he did, those legs could send him twenty feet in the air . . . but what good is that when Geronimo can fly to the top of a tree?"

"Okay," said McMaster. "I suppose it makes sense."

"You look like you have doubts," said Roosevelt.

"If *you* know Geronimo can do those things, surely *they* know,"

"Certainly," agreed Roosevelt. "But knowing he can do it doesn't mean they know how to make War Bonnet do it." He paused. "The proof is in the pudding. If he *could* change into all those things, he'd have gone after Geronimo first for the very reasons you mentioned."

Although Roosevelt was certain his reasoning was sound, he elected not to stop during the night, and the horses walked on until they began passing the abandoned silver mines on the outskirts of Tombstone the next day at noontime.

"Well, we made it, safe and sound and intact," said Roosevelt. "I want to thank you men for your help, for without you I would surely have died at War Bonnet's hands yesterday."

"Any time you need us again, Dandy, just pass the word," said Sloan. "I ain't never been nothing more than a cowboy. I *like* that I can tell people I been a Rough Rider."

"And we certainly have seen something to tell our grandchildren about," added Mickelson. "Assuming any of us lives long enough to have any."

"Got to make children before you worry about grandchildren," said Tipton. "Let's go into town and get started on that."

"Sounds good to me," said Sloan, spurring his horse into a canter. The others followed suit, leaving Roosevelt and Manitou to walk into town. He rode up to the boarding stable, dropped Manitou off, and walked the two blocks to the Grand, where he found Holliday and Masterson having dinner in the restaurant.

"Mind if I join you?" he asked, approaching their table.

"Glad to see you made it," said Masterson. "How did you kill War Bonnet?"

"I didn't."

"I didn't think you could," said Holliday. "The real question is: Why didn't he kill you?"

Roosevelt described the encounter in some detail.

"Damn!" exclaimed Masterson when he'd finished. "I was so captivated that my steak got cold."

"Mine too," noted Holliday. "Fortunately, I never gave much of a damn if they served it hot or cold." He stared at Roosevelt. "So he didn't chase after you. You know what I think?"

"What?"

"I think running him for ten minutes or so takes all the mental energy or spiritual power or whatever you want to call it that they've got."

"I agree," said Roosevelt. "But now that they know I know, they'll be making changes."

"How can they, if that's their limit?" asked Holliday.

"That's the limit for four of them. What if twenty or thirty throw their psychic abilities into him?" replied Roosevelt. "He could be bigger, stronger, faster, and stick around an hour or more."

"Should have killed those medicine men when you could," said Holliday.

"We couldn't," answered Roosevelt. "He couldn't hurt the Rough Riders, but they couldn't get past him, and when he made a break for me, they rode back to protect me instead of charging into the hut."

"Can't blame them for that," offered Masterson.

"I owe them my life," agreed Roosevelt.

"What now?" asked Holliday.

"Now I talk to Tom and Ned, and let them pick my mind about what I saw, and see if they can come up with something—*anything*—that can kill him."

"And if not?"

"If not, he'll go back East," said Masterson. "He's got a future there. He could even be governor of New York someday. No sense staying out here until War Bonnet can find a way to kill him."

"I'm not going anywhere," declared Roosevelt adamantly.

"But—"

"Bat, I know it sound egomaniacal, but someday I'm going to be the president of the United States, and I don't plan to preside over a country that stops less than halfway across the continent."

"Egomaniacal is an understatement," replied Masterson.

"I'd vote for you," said Holliday. He took a drink. "Of course, they might have to lead me to the booth and read my ballot and steady my writing hand while my other held my bottle . . ."

Roosevelt laughed. "That's years off. First things first, and the first thing is to get rid of the one obstacle that's keeping us on one side of the river. Did you notice anything at all, Doc, anything that might be useful?"

"We've been over it, Theodore," said Holliday. "You've seen him yourself now. He walks, he talks, he sees, he hears, he can't be hurt, and he can lift a two-ton rock as long as he doesn't have to throw it at anybody besides you and Geronimo."

"There's a weakness *somewhere*," said Roosevelt firmly.

"What makes you so sure?" asked Masterson.

"Because if there weren't, they'd be planning to take the war east of the Mississippi."

"How do you know they aren't?"

"If they were, Geronimo would know, and if he knew, he'd have told me."

"He barely knows you, Theodore," said Masterson.

"I'm the one he sent for," insisted Roosevelt. "If he knew, he'd have told me."

"Well, you know him better than I do," said Masterson. "I just wouldn't put any faith in that old man."

"Makes sense for you not to," offered Holliday. "After all, he turned you into a bat. But Theodore's the one white man he trusts."

"Whatever you say," said Masterson, clearly becoming annoyed. He got to his feet and left a few coins on the table. "I'm off to read a bit and then get a full night's sleep. There's a rodeo tomorrow, and I thought I might as well make a little money while I'm out here, so I'm writing it up for the *Epitaph*."

"Wonderful name for a Tombstone newspaper," commented Roosevelt.

"Useful, anyway," said Holliday as Masterson headed off to his room.

"You say that as if you've been reading it lately."

"I have," said Holliday. "John, the editor, is a friend of mine from the O.K. Corral days. The *Epitaph* hunted up witnesses, and it was the best friend Wyatt and I had during the trial. Its editorials are one of the reasons that Johnny Behan's not wearing a badge anymore."

"And how have you been using it?" asked Roosevelt.

"You've had a lot on your mind, so I don't blame you for not thinking much about it, but War Bonnet broke John Wesley Hardin out of jail a few days ago on the condition that he come to Tombstone and kill me."

"There was some talk about Hardin among the Rough Riders," said Roosevelt, appropriating Masterson's plate and his cold, half-eaten steak. "How good *is* he with a gun?"

"He's alive," answered Holliday. "Given the number of gunfights he's been in, that pretty much speaks for itself."

"Have you ever seen him in a shootout?"

"I've never seen him, period."

"But he's definitely coming this way?" persisted Roosevelt.

Holliday nodded. "The *Epitaph* has been tracking his progress for me." A grim smile. "There's no doubt who it is. Killed a man in a bar in Texas who thought it was funny to call him Hard-on." He paused. "Shot another man for not moving out of his way fast enough on a sidewalk in Lincoln County, New Mexico."

"You're kidding!"

"Check it out yourself. I'll be happy to show you."

"The man's a monster!" exclaimed Roosevelt.

"These days the man's a lawyer," said Holliday wryly. "Comes to pretty much the same thing."

"Well, we can make sure you don't have to face him alone," said Roosevelt. "I'll assemble my Rough Riders; they'll surround and protect you as they did me."

"They protected you against a magical giant with supernatural powers," replied Holliday. "Hardin is one hell of a shootist, but when all is said and done, that's all he is: a flesh-and-blood shootist."

"But why face him if you don't have to?"

"I've faced every man who ever came after me, Theodore. I faced Johnny Ringo a year after he'd been shot and killed. I've never asked anyone to fight my battles for me."

"What if you start coughing just when he's facing you?"

"Then I'll stop coughing permanently and the world will be none the worse off for it," answered Holliday. "If I were you, I'd worry about how to kill War Bonnet. After all, *I* don't plan to live long enough to be president."

Roosevelt offered a guilty smile. "It's just a fancy, a maybe-someday kind of thing. I have a lot to accomplish first."

"Well, I've done all my accomplishing. Either Hardin will put me in the grave now, or the sanitarium will plant me in a year or two. Like I said, worry about War Bonnet."

"I've been thinking about him all the way back," admitted Roosevelt. "And you know something, Doc?"

"What?"

"I'm convinced that he *can* be killed. There's a weakness there, but I'm missing it. I've gone over every one of his abilities in my mind, I've listed them all, I've examined them all, and it keeps eluding me. It's right there, so close I can almost touch it, but it keeps floating just out of my grasp." Roosevelt frowned. "I'm expressing myself badly. I really *am* a writer, you know."

"I've ordered your treatise on naval warfare," replied Holliday. "They say it's the definitive study. Should arrive in another couple of weeks."

"You really ordered it?" asked Roosevelt, clearly flattered.

"You really wrote it," was Holliday's answer.

"If it gets here before we leave, I'll inscribe it to you," Roosevelt promised.

"That's a thoughtful offer," said Holliday. "But we're either going to kill War Bonnet and Hardin or they're going to kill us before the book gets here, and I think you know it."

"I'm an optimist," said Roosevelt. "I think we'll both be here whether they arrive before the book or not."

"It'd be nice if you were right."

"If I can just see what I'm missing, I'll be right," answered Roosevelt.

"Have a drink," said Holliday, pushing his bottle across the table. "Maybe it'll clarify your thinking."

Roosevelt hesitated a moment, then shook his head. "My thinking's fine," he replied. "It's my damned perceptions that are playing havoc with me. His weakness is staring me in the face, and I'm still not seeing it."

"I understand you've been quite a few months without a woman," said Holliday. "Maybe one of Ned's metal chippies will help you relax and clarify your thinking. Kate Elder sold out when she left town, but they're still working here for the new owner."

"No," said Roosevelt firmly.

"You sure?"

"We have different moral codes, Doc. I don't tell you how to live, and I expect no less from you."

"The subject is closed," said Holliday.

"Thank you."

"Well," said Holliday, pushing his chair back from the table, "I think maybe I'll go try my luck at the poker tables." He grimaced. "I was planning to head back to Leadville after I introduced you to Geronimo, but if I'm going to face Hardin I might just as well do it where the air is thick enough to breathe."

He got to his feet, left a silver dollar on the table to pay for his dinner and his bottle, took the bottle with him, and walked out of the restaurant, past the front desk, and into the street, where he turned south and headed for the Oriental.

Roosevelt finished Masterson's steak, decided he was still hungry, ordered a small steak of his own, waited patiently for it to arrive, ate it, paid his bill, and went up to his room.

It was a hot night, and he opened the window. It almost surprised him that there was no bird waiting to fly in, become Geronimo or one of his warriors, and discuss yesterday's adventure.

He took off his coat and tie, unbuttoned the top two buttons on his shirt, stalked restlessly around the room for a few minutes, and finally sat down at the desk. He picked up a pen the hotel had supplied, dipped it in the desk's inkwell, and began writing on the hotel stationery he found in the drawer.

My Dearest Alice:

I know it is insane to write to you, who have been dead all these months, but I need to organize my thoughts, and you were always the one who acted as the perfect sounding board for them.

I find myself in a situation that nothing in my previous experience could have prepared me for. I must face, and defeat, an enormous creature, some two stories high, heavily muscled, with arms that end in flames—arms and flames that were clearly meant to engulf his enemies. By which I mean, to engulf me, for he was created solely to kill me and the Apache shaman Geronimo. He is invulnerable to bullets. I suspect he is equally impervious to knives and arrows. I find it difficult to believe that water will have any effects on his flaming extremities, nor do I know how, in this extremely dry and primitive desert town, I could find a sufficient supply of water to douse them even if I am mistaken.

All logic says that I should forget about confronting him. I should cut and run back to the eastern side of the Mississippi River. I know he won't follow me there. He was created solely to stop Geronimo and myself from coming to an agreement.

Yet if I do not deal with Geronimo, the United States will be confined to the eastern side of the Mississippi, whereas I truly believe that it is our manifest destiny to reach the Pacific as a nation. So I cannot turn tail and run, comforting as the thought of it might be to me when I sit here alone in the dark and realize what I must face.

Goliath did not tower over David the way this monster towers over normal men. And yet David brought his monster down with a single stone, and I must find the equivalent of that stone to use against my monster.

I have one advantage that David lacked: I have the greatest inventor of our age, Thomas Alva Edison, on my side. He has partnered with the inventor, Ned Buntline, to try to find weaknesses in the Indians' magic. He has succeeded here and there, in bits and pieces. If he can succeed this one last time, can create for me the equivalent of David's stone, that is the very last thing he will have to do out here in the West, and he and I can both go back to leading our normal lives.

The frustrating thing, the thing that is driving me crazy, is that I know War Bonnet's weakness. I know how to go about killing him—and yet that knowledge is buried somewhere in the back of my mind. For two days I have been trying to think of it, and have been unable to. My friend, the notorious shootist Doc Holliday, suggested that a drink might loosen the doors of my mind, and I am so frustrated that I briefly considered it. Hopefully when I talk to Edison and Buntline tomorrow, they'll ask the right question, and all will become clear.

If not, I will soon be lying beside you.

Your Theodore

25.

ROOSEVELT WAS UP WITH THE SUN, AS USUAL. He went through his calisthenics, walked down to the restaurant, and ordered some scrambled eggs and coffee. He wasn't surprised to see that Holliday wasn't in attendance, and only mildly less surprised to note that Masterson also hadn't come down to breakfast.

He finished, left some coins on the table, and went for a brisk walk around the southern end of town. Finally he found himself in front of Buntline's house, walked around it until he was facing Edison's front door, and approached it.

"One moment, Theodore Roosevelt," said a mechanical voice. A light flashed near his eyes, and by the time he'd stopped seeing spots the door opened and Thomas Edison was standing in the doorway.

"I'm sorry, Theodore," he said. "I'm trying out a new security system. I'll have to adjust the flash on that camera." He paused. "Come on in. Can I offer you anything to drink?"

"Some coffee."

"Good! I happen to have a pot on. I'll get it while I summon Ned." He stared at Roosevelt. "I assume you do want to speak to both of us?"

"I do."

"I thought so," said Edison, buzzing for Buntline. "You've been hunting the monster, haven't you?"

Roosevelt nodded, "Observing him, anyway."

"Fascinating!" said Edison, pouring the coffee. "I want to hear all about it!"

Buntline, his apron covered with soot from his furnace, where he'd been forging his super-hardened brass, entered the building through the connecting passageway. He greeted Roosevelt with a happy smile, and sat down on a shabby leather chair that had seen better days and decades.

"So, Theodore," said Edison, bringing him his coffee and then sitting down on a couch opposite him, what can you tell us about War Bonnet?"

"Most especially," added Buntline, "what can you tell us that Doc didn't tell us?"

"Everything and nothing," said Roosevelt, frowning. "I'm sure if he's got a weakness, I've seen it—but I haven't recognized it. That's what I'm hoping you two can do." He took a sip of the coffee and made a face. "Hot."

"It's just off the stove."

"Anyway, I was right that the medicine men control him, because when he had to make a split-second choice between attacking me and protecting them, he chose to protect them."

"We've pretty much figured that out," said Buntline. "Were you able to kill any of them—Dull Knife or the others?"

Roosevelt shook his head. "We may have wounded one. I'm sure we didn't kill him. And once War Bonnet got between the Rough Riders and the medicine men, he absorbed everything they threw at them."

"The Rough Riders," said Buntline with a smile. "I love that name."

"It fits them," said Roosevelt.

"Get back to the encounter, Theodore," said Edison impatiently. "Tell us everything you remember."

"He was behind a small rise when we arrived. I guess he heard us riding up in a group; he couldn't have seen us. Anyway, he got to his feet and came right at me."

"Impervious to the bullets of your men?"

"I told them not to waste time shooting at him, since based on Doc's experience it wouldn't have done any good," said Roosevelt. "Instead, I directed them to charge the medicine men's hut."

Edison grinned. "I'll bet he set a world record getting back there."

Roosevelt nodded an affirmative. "He totally ignored me—he could have reached and killed me in another ten or twelve seconds— but he raced back to get between the Rough Riders and the hut where the medicine men were."

"What makes you think you wounded one of them?" asked Buntline. "Did War Bonnet suddenly become weaker, maybe even start bleeding a little?"

"Sherman McMaster, one of my men, took a blind shot through the wall of one of the huts and we all heard a scream from within. War Bonnet screamed, too. He clutched his shoulder, and moved to protect the hut with his body. He was still absorbing all the bullets, so he didn't seem to be weakened at all . . . but from his actions, we felt sure that we'd chosen the right hut, and from the scream it seems safe to assume that we wounded *something*."

"All right," said Edison. "Once he got there, you couldn't do the inhabitants of the hut any more harm."

"Not *much* more," qualified Roosevelt.

"So at some point either your men retreated or War Bonnet assumed the medicine men were safe—"

"Or was *told* they were safe," interjected Buntline.

Edison nodded. "Or was told they were safe." He paused, frowning. "And then he went after you?"

Roosevelt shook his head. "It didn't happen quite that way. It was when other warriors—*normal* warriors, not medicine men and not monsters—joined the battle that my Rough Riders realized the medicine men were temporarily safe, and that meant I was exposed. So they raced back to me, dismounted, and surrounded me before War Bonnet could reach me. They knew from Doc's account, and their own battle just seconds ago, that he couldn't hurt them, couldn't even touch them with those fiery hands, so they had me kneel down and War Bonnet, try as he could, couldn't reach through or around them to get to me."

"Fascinating!" said Buntline. "But of course you couldn't stay like that all day. What changed?"

"I instructed Luke Sloan, one of my men, to mount up while the other five tightened the circle around me, and to ride, firing his guns, toward the medicine men's hut. War Bonnet immediately raced back to protect them, we mounted up and rode off, and Luke caught up with us later."

"And War Bonnet?" asked Buntline.

"Never saw him again," answered Roosevelt. He leaned back and finished his coffee. "And that's the whole story."

Edison rubbed his chin with his right hand. "Interesting," he said.

"Have you spotted something?" asked Roosevelt.

"Only the obvious, so far."

"Nothing's obvious to me," said Roosevelt. "What have you got?"

"He's not the brightest Indian you ever came across," said Edison. "Consider: he's standing almost within arm's reach of you. One of your men rides back toward the medicine men, and he promptly ignores you and races back, and by the time he's gotten there and scared Sloan away—I assume that's all he could do, that he couldn't actually harm or even touch your man—you've mounted up and gone. Right?"

"Right."

"Well, there you have it," said Edison.

Roosevelt frowned. "Maybe *you* have it. *I* don't."

"Think about it, Theodore. Your six men retreated, not because War Bonnet was decimating or even hurting them, but because *other* warriors showed up and drove them off. And suddenly he leaves you because one man is riding back to the very spot those warriors are stationed? He left the man he was created to kill to protect some medicine men who were in no need of his protection."

"Damn!" exclaimed Roosevelt. "I never thought of that."

"Don't let it bother you," replied Edison. "It's probably of little or no use to us. After all, we want to kill him. We already know that he's stupid."

"And nothing you shot at him—guns, rifles, *nothing*—got any reaction?" asked Buntline.

"Nothing," Roosevelt affirmed.

Edison rose and walked to the kitchen. "This sounds like a two-pot problem," he said, returning with the pot and refilling their coffee cups. "But we won't quit thinking and planning until we've got a solution."

"*Is* there a solution?"

"If I can electronically light the whole of Tombstone and find a way to power Ned's horseless stagecoaches, I promise you I can find a way to kill a monster who can only appear for a few minutes at a time and can only make physical contact with two men in all the world," said Edison. "Now let's go over what happened again."

And so they did, and then a third time, and then a fourth.

"You know, Theodore," said Edison ninety minutes later, "I'm starting to feel exactly like you. I have a feeling that I know everything I need to know, but I just haven't put it together yet." He went back to the kitchen and started brewing a new pot of coffee.

"Will you find him in the same place?" asked Buntline.

Roosevelt shrugged. "It depends. I think they're going to want more warriors to protect the medicine men in case I come back with a bigger group of Rough Riders—or they may want more medicine men if that'll make War Bonnet stronger. I don't imagine they'll move any closer."

"So you've got at least a day and a half's ride to confront him again."

"Not necessarily," replied Roosevelt. "Don't forget, he showed up just outside of Tombstone when Doc faced him. I imagine if Geronimo sends the word—and he doesn't need a runner or a telegraph to send it—that we're together and waiting for him, he'll show up there, wherever *there* is, a couple of minutes later."

"Does Geronimo contact him or the medicine men?"

"Beats me," said Roosevelt. "If I was to guess, I'd say the medicine men. *They* control *him*; I'm sure it doesn't work the other way around."

"No, that makes sense," agreed Buntline. "If he was a fifty-foot-high gorilla, I could build a cannon in two days' time that could put a hole in him the size of a bar stool. But a creature that's invulnerable . . ." He shook his head. "It's a mystery to me."

"We were sent out here to solve just such mysteries," said Edison, returning to the room with a coffee pot and three clean cups on a tray. He placed the tray on a table, took a cup, and sat down.

"I can go over the incident again," offered Roosevelt.

"No, Theodore," said Edison. "Four times is enough for both of us. Now it's a matter of finding the right way to look at the problem."

"I'm not sure I follow you, Tom," said Roosevelt.

"Don't let it distress you," said Buntline. "When he starts thinking, no one can follow him. That's why he's Thomas Alva Edison."

"We've put enough thought into this to realize that we're examining it from the wrong angle," said Edison.

"I still don't follow you," said Roosevelt.

"What have we been doing? Looking for a way to kill an invulnerable monster. Bigger bullets? A bigger cannon? Something sharp?" He sighed deeply. "None of that will work, and we're wasting our time trying to find a way, to put it bluntly, to puncture skin that is protected by magic and can't be punctured."

"Okay, I can agree with that," said Roosevelt. "But if we can't puncture his skin, how do we kill him?"

"We have to find a way," answered Edison, "and at least we know what *won't* work. I don't suppose asphyxiation will work either. Doc had a feeling that even though he has a nose and a mouth, he doesn't breathe—and even if he does, I don't see any way to cut off his air that he can't overcome. You can't gag him—he'd rip you apart before you got close enough."

Roosevelt walked over to the table, poured himself a cup of coffee, and returned to his seat.

"Too bad he doesn't eat," he remarked. "We could save a lot of trouble by poisoning his food."

Suddenly Edison smiled. "Say that again, Theodore."

"About poisoning his food?" repeated Roosevelt, frowning. "But we can't, and like I say, even if we could, he doesn't eat, or at least no one's ever *seen* him eat."

"I know," said Edison, the smile growing larger. "What a stupid way to hit upon a solution."

Roosevelt stared at him. "Are you quite well?"

Edison chucked. "Quite."

"Then I don't know what—"

"Give me just a second to work it out, Theodore."

Edison closed his eyes, placed an elbow on his knee, formed a fist, and propped his chin up with it.

"It's okay, Theodore," said Buntline softly, so as not to disturb his partner. "I've seen him like this before. He'll be fine in a minute. He'll sit so still you think he's gone catatonic, and then he'll open his eyes and explain whatever he's figured out in terms you and I can understand." He smiled reassuringly. "You'll see."

"It must drive you crazy," said Roosevelt.

"The results are worth it."

They sat in silence for almost two minutes, staring at the motionless Edison, who finally opened his eyes and sat erect.

"Let me ask you a couple of very simple questions, Theodore," he said.

"Go right ahead," said Roosevelt. "I'm dying to learn what I missed."

"Did you speak to him?"

Roosevelt frowned, trying to remember. "I don't think so," he said at last. "He yelled a threat or two, but I was talking to my Rough Riders. No, I don't think any of us spoke directly to him."

"Doesn't really matter," said Edison. "We know Doc spoke to him. Next question: Why did he stop coming after you and race off to protect the medicine men's hut?"

"My men were attacking it."

"How did he know?"

"They were screaming and shooting and riding directly toward it. He couldn't have missed that, not with all the shooting."

"One more question," said Edison. "When your men encircled you and you were kneeling on the ground, did he try to reach over them for you?"

"Yes," said Roosevelt. "They couldn't hurt him or drive him back, but he couldn't move them either."

"That's not what I meant," replied Edison. "He knew where you were. When one of them told you to kneel down, did he change his means of attack in any way? Which is to say, did he lean over and try to reach down to grab you?"

"Yes, but they kept pushing his arms away."

"But he knew you were kneeling?" persisted Edison. "He tried to reach you where you were, not where you'd been standing."

"That's right."

"Good."

"Good?" repeated Roosevelt, surprised. "That's all?"

Edison smiled. "That's all. The rest is up to Ned and me."

"I don't understand at all," said Roosevelt.

"Remember what I said: we were wasting our time trying to think of ways to pierce his skin, because he is invulnerable."

"Right."

"And we also decided there was no sense going after the medicine men again, that they'd be better protected this time."

"I know . . ." said Roosevelt, trying to follow Edison's chain of reasoning.

"It comes down to facing War Bonnet," said Edison. "We know that his body is invulnerable to bullets, and we can conclude based on both your and Doc's experiences with him that he's impervious to pain. There's every likelihood that he doesn't eat—that he's not in this plane of existence long enough to work up and satisfy an appetite. And there's a chance that he doesn't breathe, though I personally doubt that, because you need air to force out words, and we know he talks." Another smile. "Do you see it yet?"

"Oh, hell!" bellowed Roosevelt. "Of course I do. How could I have been so stupid?"

"It wasn't stupidity, Theodore," said Edison. "You are a remarkably adept problem-solver. This problem is just a long way beyond your area of expertise."

"It's still beyond mine," growled Buntline. "Will one of you two geniuses please enlighten me?"

"You go ahead, Theodore," said Edison.

Roosevelt leaned forward, facing Buntline directly. "What that litany Tom just recited did was list everything that was magical or supernatural about War Bonnet. He can't be hurt. He can't feel pain. He probably doesn't eat. He may not breathe. The trick," continued Roosevelt, smiling triumphantly, "the step I couldn't take when I was thinking about it last night, was to find if he has any trait or talent that *isn't* magical or supernatural, and to attack *it*." He paused, still grinning. "And since he can speak and hear and see, *that's* what we have to attack."

"We can't shoot him in the eyes," said Buntline. "The bullets will just bounce off. So we need another tactic."

"Same with his hearing," said Edison. "Unless you think Theodore can bite his ear off," he added with a laugh.

"How long will you need to make whatever it is you're going to make for me to use against him?" asked Roosevelt.

"I'd like a week," said Edison. "But we'll do it in two days if we have to."

"So if I were you," added Buntline, "I'd make myself mighty scarce for the next forty-eight hours."

"He can find me anywhere I hide," said Roosevelt. "I mean, hell, if a bloodhound could find me, it should be child's play for a creature of the medicine men."

"I don't think we can produce what you need any sooner, Theodore," said Buntline.

"That's all right," said Roosevelt. "I've got an idea that ought to work."

26.

OLLIDAY WAS HAVING A LUCRATIVE NIGHT at the Oriental, as Geronimo had promised. He was up four thousand dollars, and he'd won half of it on the preceding hand when he'd had nothing but a pair of deuces but bet his entire pile of chips and bluffed his four opponents into tossing in their hands rather than paying to see what he held.

He'd decided it was time to take a ten-minute break and celebrate with some imported Scotch. Not that he preferred it, but since it cost twice as much, it was what he drank when he was celebrating.

The usual crowd was there—all of Roosevelt's Rough Riders, plus Charlie Bassett, Loose Martinez, even Henry Wiggins, who rarely drank and never gambled. John Behan walked past the window, looked in, didn't like what he saw, and kept walking.

"Bartender!" said Holliday.

"Come on, Doc," said the bartender. "You know perfectly well that my name is Tom."

"True," agreed Holliday. "But 'Bartender' sounds so much more dramatic. However, let's split the difference." He cleared his throat. "Bartender Tom, drinks for the house."

"Scotch?" asked the bartender.

"I'm merely generous, not philanthropic," replied Holliday. "Make it whiskey." He looked out the window into the street. "And if the gentleman I see approaching the Oriental actually enters, get him a glass of milk or sarsaparilla, whichever comes first."

Roosevelt entered the saloon, waved to his men, and sat down at a table. "I'll have some tea, please."

"You sure you don't want milk?" asked the bartender.

"No, thanks."

"Or sarsaparilla."

"Never tried it," replied Roosevelt. "Is it any good?"

"Beats me," said the bartender with a shrug.

"Might as well find out," said Roosevelt. "Bring me a bottle."

"There's saloons where you put your life in danger just ordering a bottle of that," noted Holliday.

"Well, hopefully this isn't one of them," answered Roosevelt. "Right now my life is in Tom and Ned's hands."

"They think they'd found a way to kill War Bonnet?" asked Holliday, and suddenly all other talk ceased.

"It's possible," said Roosevelt. "The problem is, it'll take them two days to make the weapon I need. I thought, just in case he shows up before I'm ready for him, I might prevail upon the brave men who just returned with me to perform the same service here that they did when he tried to attack me in Indian country."

"You can count on me, Dandy," said Sloan.

"And I," added Mickelson.

Soon all six Rough Riders had pledged their support.

"I'm sorry I couldn't ride with you before, but I'll do whatever I have to—if you'll have me," said Charlie Bassett.

"I appreciate that, Mr. Bassett—"

"Charlie."

"Charlie," corrected Roosevelt. "And from everything I've heard about you, you're a man whose help would be most welcome."

"I've never fired a gun in my life," said Wiggins, "but I'll lend all the moral support I can."

"That will be more than sufficient, Henry," said Roosevelt.

"What the hell," said Martinez. "Count me in too."

"This is precisely the reaction I'd hoped for," said Roosevelt. "It's only for two days, and in all likelihood nothing will come of it. Once the weapon is completed, your job is done and mine begins."

"Are you planning on facing this monster alone?" asked Bassett.

Roosevelt nodded his head. "Either the weapon will work or it won't. If it works, I won't need any help, and if it doesn't, I'll be past needing help by the time I know it."

He pulled a book out of his pocket and began to read.

"Ben , , , something," said Wiggins, looking at the cover.

"*Ben-Hur*," replied Roosevelt.

"Good book?"

"Not to my taste, but reasonably well written."

"If it's not your taste, why read it?" asked Mickelson.

"Because it's written by General Lew Wallace," answered Roosevelt.

Mickelson frowned. "I know that name."

"You sure as hell ought to," said Holliday. "He was the Governor of the New Mexico Territory."

"Why should that matter?"

"He's the man who pardoned Billy the Kid. If he hadn't, the Kid would still be rotting in jail and a lot less men would be dead."

"And Pat Garrett would be a damned sight poorer."

"Right," said Holliday with an amused smile that only Roosevelt understood. Initially he'd been surprised that Holliday made no attempt to set the record straight, until he realized that the last thing the consumptive dentist needed was to face an unending line of young guns who wanted to go up against the man who'd killed Billy the Kid. He'd had enough of that already.

"Why don't you put that book down for a while and play a man's game with us, Theodore?" said Turkey Creek Johnson.

Roosevelt smiled. "Tombstone's already got a mayor."

"What the hell are you talking about?"

"Politics is a man's game," said Roosevelt. "Poker is a gambler's game."

"What about war?" asked Mickelson.

"War," replied Roosevelt, "is a fool's game."

"Damn!" said Holliday with a chuckle. "I can see that drawing a standing ovation at a political rally. Especially from those who have never had to participate in one."

"Or those who have," said Roosevelt.

"You gonna run for office again, Theodore?" asked Hairlip Smith.

"Let's see if I survive the next few days," answered Roosevelt. "Then I'll worry about it."

"Got to admit he answers like a politician," said Mickelson. "I'd vote for you myself if I'd ever bothered to become a citizen."

"You don't have to be a citizen to vote on this side of the river," said Johnson. "We're not officially a country, you know."

"Keep me alive for two days and I have every intention of changing that," said Roosevelt.

"I can think of a lot of reasons to keep you alive, Theodore," said Sherman McMaster, "but turning this place into another Boston sure as hell ain't one of them."

There was general laughter, and then Holliday took his Scotch back to the table.

"We ready to start again?" asked Sloan.

"You got any money left?" asked Holliday. "Any at all?"

"Yeah."

Holliday smiled. "Then we're ready to start again."

Hairlip Smith dealt the cards, and as the game took their attention, Wiggins walked over to Roosevelt's table.

"Care for a little company?" he asked. "I just never got in the habit of wasting my money at poker or faro."

"Certainly," said Roosevelt, closing his book and pushing it aside.

"They've been talking about War Bonnet all evening," said Wiggins. "Problem is, they've been drinking all evening, and every time they describe him he gets bigger and more terrifying. What was he really like?"

"Big and terrifying," said Roosevelt with a smile. "I hardly saw him at all. For most of the time he had his back to me, and when he didn't, my men had me surrounded while I knelt on the ground, so I never got a good look at him. The man to talk to is Doc, who was as close to him, face-to-face, as I am to you."

"I've heard Doc. If this War Bonnet is half what Doc says and even a quarter of what the others say, why are you sitting here waiting for him? Why not go back to New York? He won't follow you across the Mississippi. From what I understand, all he wants is to stop you from making a deal with Geronimo."

"There are a lot of wrong assumptions in that statement, Henry," said Roosevelt. "First, I came here from the Dakota Badlands, not New York. Second, there is no reason to believe that he either can't or won't follow me anywhere I go. And third, I'm here because there are some things worth risking my life for, and doubling the size of the United States—more than doubling it—is certainly one of them."

Wiggins stared down at his folded hands and made no reply.

"Is something wrong?" asked Roosevelt after a moment.

"I'm used to the fact that you make me feel totally unaccomplished," replied Wiggins. "But this is the first time you've made me feel like a coward. Even Doc and Wyatt never managed that."

"I'd no intention of doing that," said Roosevelt. "Nor do I think you're a coward. You've come out to a lawless land, and you've made a life for yourself. You walk among shootists without carrying a weapon. And I have no doubt that faced with a choice, there are half a dozen things you'd put your life on the line for. There's no reason why you should share my views about the expansion of the United States. But if your children were threatened, or even Tom and Ned, who befriended you and employed you, I think you'd find that you are far braver than you think you are."

Wiggins stared thoughtfully into space for a few seconds. "Yes," he said. "Yes, I *would* risk my life for my children. And for some other things." He extended his hand across the table. "Thank you, Theodore. Thank you for giving my self-esteem a good hard kick in the pants."

Roosevelt grinned. "That's what politicians are for."

Suddenly a well-dressed man Roosevelt had never seen before entered the Oriental, a folded piece of paper in his hand. He looked around and then walked up to the table Holliday was seated at.

"I've been looking all over for you, Doc," he said.

"I thought everyone knew where to find me after dark," said Holliday, getting to his feet and facing the man. "John, this distinguished-looking young man at the next table is Theodore Roosevelt, about whom you've doubtless been hearing. Theodore, say hello to John Clum, editor of the *Tombstone Epitaph*."

Roosevelt got up, walked over, and shook Clum's hand. "I'm pleased to meet you. Doc has been praising you since I got here. I take it you write a splendid editorial."

"I also write obits," answered Clum, "and if Doc stays in Tombstone there's every likelihood I'll be writing *his* in a few days."

"Can't be a parade of jealous husbands," said Holliday with a smile. "I'm not the man I used to be." He paused. "Probably I never was."

"I'm serious, Doc." He pulled the paper out of his pocket, unfolded it, and held it up. "He's just a couple of days away, and he's killing his way to Tombstone."

"This is John Wesley Hardin you're speaking of?" asked Roosevelt.

Clum nodded. "This mystical Indian everyone's talking about seems to have broken him out of jail on the condition that he kill Doc."

"First he's got to get here," said Holliday. "Then he has to beat me in a gunfight. It's never been done yet."

"He's never lost yet either," said Clum in frustrated tones. "Doc, you're a good man despite your reputation, and I consider you a friend, so please listen to me. You've survived the O.K. Corral, and the thing that used to be Johnny Ringo, and Billy the Kid, and a disease that would have killed most men a decade ago. Just how long do you think you can stay lucky?"

"Another week ought to do it," answered Holliday.

"Bah!" Clum growled, stalking toward the swinging doors. "I did my best."

Then he was gone.

"You know, Doc," said Roosevelt, "I've got my Rough Riders now, and I'll have a weapon in two days. There's no reason for you to stick around."

"You think I should go back to Colorado?" asked Holliday.

"Why not?"

"He's already killed forty-two men before they locked him away, and five more since he broke out. Do you want him to follow me to

Leadville shooting everyone and everything he sees there, starting with Kate Elder and the staff of the sanitarium?" snapped Holliday. "Damn it, Theodore, I'm going to have to face him sooner or later. No one else can stop him."

"You're right," said Roosevelt. "I hadn't thought it through. I apologize."

Holliday turned back to his table and began dealing the cards, Roosevelt sat down and began reading his book again, and both of them tried to pretend that their minds weren't dwelling almost exclusively on their confrontations to come.

27.

ROOSEVELT SPENT THE NEXT TWO DAYS IN THE ORIENTAL. He ate his meals there, he slept there, he frequently cursed the fact that he couldn't bathe there, and he waited there, surrounded by his Rough Riders and other friends standing guard in rotation. Buntline had even sent over a reconditioned robotic prostitute, which was now his cook and housemaid, to patrol the outside of the building.

"She can see in almost total darkness," explained Buntline when he brought the robot to the Oriental, "she can hear sounds that are even beyond a dog's ability to hear, and since she has no emotions—I removed the more primitive ones that people paid for—I guarantee neither War Bonnet nor anything else the medicine men can produce is going to scare her."

Roosevelt was picking at some fried eggs when the robot entered the saloon. He looked up at her curiously.

"He wants you," said the robot.

"He's finally got it built—whatever it is?" asked Roosevelt, getting to his feet.

"All I know is that he has sent for you."

"I'm on my way," said Roosevelt, grabbing his hat from where he'd hung it on the back of the chair and heading for the swinging doors with the robot following him.

"Hey, honey, don't be in such a hurry to leave," said Luke Sloan.

"My duties have ended," replied the robot. "There is no reason to remain."

"I could show you one or two," said Sloan as Roosevelt walked out the door and hurried down the street. A moment later he heard a crash and turned to see Sloan hurled through the plate-glass window, landing past the raised sidewalk and into the dirt street with a *thud*.

Roosevelt smiled but kept walking, and a few moments later came to Edison's house. The door was open, and he walked right up to it.

"Is this thing working?" he called out, stopping a few feet short of it.

"It's working just fine," said Edison's voice through a crude metal speaker that was positioned above the door.

"It's wide open."

"That's because it's been told to let you in. If you were anyone else, even Doc, it would have slammed in your face. Now, are you going to stand out there in the sun all day, or are you going to come in and see what we've got for you."

Roosevelt entered the house, saw that the living room was empty, and made his way to the office, where Edison and Buntline were waiting for him.

"From what I saw over at the Oriental, all I really need is one of those metal harlots to protect me," said Roosevelt. "She packs quite a wallop."

"They should have left her alone," said Buntline. "She's not programmed for that kind of thing anymore." He paused. "I assume someone laid lecherous hands on her?"

"All I saw was the aftermath," replied Roosevelt. "A body flying through the window into the street. You wouldn't know she was that strong to look at her."

"She has that in common with a lot of women," said Edison with a smile.

"I need her to be that strong," said Buntline. "She can lift an entire brass stagecoach if she has to."

"You make her sound like Kate Elder," commented Roosevelt with a grin.

"Doc's Kate?" replied Buntline. "If this one had Kate's temper, she'd probably have killed *both* sides by now—us and the Indians."

"Hard to imagine her as a prostitute."

"That is definitely *not* what she and the others were created for," said Buntline heatedly. "Medical science is making progress, but the War between the States left us a nation of cripples. If you were shot in an arm or a leg, the odds were fifty-fifty that they were going to have to amputate that limb if you were to live."

"Ah!" said Roosevelt. "I'm starting to understand."

"The first few successful experiments weren't robots like you saw, Theodore," said Edison. "We created them just to offset the costs, since the government was paying me to learn how the Indians worked their magic and to combat it, not to find out how to replace amputated limbs. Anyway, the first few were women with metal legs or arms. Some of them wound up working for Kate Elder, who offered us a very healthy fee if we could make one hundred percent robotic prostitutes for her brothel. Not only were they a unique attraction, but they never got sick, they never asked for more money, they were never bought away by rival establishments, they worked twenty-four hours each and every day, they never had periods, they—"

"Stop, Tom," interrupted Buntline. Edison turned to him questioningly. Buntline smiled. "You were getting too enthused."

Edison actually blushed. "Anyway," he concluded, "it was quite a breakthrough. Once we're back East, I plan to present papers and demonstrations at the leading medical colleges—with Ned's assistance, of course."

"That's fascinating," said Roosevelt. "It truly is."

"Thank you."

"But I have a more pressing problem," he continued. "I believe you summoned me here to talk about it."

"More than talk, Theodore," said Edison. "As I said two days ago, there is no sense going after War Bonnet's supernatural strengths, so we're going after his very human weaknesses." He turned to Buntline. "Ned? The clip-ons?"

"What's a clip-on?" asked Roosevelt.

"You'll see," said Edison, as Buntline reached into a pocket and pulled out a pair of dark, almost black lenses attached to a metal frame.

Edison took them from him, held them up to the light, and tried to peer through them. "Good job," he said approvingly, then turned to Roosevelt. "Theodore, the fact that you wear glasses may actually prove to be a benefit in your coming confrontation."

"That'll be a first," said Roosevelt.

"Trust me, it'll buy you a couple of seconds, and you just may need those seconds in a life-and-death battle with War Bonnet."

"I need every advantage I can get when I go up against him," said Roosevelt with conviction. "As awesome as I made him sound, he's even more so in person."

Edison walked over, lenses in hand, and reached out for Roosevelt's glasses. Roosevelt instinctively pulled his head back.

"It's all right, Theodore," said Edison. "I'm not going to hurt you."

"I know that, Tom," replied Roosevelt. "I just have this tendency to protect my eyes." He reached up to remove his glasses. "Here, you can have them."

"No," said Edison. "Leave them on—and believe me, I'm not about to poke your eye out."

Roosevelt held still while Edison reached out with the lenses, and clipped them onto the top of the glasses' frame.

"It works," he said happily.

"I told you it would," said Buntline. "Now flip them down."

Edison lowered the darkened lenses on tiny hinges until they totally covered Roosevelt's own lenses.

"Works perfectly," announced Buntline.

"I don't want to disillusion you," said Roosevelt. "But I can't see a damned thing."

"Better now than later," said Buntline.

"What the hell are you talking about?" demanded Roosevelt.

"I'll explain it in a moment," said Edison. "Now, gently, so you don't break them or detach them, flick the dark lenses up so that you're looking at me through your regular glasses again."

Roosevelt did as he was told.

"What do you think?" asked Edison.

"Perfect," said Buntline. "If they didn't work, we'd have had to put them in real frames, he couldn't have worn his own glasses, and who knows how blind he is without them?"

"Follow me, Theodore," said Edison, walking through his living room and out into his front yard with Roosevelt and Buntline falling into step behind him.

"Just about high noon, wouldn't you say?" asked Edison.

"Give or take ten minutes," agreed Roosevelt.

"Good. Look up into the sun."

"Really?" said Roosevelt, frowning. "Why?"

"Just do it, please."

Roosevelt looked up. Within ten seconds his eyes were watering, and in another five he had to shut them and turn away.

"Thank you, Theodore."

"What was *that* all about?" demanded Roosevelt.

"You'll see in a moment. Now fold those black lenses down over your glasses."

"All right," said Roosevelt.

"Can you see me?"

Roosevelt shook his head.

"And of course you couldn't see me in the house."

"That's right."

"Good. Now look up at the sun."

Roosevelt looked straight overhead.

"Can you see it?" asked Edison.

"Just barely," said Roosevelt. "As if it's three times as far away as usual on a very foggy day."

"Keep looking," said Edison, staring at his watch.

"What's this all about, Tom?"

"Soon. Just keep looking."

Roosevelt stood motionless, his head tilted back.

"Okay," said Edison. "You're done. Take 'em off and let's go back into the house."

Roosevelt followed Edison and Buntline back inside. This time they didn't go into the office but seated themselves in the living room, and he followed suit.

"What do you think?" asked Edison.

"I think he'll be all right."

"Well, that's the first half of it."

"Would one of you mind telling me what you're talking about, and what the purpose of my staring into the sun through those things was?"

"You want to get it, Ned?"

Buntline got up. "I'll be right back," he said, heading off to the enclosed passageway between the two houses.

"As I said, Theodore, there was no sense trying to find something that could pierce War Bonnet's skin, or even give him some massive electric shock. You say he's invulnerable, Geronimo says so, and based on my observations of Indian magic, I have no trouble believing it. But based on everything you and Doc have told me from your separate encounters with him, he can see."

Roosevelt frowned. "Of course he can."

"The eye is a very complex organ, but it functions pretty much the same in all living things—men, horses, fish, dogs, birds, you name it."

"All right," said Roosevelt. "Eyes operate the same."

"Then believe me when I tell you that no living thing can stare into the sun for much longer than you did a few moments ago, at least not without the kind of protection we created for your glasses."

"You're not suggesting that you've found a way to make him stare into the sun," said Roosevelt.

"Almost," said Edison with a smile as Buntline returned to the room, carrying a device that was cylindrical, perhaps two feet long and six inches in diameter. There was a trigger mechanism beneath it, and a cord emanating from the back.

"Looks heavy," remarked Roosevelt.

"It has to be, for what it's got to do," said Buntline. "And it's got an even heavier battery. I hope you're in good shape, Theodore."

Roosevelt took the weapon from Buntline, hefted it, spun around once with it. "I can handle it," he announced.

"Can you handle it with thirty or forty pounds strapped to your back?" asked Buntline.

"I suppose I'll have to."

"Try holding it up, aimed right at me, with one hand."

Roosevelt did so. "Now perhaps you'll tell me *why* I'll have to, which is to say, what does this weapon do?"

"Theodore," explained Edison, "this mechanism produces a light that will affect the eyes the way staring into the sun effected yours, and it'll do it within two seconds. If War Bonnet saw you, and of course he did, if he avoided things that were in his way, if he saw the rock that Doc says he lifted, then we have to assume his eyes will react to light like anyone else's—and that means the three or four seconds after you start firing this, he'll be blind, and stay blind for quite some time. You don't fire time and again like a six-gun; you depress the trigger and hold it down. But *not*," concluded Edison, "before you flip those black lenses down over your glasses. Even from a position behind the gun, the world around you will get so bright so fast that you will literally go blind in seconds, and since you're not a supernatural creature whose eyes can be remade by your creators, you'll *stay* blind. So you *must* remember to flip those lenses down before you fire. The world will become so bright in your immediate vicinity that you'll have no difficulty seeing through them. It really won't look like a foggy night to you."

Roosevelt handed the weapon back to Buntline.

"You look less than enthused," noted Edison.

"Maybe you know something I don't know," said Roosevelt, "but I agree with your statement that he'll only be temporarily blind, and that Dull Knife and the others can fit him out with a new pair of eyes easier and faster than you and Ned could fit a wound victim out with a new arm or leg."

Edison smiled.

"What's so funny?" demanded Roosevelt.

"You're right. We do know something you don't know."

"Perhaps you'll enlighten me and then we'll all know it," said Roosevelt irritably.

"That weapon," began Edison, "that focused sunshine, was never intended to be a long-term solution. Its entire purpose is to temporarily blind War Bonnet so he cannot attack or destroy the weapon that *will* kill him."

"Just what the hell are you talking about?" demanded Roosevelt.

Edison turned, walked into his office, opened a cabinet, withdrew another cylindrical device, and returned to the living room with it.

"It looks like the other one's little brother," remarked Roosevelt, staring at it.

"It's the ultimate weapon, Theodore," said Edison. "Our biggest problem was how to protect *you* from it."

Roosevelt took the weapon from Edison, hefted it, noticed that it, too, had a cord in the back.

"Okay," said Roosevelt. "I've blinded War Bonnet before he can get his hands on me. Now what?"

"Now you fire this baby," said Buntline, "and unless I miss my guess, you're going to be looking at one dead giant Indian."

"It clearly doesn't shoot bullets," said Roosevelt, studying it. "What *does* it shoot?"

"Same thing we were talking about two nights ago, and just a few minutes ago," answered Edison. "He has superhuman, supernatural strength. He's invulnerable. But he has human senses. Vision is one of them. Hearing is the other."

"This weapon will make such a sound as has never been heard before, Theodore," said Buntline. "In fact, I'd hesitate to call it a sound at all. Just as there are sounds so high we can't hear them but dogs can, and sounds they can't hear but that certain insects will react to . . . well, this will produce the Ultimate Sound. You won't hear a thing, and neither will War Bonnet . . . but if we're right, it'll burn out every circuit in what passes for his brain."

"Just like that?" said Roosevelt.

"Just like that," replied Buntline.

"Well, not *quite* like that," interjected Edison. "First, those black lenses have to work. You have to not only be able to see him, but to protect yourself if he's thrashing around blindly and he stumbles in your direction."

"And second?"

"Second, I can protect you by chemically sealing your ears before you set out to meet him, but once they *are* sealed, you won't understand a word he or anyone else is saying unless you're a lip reader. And of course that condition will remain until you make it back here and I unseal them. It's a delicate process; if anyone else attempts to work on your ears, you could go permanently deaf, so even if you're wounded and can't return here for weeks or even months, don't let anyone else work on your ears."

"Is there any third thing I should know?"

"I'll show you how to connect both weapons to the battery. Then, whenever you're ready, I'll go to work on your ears. It'll probably take an hour."

"Might as well start as soon as you show me the batteries," said Roosevelt. "I don't plan to have a conversation with that supernatural bastard anyway."

"Have you thought about how you'll find him?" asked Edison. "You won't want to go around deaf, carrying two weapons, with a massive battery strapped to your back, for days or even weeks."

"It won't take that long," said Roosevelt. "As soon as you're done with me, I'll start riding toward Geronimo's lodge. He'll probably be watching me as a bird or a snake or a rat even as I'm leaving town, and as soon as no one's around he'll manifest himself to find out where I'm going. And if I'm wrong and I have to ride all the way to his lodge, it's only a few hours."

"Why go at all?" asked Buntline. "He has no means of combating War Bonnet."

Roosevelt grinned. "Can you think of a better way to draw War Bonnet here than to present him with a chance to kill both of us at once?"

28.

ROOSEVELT DECIDED THAT IF EDISON WAS RIGHT about his weaponry, the sound would instantly kill Manitou, so he left him stabled in Tombstone and rented a swaybacked old gelding, then stopped by the inventor's house briefly to have his ears plugged.

Half an hour later he was riding south out of town, heading in the general direction of Geronimo's lodge. He wasn't sure he could pinpoint the location, but he was sure the Apache would know he was coming and was probably watching him already.

An hour out of town he stopped at the one water hole he remembered, and after he filled his canteen and stood aside to let his horse drink, a brown hawk that had been circling high above him gently soared down, landed lightly on the ground, and immediately became Geronimo.

"I see you have been with the man Edison," noted the Apache.

Roosevelt smiled, shook his head, and pointed to his ears. "I can't hear you."

"What is wrong with you?" asked Geronimo.

Roosevelt shrugged and pointed to his ears. "I'm sorry. I can't hear you. Edison closed my ears."

And then it seemed to Roosevelt that he could *feel* Geronimo's voice inside his head.

"*I understand*," said the medicine man. "*This has to do with the weapon.*"

"Yes," said Roosevelt.

"*You think to find War Bonnet out here, in the desert?*"

"I hope to," replied Roosevelt. "I can't go around deaf for weeks waiting for him to show up, and I can't lug these weapons everywhere. I don't even know how long the battery holds a charge."

"*The battery?*"

"Don't worry about it. It powers the weapons." Roosevelt wiped some sweat from his brow. "I was hoping to draw War Bonnet out, that if he thought he'd find the two of us together he might attack—or if he thought I'd learned something from Edison or anyone else that might prove detrimental to him, he might want to attack me before I could contact you." He paused. "At any rate, my idea was to get him to attack while I'm ready for him."

Geronimo closed his eyes for a moment and frowned, as if concentrating on something. Finally he opened them. "*You are about to get your wish, White Eyes.*"

"Get away from here as fast and as far as you can!" said Roosevelt. "Even you are not safe from these weapons."

Suddenly Roosevelt was speaking to empty air. He decided there was no sense getting back onto his horse, that the weapons were hard enough to handle when he was on solid ground. Besides, there was no question that the light would blind and probably panic the horse, and the sound would kill it, and he didn't need to have a horse bucking in terror or falling over dead on him while he was training his large, awkward weapons on War Bonnet.

He slipped into the harness Edison had made that held the heavy battery onto his back, lay the weapon he'd dubbed "the deafener" gently on the ground, and held the one he called "the blinder" across his chest after making sure it was connected to the battery.

He stood motionless for a long moment in the blazing sun, wondering if Geronimo had finally been wrong about something. But then a huge shadow fell across the ground just ahead of him, and he found himself facing War Bonnet, who seemed to have gotten even taller and more massive since their last encounter.

"I have come for you, Roosevelt!" thundered the creature. "And this time there are none to protect you."

Roosevelt tried to lip read, but it was futile; the monster had no discernible lips. So he simply pointed the blinder at War Bonnet and prepared to fire.

At the last second he realized he hadn't flipped down his special lenses. He reached up, lowered them in front of his glasses, hoped War Bonnet was either standing still or approaching in a straight line, because he couldn't see a thing, and then he pulled the trigger.

Roosevelt couldn't hear it, but War Bonnet's scream of surprise and anger could be heard within a radius of five miles—and suddenly he could see, plain as day, through the almost-opaque black lenses. He depressed the trigger for another four seconds, then laid the weapon on the ground, removed the clip-ons, and saw the creature staggering blindly around, some thirty feet away.

Roosevelt knelt down, picked up the deafener, attached it to the battery cord, and pressed the firing mechanism. War Bonnet screamed, though Roosevelt couldn't hear him, took a blind step toward his enemy, then clasped his hands to his ears and screamed again. Roosevelt kept the mechanism depressed, War Bonnet kept screaming and clasping his ears, and then, about ten seconds later, he literally exploded in a thousand pieces.

Roosevelt lay the deafener down next to the blinder and walked around the area, making sure there was nothing alive and moving where War Bonnet had been. Satisfied that the creature was totally gone, he turned to load the weapons onto his gelding, only to realize that of course the sound had killed the horse, too.

"Damn!" he muttered. "It's going to be a long walk."

"You have done a service to your country and saved both our lives. You will not have to walk alone."

And suddenly Geronimo was beside him, picking up the smaller of the two weapons. Roosevelt, the battery still on his back, retrieved the blinder, and the two men walked back to town, ignoring the burning rays of the desert sun as best they could.

As they came within sight of Tombstone, Geronimo came to a stop.

"Is something wrong?" asked Roosevelt.

"I will see you one more time before you return home. And again, many years from now."

Before Roosevelt could ask what he had meant, Geronimo, the chief medicine man of the Apache nation, had vanished.

29.

HOLLIDAY DRAGGED HIMSELF OUT OF BED, turned a handkerchief red with the blood he coughed up, walked painfully to the sink in the corner and splashed some water on his face, then stared blearily into the mirror on the wall.

"You look worse than usual," he managed to croak, and was sure his image agreed.

He was getting ready to put on his clothes when he realized that he hadn't taken them off the night before. He seemed to remember getting back to his room just about the time the sun was rising, and he thought he'd won something like three thousand dollars, but he wasn't sure of anything. Everything would become clear after his first drink of the day, as usual.

He retied his tie, felt for his Derringer, realized it wasn't in his pocket, looked around, and saw that he'd left it on the nightstand. Just as well. The safety catch was off, and he might have blown a hole in his chest if he had rolled the wrong way.

"It's so easy to go to bed," he muttered. "Why is it so goddamned hard to get out of it?"

He found his holster on the floor where he'd let it drop, put it back on, checked to make sure his gun was loaded, then looked around for his hat. It lay against a wall, and he figured he'd aimed at the chair and missed. He picked it up, dusted it off, and donned it, then decided that the rest of him needed dusting as well.

Finally he was ready to face the world, and he opened the door, walked out into the corridor, followed it to the top of the stairs, and climbed down to the main floor, where he saw Masterson at the front desk.

"Good morning, Doc," said Masterson.

"Well, it's morning, anyway," replied Holliday. "I see you've got your carpet bag. Where are you off to?"

"Home."

Holliday frowned. "Home?"

"Haven't you heard the news?" said Masterson. He studied Holliday's face for a moment. "No, of course you haven't. You've been asleep all day."

"What news?"

"Theodore killed War Bonnet," said Masterson.

"How?"

"You'll have to ask him. He's telling his Rough Riders all about it over at the Oriental."

"So why aren't you there?" asked Holliday.

"This life isn't for me, Doc, not anymore," replied Masterson. "I brought Theodore out here, and I stuck around until he met Geronimo and killed War Bonnet, but I belong back in New York, writing about a horse race or a baseball game. I served my decade out here fighting bad guys. It cost me a brother and ten years of any reasonable income. Now I'm a writer and enjoying the hell out of it."

"I'm sure you'll be writing about your pal Theodore one of these days," said Holliday. "That young man has a hell of a future ahead of him." He paused. "He really killed War Bonnet?"

"He really did."

"Son of a bitch," said Holliday. "I do believe you woke me up."

Masterson chuckled. "Anyway, he doesn't need me to guide him back. Anyone who can do what he's done can find the Badlands or New York City on his own when he's ready to go back home."

"True enough," agreed Holliday. He extended his hand. "Take care, Bat."

"You too, Doc," said Masterson. "Theodore killed *his* monster. I hear that yours is still making his way here."

"He's just a man."

"And John L. Sullivan is just a guy with a temper. Don't give him any kind of edge, Doc."

"You can bank on that," said Holliday.

Then Holliday was out the door and walking over to the Oriental. When he got there he saw Manitou tied to hitching post out front, with Edison's weapons hanging from his saddle.

He entered the saloon and walked over to his usual table.

"Breakfast!" he grated.

"In a glass or a bottle?" asked the bartender.

"Yes."

"Damn it, Doc . . ."

"A bottle."

The bartender brought a bottle over, Holliday took a swallow, and as he did so Roosevelt, who had been conversing with Hairlip Smith, Luke Sloan, and Morty Mickelson got up and walked over to Holliday's table.

"Good morning, Doc."

"If you say so."

"Well, it's *was*," chuckled Roosevelt. "Actually, it's about five in the afternoon." He stared at Holliday. "You look like death warmed over."

"That good, huh?" said Holliday.

"Have you heard that I killed War Bonnet?"

"Yeah, Bat told me. But I still don't know how the hell you did it. I shot that bastard from point-blank range and never made a dent in him."

"Tom and Ned crafted a pair of weapons that did the trick."

"I saw them hanging on your saddle."

"No one's going to take them. I've got the Rough Riders keeping watch on them through the window."

"So when are you going back East?" asked Holliday, taking another long swallow and starting to feel more human.

"Very soon," said Roosevelt. "I have to say good-bye to Tom and Ned first." He flashed Holliday a guilty smile. "I haven't even been to their houses since the battle. I've been too intent on telling my Rough Riders all the details of what happened. After all, Tom and Ned made the weapons, but it was the Rough Riders who faced War Bonnet and kept him from killing me."

"Buy 'em all a drink," suggested Holliday.

"I bought a bottle for each of them," said Roosevelt, flashing the grin that Holliday was getting used to. "Anyway, in answer to your question, I'll be going East tomorrow or the next day, but I haven't decided how far east."

"If your hat floats, you've gone too far," said Holliday.

"Very funny," replied Roosevelt. "Anyway, I don't know if I'm going to stop at Elkhorn—that's my ranch near Medora—or go all the way back to New York." He sighed deeply. "Nothing's going to bring my Alice back to me, and there's so much that needs doing. I can't hide from the world in the Badlands all my life."

Holliday smiled. "I have a feeling that the world has a way of finding men like you wherever you hide."

"There are important things to be done," agreed Roosevelt. "Things that can't be done from Medora. Would you think I was crazy if I told you that someday I plan to open a channel through Panama, so our ships don't have to sail all the way around the tip of South America to get from one ocean to another?"

"If you plan to do the shoveling yourself, I'd say you were crazy," answered Holliday. "Otherwise, I'd say that's a damned useful project."

"And I have so many more, so many that we truly *need*."

"Can I offer a word of advice, Theodore?"

"Certainly."

"Forget the Badlands *and* New York. Go right to Washington, DC."

Roosevelt uttered a hearty laugh. "The thought has crossed my mind."

"Hang on to it," said Holliday. "The country needs someone like you running things, especially if it's going to more than double its area."

"I appreciate the thought, and I'll admit it has crossed my mind as well, but I've got things to do first."

"And I've got one thing to do last," said Holliday grimly.

"Hardin? Is there any word on when you can expect him?"

Holliday shook his head. "He could have been here two or three days ago if he'd just take some time off from all his killing."

"What makes someone kill like that?" asked Roosevelt.

"Seriously?" asked Holliday.

"Seriously."

"The fact that he can."

"That's a hell of an answer, Doc," said Roosevelt disapprovingly.

"It's an answer based on all the killers I've known, Theodore," replied Holliday. "If you can't, you don't even get started. But if you can, and there's no one who can stop you, then you either kill when you have to, like me, or when you want to, like Hardin."

"Do you remember the first man you ever killed?"

"I remember all of them, Theodore," said Holliday. "That's not to say that they haunt me; they don't. Every last one of them is better off dead. But when a man puts his own life on the line to kill you, even if he's just some empty-headed punk kid out to make a reputation, you remember him. Sometimes you forget the details, and often you forget the reasons, since almost as often there weren't any real reasons, but you remember the faces, and usually the names." Suddenly he smiled. "Do you remember who you beat in your New York elections?"

"Of course."

"Same thing."

"You are one of the most interesting men I have ever met, Doc," said Roosevelt.

"Clearly your circle of acquaintances is too small."

Roosevelt chuckled at that. "Well, maybe one of these days I'll return to public life and make it larger."

"If you're too young to run for president, and I suspect you are by a decade, then perhaps you'll stay out here and run for governor, because if Geronimo keeps his word, we're going to need one."

"He'll keep it," said Roosevelt with certainty. "He's an honorable man."

"I've always found him so," agreed Holliday, "but never forget that he's an honorable man who's responsible for twenty times as many deaths as Hardin."

"He's a warrior, protecting his people," responded Roosevelt. "Hardin is just a killer, like . . ."

"Like me?"

"I was going to say like Billy the Kid."

"A nice young man, in his way," said Holliday.

"But you killed him."

"You don't have to hate what you kill," answered Holliday. "Johnny Ringo—or what was left of him, or what he'd become, or however you want to say it—was the most educated and interesting man I've met out here until you came along. But sometimes liking someone isn't enough."

"What was it about them that you liked?" asked Roosevelt. "As far as everyone knows, they were cold-blooded killers."

"Well, the Kid was," agreed Doc. "But Ringo only became a killer when he was drinking, so I guess you'd call him a hot-blooded killer. Anyway, I could discuss Chaucer and Descartes and Cicero with Ringo, and I've never been able to do that with anyone else out here."

"You never brought them up with me," said Roosevelt.

"If you stay, we'd get around to it. We've had more pressing business. Anyway, Ringo was a fascinating man to talk to when he was sober."

"And the Kid?"

Holliday shrugged. "He reminded me of someone."

"Oh? Who?"

A smile. "Me."

"So if Hardin actually shows up, you'll probably like him too," suggested Roosevelt.

"Probably," agreed Holliday. "And he'll probably like me too. But it won't stop one of us from killing the other."

Holliday took another drink from the bottle.

"Well," said Roosevelt, "I think I'd better be taking these weapons back to Tom and Ned, and saying my good-byes. I figure I'll spend the night in the Grand, and set out right after sunrise."

He extended his hand and Holliday took it.

"I'm glad we met," said Roosevelt.

"It's been a privilege to know you," replied Holliday.

"And now I'll be able to correct all the dime-novel writers and artists," added Roosevelt with a grin.

"Heads up, Doc!" said Hairlip Smith.

Holliday looked across the saloon at him.

"I think your company just arrived," said Smith, pointing out the window.

Holliday turned and looked into the street, where a tall, lean man, dressed all in black, was dismounting. He had a rifle slung over his shoulder, a sword with an umbrella handle attached to the left side of his belt, and a well-used pistol tucked into his belt. He wore a broad-brimmed black hat that had a thin headband with a couple of feathers hanging down from it. A bunch of fringe, taken from some dead Union soldier's dress uniform, was sewn onto his right shoulder and arm.

"That's him, all right," said Holliday. He turned to Roosevelt. "Theodore, he doesn't want you. Go over there with your Rough Riders."

"But—"

"Damn it, Theodore!" snapped Holliday. "You can't beat him, and I'm going to be too busy protecting myself to worry about you too."

Roosevelt seemed about to object again, thought better of it, got up, and walked over to sit at a table with Mickelson, Sloan, and the others.

An instant later, John Wesley Hardin walked through the swinging doors, looked around the tavern, and walked over to stand in front of Holliday.

"It has to be you," he said.

"Have a seat, John Wesley," said Holliday. "Bartender, a glass for my guest."

Hardin sat down and glared at him. "You can't weigh much more than a hundred, a hundred and ten pounds," he said. "How the hell did you kill all those men?"

"Force of personality," said Holliday with a smile. The glass arrived, he filled it, and placed it in front of Hardin.

"They say you're a lunger, too."

"True enough," replied Holliday. "They say you're a lawyer."

"I am now."

"Then you know that the law tends to frown on murder."

"This isn't murder," said Hardin. "You can go for your gun whenever you want."

"Perhaps later," said Holliday, taking another swig from the bottle. "Tell me about Texas. Has it changed much since I had to leave it in a hurry?"

"Cows and dust, same as ever." Suddenly Hardin grinned. "I heard about why you left Dallas."

"Well," said Holliday, returning his smile, "the sheriff was running me out of town in the morning anyway for practicing a vigorous brand of self-defense."

"I wasn't talking about that. It was the teeth."

Holliday's smile became even broader. "He gave me twelve hours to get out of town. But then that night he had an abscessed tooth, and I was the only dentist he knew, so he hunted me up to have me pull it." Holliday chuckled. "I put him under with laughing gas, pulled every tooth in his goddamned head, and decided to leave town without waiting for the stagecoach."

Hardin threw back his head and laughed. "Damn! I *knew* we could be friends if we ever met!"

"No reason why not," agreed Holliday.

Suddenly Hardin's smile vanished. "Except that I got to kill you."

"No, you don't."

"That was the deal. This huge critter, I guess he was an Indian but he sure as hell wasn't like any I ever saw, tore the brick wall right out of my cell and set me free, but the deal was that he'd only do it if I promised to kill you."

"You don't owe him anything," said Holliday. "He's dead."

Hardin frowned. "Are you kidding me, Doc?"

"Ask anyone here," said Holliday. "See the guy in the store-bought buckskins and the spectacles? He killed him."

"Really?"

"Really," said Holliday, pulling a pack of cards out of a pocket. "So drink up and let's play a little serious blackjack."

Hardin stared at Roosevelt for another few seconds.

"*Him?*" he said disbelievingly.

"Him," replied Holliday.

"Well, I'll be damned!"

"Probably we both will be," agreed Holliday.

Hardin downed his drink. "Deal," he said.

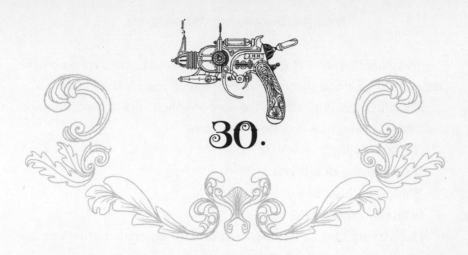

30.

"NICE LITTLE TOWN," remarked Hardin after they'd been playing for about twenty minutes and had pretty much broken even.

"Used to be even nicer, before the silver mines played out," replied Holliday. "I think it lost better than half its population in the last thirty months."

"Too bad. As famous as you and the Earps made it, you kinda hate to see it die."

"As long as people will pay good money to see the corral where the fight wasn't, it'll stay alive."

Hardin frowned. "Where it *wasn't*?"

"It's easier to call it the Gunfight at the O.K. Corral than the Gunfight in the Alley Backing Up to the O.K. Corral," said Holliday.

"A telling point," agreed Hardin. "Still, it's a shame. I could have settled down here and gone to work."

"That's right," said Holliday. "With your law degree."

Hardin smiled. "Can you picture that, Doc—me defending killers?"

"Why not?" replied Holliday. "If you got your degree, you know the law, and I don't think anyone would deny that you know shootists."

Hardin laughed at that. "You've got a hell of a sense of humor, Doc. Why do you look so damned grouchy?"

"I resent dying."

"I ain't going to kill you."

"I'm dying just the same."

"The consumption?"

Holliday nodded. "I'll be heading back to Colorado in the next few days to die."

"Colorado makes dying more pleasant, does it?"

"The sanitarium I plan to check into does," answered Holliday.

"Is this sanitarium in Denver?"

Holliday shook his head. "Leadville."

"Well, maybe we'll become almost-neighbors," said Hardin. "Got to be a lot of lawbreaking going on in Denver. Place like that must need a good lawyer who knows all there is to know about lawbreaking."

"Especially if there aren't any warrants out for you in Colorado."

"Never been to Colorado," answered Hardin. "And after living in hellholes all over the Texas, New Mexico, and Arizona Territories, it might be nice to step outside at night and feel the need of a coat."

"Leadville was a hundred four degrees when I left it," said Holliday with a rueful smile.

"Surely it's not like that all the time."

"No, it's not," admitted Holliday. "I have a hard time breathing that thin mountain air, but hell, these days I have a hard time breathing *any* air."

"Cool mountain air," mused Hardin. "It's worth considering, anyway."

"I'd be happy to have you ride along with me."

Hardin paused, considering the offer. "It's tempting, Doc," he said at last. "Damned tempting."

"But?" said Holliday. "Sounds for sure like you've got a 'but' coming at the end of that sentence."

"I got a couple of men who have offered to set me up with a law office back in El Paso." He grinned. "Might even hire me one of those dance-hall girls as a secretary. I'll get up to Colorado one of these days, but as long as there's money waiting for me in El Paso . . ."

"I'd do the same thing if I were you," said Holliday. "And if I ever need a lawyer, I'll know where to go."

"Well, I reckon I'll be moving on," said Hardin. "It's been a pleasure talking with you, Doc, and I'm glad it didn't come down to a gunfight."

"My sentiments exactly," said Holliday, getting to his feet. "Come on, I'll walk you to your horse."

Hardin made a circular route to the door, passing by Roosevelt's table. "Nice shooting—or whatever the hell you did to him."

"Thank you," said Roosevelt.

"Maybe we *all* ought to wear specs," said Hardin with a chuckle. He joined Holliday at the door and the two men walked out to the street, where Hardin's sorrel mare was tied to a hitching post.

Suddenly Holliday was aware that they weren't alone. Four Indians, none of them young, stood between them and Hardin's mare.

"You men are blocking my way," said Hardin ominously.

"You are going nowhere, John Wesley Hardin," said the nearest of them.

"Get out of my way," growled Hardin. "I won't ask you again."

"You made a bargain. You are not leaving until you keep it."

"You want me to shoot him?" he said, jerking his thumb at Holliday.

"That is correct."

"Okay," said Hardin. "But let me make sure my gun is working first."

He drew his gun and fired four quick shots at the Indians. The bullets turned to dust and floated to the ground before they reached their targets.

"Would I be correct in assuming that you're Dull Knife, Spotted Elk, Tall Wolf, and Cougar Slayer?" asked Holliday as the Oriental emptied out into the street at the sound of the gunshots.

"We do not speak to dead men," answered the closest one, "and you are all but dead, Holliday."

"I hope you're not trying to frighten me," replied Holliday. "Hell, I've been all but dead for years."

The Indian turned to Hardin. "If you wish to live, you know what you must do."

"No one gives me orders!" growled Hardin, emptying his second gun into the Indians. Again, the bullets turned to dust as they left his six-gun.

Holliday knew his gun wouldn't work against the medicine men either, but he couldn't think of what else to do, so he pulled it and fired off three quick shots to no effect.

"You are not the fastest learner I ever met," said a familiar voice from behind him. He turned and saw Roosevelt, the black lenses clipped onto his glasses but raised so he could see, the battery slung over his back, carrying Edison's two weapons, one in each arm, both attached to the battery. "Here," he said, thrusting the deafener into Holliday's hands. "And understand: if you use it, they're going to die, but so will every man and animal within a mile or more."

Holliday took the deafener, handling it *very* gently, while Roosevelt pointed the blinder at the four medicine men.

"Now, you gentlemen are going to let Mr. Hardin leave right now, aren't you?"

And with that, the hawk swooped down and landed in front of the medicine men, and instantly morphed into the Apache. He spread his arms, and suddenly a transparent dome covered the five of them. They spoke for less than a minute, their words unheard by any of the combatants or observers. Then the dome vanished, and so did the four medicine men.

"It is settled," announced Geronimo. "Tomorrow the spell will be lifted, and the White Eyes and their armies may cross the great river." He turned to Hardin. "Ride on!" he ordered him.

Hardin stared at him for just a second, then tipped his hat, climbed onto his mare, uttered a yell of triumph, and galloped off in the general direction of El Paso.

"Maybe we should have had it out after all," said Holliday. "He's going to kill a lot more men."

"He is not," answered Geronimo. "He will work as a lawyer, and less than a month later he will be shot in the back and killed."

"You know how everyone's going to die, do you?" asked Luke Sloan, who was standing in front of the Oriental's swinging doors.

Geronimo stared at him as one might stare at an insect, and did not deign to answer him.

"You will leave now," he said to Roosevelt.

"After I return the weapons to Edison and Buntline."

Geronimo nodded.

"Thank you," said Roosevelt, extending his hand, and the old medicine man took it. "I hope someday we will meet again."

"As I told you, we will," answered Geronimo. "Many years and many weeks' march from here."

Roosevelt took the smaller weapon from Holliday, climbed aboard Manitou, and headed off to Edison's house, trying without success to figure out what Geronimo had meant by his final sentence.

31.

HOLLIDAY WAITED FOR THE LENS ABOVE THE DOOR to identify him and allow the portal to swing open, then he walked into Edison's living room, where the inventor and Ned Buntline were waiting for him.

"We got your message," said Edison.

"I just wanted to stop by to thank you for what you did for Theodore," said Holliday. "Hell, for the whole damned country."

"Which is going to be a much bigger country now," said Buntline with a satisfied air.

"I wish I could stick around to see it."

"Why don't you?" asked Buntline.

"No," replied Holliday. "It's time to go to Leadville and die."

"My God, that's a morbid way to put it!" said Edison.

"If it was my choice, I'd live another twenty or thirty years and see what young Roosevelt can accomplish with his new nation. Hell, if I could lift a sixth of a coffin, I'd mosey down to El Paso and be a pall-bearer when Hardin finally gets backshot—he's too good for anyone except maybe me to take him in a fair fight. But I'm not going to live twenty years, and I can't lift a sixth of a coffin, and I'm running out of handkerchiefs, so it's time to go back to Leadville."

"We have an office up there," said Edison. "Maybe we *will* see you again."

"I won't be much to look at," said Holliday. Suddenly he grinned. "But then, I never was."

"Can I get you anything before you leave?" asked Buntline.

"I've already drunk my breakfast, but if you've got something wet before lunch . . ."

Buntline shook his head. "Neither of us drink whiskey."

"If you're not careful, you just might live to be a hundred." Holliday walked across the room and shook hands with each of them. "Thanks, again. You are the only two men I've ever been able to count on."

Then he was gone, and a few minutes later he was riding north in one of the Bunt Line's horseless coaches. He leaned back, sighed, pulled a flask out of his lapel pocket, uncapped it, and took a drink—and was suddenly aware that he wasn't alone any longer.

"I know, I know," he said. "This stuff'll kill me."

"You are dying anyway, so drink what you want," said Geronimo.

"You magicked yourself here just to tell me that?"

"And to tell you that no matter what others say, you are a good man." He paused. "Roosevelt will get the credit."

"He's welcome to it," said Holliday. "It's not going to do me any good where I'm going."

"You are dying," repeated Geronimo. "But you are not dead yet."

And with that he was gone.

Holliday stared out the window, shading his eyes and trying to imagine the Mississippi some two thousand miles distant. They'd start crossing it in the coming weeks and months—settlers, farmers, soldiers, everyone. There would be a mad rush to the West.

And, unknown to him, there would be two brilliant and half-crazed millionaires, one from Philadelphia and one from New Haven, who would rewrite the history of American science as their lives intertwined with his.

Appendix 1

THERE HAS BEEN QUITE A LOT written about Doc Holliday, Theodore Roosevelt, Geronimo, John Wesley Hardin, and the so-called Wild West. Surprisingly, a large amount takes place in an alternate reality in which (hard as this is to believe) the United States did not stop at the Mississippi River, but crossed the continent from one ocean to the other.

For those of you who are interested in this "alternate history," here is a bibliography of some of the more interesting books:

L. F. Abbott, *Impressions of Theodore Roosevelt*, Doubleday, Page (1919)

Alexander B. Adams, *Geronimo: A Biography*, Da Capo Press (1990)

C. E. Banks and R. A. Armstrong, *Theodore Roosevelt: A Typical American*, S. Stone (1901)

Stephen Melvil Barrett and Frederick W. Turner, *Geronimo: His Own Story*, Penguin (1996)

Bob Boze Bell, *The Illustrated Life and Times of Doc Holliday*, Tri Star-Boze (1995)

Glenn G. Boyer, *Who Was Big Nose Kate?* Glenn G. Boyer (1997)

H. W. Brands, *T. R.—The Last Romantic*, Basic Books (1997)

William M. Breakenridge, *Helldorado: Bringing the Law to the Mesquite*, Houghton Mifflin (1928)

E. Richard Churchill, *Doc Holliday, Bat Masterson, & Wyatt Earp: Their Colorado Careers*, Western Reflections (2001)

Michael L. Collins, *That Damned Cowboy: Theodore Roosevelt and the American West, 1883–1898*, Peter Lang (1989)

O. Cushing, *The Teddysey*, Life Publishing (1907)

Paul Russell Cutright, *Theodore Roosevelt—The Making of a Conservationist*, University of Illinois Press (1985)

Jack DeMattos, *Masterson and Roosevelt*, Creative Publishing (1984)

Mike Donovan, *The Roosevelt That I Know: Ten Years of Boxing with the President*, B. W. Dodge (1909)

G. W. Douglas, *The Many-Sided Roosevelt: An Anecdotal Biography*, Dodd, Mead (1907)

E. S. Ellis, *From the Ranch to the White House: Life of Theodore Roosevelt*, Hurst (1906)

T. T. Handford, *Theodore Roosevelt, the Pride of the Rough Riders*, M. A. Donohue (1897)

John Wesley Hardin, *The Life of John Wesley Hardin, as Written by Himself*, Smith & Moore (1896)

Albert Bushnbell Hart and Herbert Ronald Ferleger, eds., *Theodore Roosevelt Cyclopedia*, Theodore Roosevelt Association and Meckler Corporation (1989)

Pat Jahns, *The Frontier World of Doc Holliday*, Hastings House (1957)

Sylvia D. Lynch, *Aristocracy's Outlaw—The Doc Holliday Story*, Iris Press (1994)

Paula Mitchell Marks, *And Die in the West: The Story of the O.K. Corral Gunfight*, William Morrow (1989)

Leon Metz, *John Wesley Hardin: Dark Angel of Texas*, Mangam Books (1996)

Edmond Morris, *The Rise of Theodore Roosevelt*, Coward, McCann, and Geoghegan (1979)

Edmond Morris, *Theodore Rex*, Random House, 2001

John Myers Myers, *Doc Holliday*, Little, Brown (1955)

Frederick Nolan, *The Lincoln County War, Revised Edition*, Sunstone Press (2009)

Fred E. Pond, *Life and Adventures of Ned Buntline*, Camdus Book Shop (1919)

Gary Roberts, *Doc Holliday: The Life and Legend*, John Wiley & Sons (2006)

Theodore Roosevelt, *An Autobiography*, MacMillan (1913)

Theodore Roosevelt, *Hunting Trips of a Ranchman*, Putnam's (1885)

Theodore Roosevelt, *Ranch Life and the Hunting-Trail*, Century (1888)

Theodore Roosevelt, *The Rough Riders*, Scribner's (1899)

Theodore Roosevelt, *The Strenuous Life*, Century (1900)

Theodore Roosevelt, *The Winning of the West*, 4 vols., Putnam's, (1888–1894)

Karen Holliday Tanner, *Doc Holliday—A Family Portrait*, University of Oklahoma Press (1998)

Paul Trachman, *The Old West: The Gunfighters*, Time-Life Books (1974)

Ben T. Traywick, *John Henry: The Doc Holliday Story*, Red Marie's (1996)

Ben T. Traywick, *Tombstone's Deadliest Gun: John Henry Holliday*, Red Marie's (1984)

R. L. Wildon, *Theodore Roosevelt—Outdoorsman*, Trophy Room Books (1994)

APPENDIX 2

IN THAT "ALTERNATE HISTORY" in which the United States extended all the way to the Pacific, there are also a number of films made about the principals in this book, and a number of very popular actors portrayed them. Here's a list of them:

SOME MOVIE DOC HOLLIDAYS:

Victor Mature

Kirk Douglas

Jason Robards Jr.

Cesar Romero

Stacey Keach

Dennis Quaid

Val Kilmer

Walter Huston

Arthur Kennedy
Randy Quaid (TV)
Douglas Fowley (TV)
Gerald Mohr (TV)

SOME MOVIE THEODORE ROOSEVELTS:

Brian Keith
Tom Berenger
Karl Swenson
Robin Williams
Frank Albertson (TV)
Peter Breck (TV)
Len Cariou (Broadway musical)

SOME MOVIE THOMAS ALVA EDISONS:

Spencer Tracy
Mickey Rooney

SOME MOVIE NED BUNTLINES:

Lloyd Corrigan
Thomas Mitchell

SOME MOVIE GERONIMOS:

Chuck Conners
Wes Studi
Jay Silverheels (four times)
Monte Blue

SOME MOVIE JOHN WESLEY HARDINS:

Rock Hudson
John Denher
Jack Elam
Max Perlich
Randy Quaid (TV)

SOME MOVIE BAT MASTERSONS:

Albert Dekker
Randolph Scott
George Montgomery
Joel McCrea
Tom Sizemore
Gene Barry (TV)

Appendix 3

This is a "who's who" of the book's participants in that fictional alternate reality where the United States extended to the West Coast.

Doc Holliday

He was born John Henry Holliday in 1851, and grew up in Georgia. His mother died of tuberculosis when he was fourteen, and that is almost certainly where he contracted the disease. He was college-educated, with a minor in the classics, and became a licensed dentist. Because of his disease, he went out West to drier climates. The disease cost him most of his clientele, so he supplemented his dental income by gambling, and he defended his winnings in the untamed cities of the West by becoming a gunslinger as well.

He saved Wyatt Earp when the latter was surrounded by gunmen in

Dodge City, and the two became close friends. Somewhere along the way he met and had a stormy on-and-off relationship with Big Nose Kate Elder. He was involved in the Gunfight at the O.K. Corral, and is generally considered to have delivered the fatal shots to both Tom and Frank McLaury. He rode with Wyatt Earp on the latter's vendetta against the Cowboys after the shootings of Virgil and Morgan Earp, then moved to Colorado. He died, in bed, of tuberculosis, in 1887. His last words were: "Well, I'll be damned—this is funny." No accurate records were kept in the case of most shootists; depending on which historians you believe, Doc killed anywhere from two to twenty-seven men.

THEODORE ROOSEVELT

Theodore Roosevelt was born in New York City in 1858. A sickly child, suffering from extreme asthma, he worked at strengthening his body through exercise and swimming, and by the time he attended Harvard he was fit enough to become the college's lightweight boxing champion. Even prior to that he was a devoted naturalist, and was acknowledged—even as a teen—as one of America's leading ornithologists and taxidermists.

His *The Naval War of 1812* was (and is) considered the definitive book on that battle. Shortly thereafter he developed an interest in politics and became the youngest-ever minority leader of the New York State Assembly. His wife and mother died eight hours apart in the same house in 1884, and he quit politics, headed out to the Dakota Badlands, and bought two ranches. He signed a contract to write the four-volume *The Winning of the West*, became a lawman, and caught and captured three armed killers during "the Winter of the Blue Snow."

Coming back East, he married again, served as police commissioner of New York City, later was secretary of the navy, assembled the Rough Riders and took San Juan Hill during the Spanish-American War, became governor of New York, was elected vice president in 1900, and became president less than a year later with the assassination of President McKinley.

As president, Roosevelt fought the trusts, created the National Park System, won the Nobel Peace Prize, and turned the United States into a world power. When he left office in 1908 he embarked on a year-long African safari. He ran for president in 1912, was wounded by a would-be assassin, lost, and spent a year exploring and mapping the River of Doubt (later renamed the Rio Teodoro) for the Brazilian government. He was a strong advocate for our entry into World War I, and it was assumed the presidency was his for the asking in 1920, but he died a year before the election.

During his life, he wrote more than twenty books—many of them still in print—and over 150,000 letters.

THOMAS ALVA EDISON

Born in Milan, Ohio, in 1847, Edison is considered the greatest inventor of his era. He is responsible for the electric light, the motion picture, the carbon telephone transmitter, the fluoroscope, and a host of other inventions. He died in 1931.

NED BUNTLINE

Buntline was born Edward Z. C. Judson in 1813, and gained fame as a publisher, editor, writer (especially of dime novels about the West), and for commissioning Colt's Manufacturing Company to create the Buntline Special. He tried to bring Wild Bill Hickok back East, failed, and then discovered Buffalo Bill Cody, who *did* come East and perform in a play that Buntline wrote.

BAT MASTERSON

William "Bat" Masterson was born in 1853. In his late teens, he and brothers Ed and James left their family home to go out west as buffalo hunters. He spent some time as an army scout, seeing action against the Kiowa and Comanche Indians. He moved to Dodge City, Kansas, in 1877, and shortly afterward became Wyatt Earp's deputy, after which he was elected sheriff of Ford County.

Brother Ed was also a lawman. Masterson saw him murdered and instantly responded with deadly force, killing his killer. He then became a gambler, and was in Tombstone just before the Gunfight at the O.K. Corral. After a few more gunfights, always on the side of the law (or *as* the law), he became a writer, wound up in New York, and became friends with Theodore Roosevelt, who appointed him marshal of New York from 1905 to 1909. He died at his typewriter in 1921.

JOHN WESLEY HARDIN

John Wesley Hardin, like Bat Masterson, was born in 1853. He was a killer from a very early age, had at least one encounter with Wild Bill Hickcock, and when he was finally apprehended and tried in 1878, he was convicted of killing forty-two men. He wrote his autobiography and obtained his law degree while in jail, was released in August of

1895, set up a law practice, and was killed shortly thereafter by John Selman Sr.

TEXAS JACK VERMILLION

A friend of both Holliday and Wyatt Earp, Texas Jack Vermillion (later known as Shoot-Your-Eye-Out Vermillion) participated in Wyatt Earp's Vendetta Ride, and was saved in at least one shoot-out by Holliday.

GERONIMO

Born Goyathlay in 1829, he was a Chiricahua Apache medicine man who fought against both the Americans and the Mexicans who tried to grab Apache territory. He was never a chief, but he *was* a military leader, and a very successful one. He finally surrendered in 1886, and was incarcerated—but by 1904 he had become such a celebrity that he actually appeared at the World's Fair, and in 1905 he proudly rode in Theodore Roosevelt's inaugural parade in Washington, DC. He died in 1909 at the age of eighty.

Appendix 4

THIS IS WYATT EARP'S DESCRIPTION and recollection of Doc Holliday, in his own words:

By the time I met him at Fort Griffin, Doc Holliday had run up quite a record as a killer, even for Texas. In Dallas, his incessant coughing kept away whatever professional custom he might have enjoyed and, as he had to eat, he took to gambling. He was lucky, skillful, and fearless. There were no tricks to his new trade that he did not learn and in more than one boom-camp game I have seen him bet ten thousand dollars on the turn of a card.

Doc quickly saw that six-gun skill was essential to his new business, and set out to master the fine points of draw-and-shoot as cold-bloodedly as he did everything. He practiced with a Colt for hours at a time, until he knew that he could get one into action as effectively as any man he might meet. His right to this opinion was justified by Doc's achievements. The only man of his type whom I ever regarded as anywhere near his equal on the draw was Buckskin Frank Leslie of Tombstone. But Leslie lacked Doc's fatalistic courage, a courage induced, I suppose, by the nature of Holliday's disease and the realization that he hadn't long to live, anyway. That fatalism, coupled with his marvelous speed and accuracy, gave Holliday the edge over any out-and-out killer I ever knew.

Doc's first fight in the West ended a row over a Dallas card-game. He shot and killed a topnotch gunman, and as Doc was comparatively a stranger where his victim had many friends, Doc had to emigrate. He went to Jacksborough, at the edge of the Fort Richardson military reservation, where he tangled with three or four more gunmen successfully, but eventually killed a soldier and again had to take it on the run. Next, he tried the Colorado camps, where he knocked off several pretty bad men in gun-fights. In Denver, Doc encountered an ordinance against gun-toting, so he carried a knife, slung on a cord around his neck. Bud Ryan, a gambler, tried to run one over on Doc in a card game, and when Doc objected, Ryan went for a gun he carried in a concealed holster. Doc beat him into action with his knife, and cut him horribly.

Doc gambled in the Colorado and Wyoming camps until the fall of '77, and fought his way out of so many arguments that, by the time he hit Fort Griffin, he had built up a thoroughly deserved reputation as a man who would shoot to kill on the slightest provocation. That reputation may have had some bearing on the fact that when I first met him, he had not yet found anyone in Fort Griffin to provide him with a battle.

It was in Shanssey's saloon, I think, that Doc Holliday first met Kate Elder, a dancehall girl better known as "Big-Nosed Kate." Doc lived with Kate, off and on, over a period of years. She saved his life on one occasion, and when memory of this was uppermost Doc would refer to Kate as Mrs. Holliday. Their relationship had its temperamental ups and downs, however, and when Kate was writhing under Doc's scorn she'd get drunk as well as furious and make Doc more trouble than any shooting-scrape.

Perhaps Doc's outstanding peculiarity was the enormous amount of whiskey he could punish. Two and three quarts of liquor a day was not unusual for him, yet I never saw him stagger with intoxication. At times, when his tuberculosis was worse than ordinary, or he was under a long-continued physical strain, it would take a pint of whiskey to get him going in the morning, and more than once at the end of a long ride I've seen him swallow a tumbler of neat liquor without batting an eye and fifteen minutes later take a second tumbler of straight whiskey which had no more outward effect on him than the first one. Liquor never seemed to fog him in the slightest, and he was more inclined to fight when getting along on a slim ration than when he was drinking plenty, and was more comfortable, physically.

With all of Doc's shortcomings and his undeniably poor disposition, I found him a loyal friend and good company. At the time of his death, I tried to set down the qualities about him which had impressed me. The newspapers dressed up my ideas considerably and had me calling Doc Holliday "a mad, merry scamp with heart of gold and nerves of steel." Those were not my words, nor did they convey my meaning. Doc was mad, well enough, but he was seldom merry. His humor ran in a sardonic vein, and as far as the world in general was concerned, there was nothing in his soul but iron. Under ordinary circumstances he might be irritable to the point of shakiness; only in a game or when a fight impended was there anything steely about his nerves.

To sum up Doc Holliday's character as I did at the time of his death: he was a dentist whom necessity had made into a gambler; a gentleman whom disease had made a frontier vagabond; a philosopher whom life had made a caustic wit; a long, lean, ash-blond fellow nearly dead with consumption and at the same time the most skilled gambler and the nerviest, speediest, deadliest man with a six-gun I ever knew.

Appendix 5

T HIS IS AN ARTICLE THAT I ORIGINALLY WROTE FOR *Oval Office Oddities*, edited by Bill Fawcett.

The Unsinkable Teddy Roosevelt

His daughter, Alice, said it best:

"He wanted to be the bride at every wedding and the corpse at every funeral."

❦

Of course, he had a little something to say about his daughter, too. When various staff members complained that she was running wild throughout the White House, his response was: "Gentlemen, I can either run the country, or I can control Alice. I cannot do both."

~⁓

He was Theodore Roosevelt, of course: statesman, politician, adventurer, naturalist, ornithologist, taxidermist, cowboy, police commissioner, explorer, writer, diplomat, boxer, and president of the United States.

John Fitzgerald Kennedy was widely quoted after inviting a dozen writers, artists, musicians and scientists to lunch at the White House when he announced: "This is the greatest assemblage of talent to eat here since Thomas Jefferson dined alone." It's a witty statement, but JFK must have thought Roosevelt ate all his meals out.

~⁓

Roosevelt didn't begin life all that auspiciously. "Teedee" was a sickly child, his body weakened by asthma. It was his father who decided that he was not going to raise an invalid. Roosevelt was encouraged to swim, to take long hikes, to do everything he could to build up his body.

He was picked on by bullies, who took advantage of his weakened condition, so he asked his father to get him boxing lessons. They worked pretty well. By the time he entered Harvard he had the body and reactions of a trained athlete, and before long he was a member of the boxing team.

It was while fighting for the lightweight championship that an incident occurred which gave everyone an insight into Roosevelt's character. He was carrying the fight to his opponent, C. S. Hanks, the defending champion, when he slipped and fell to his knee. Hanks had launched a blow that he couldn't pull back, and he opened Roosevelt's nose, which began gushing blood. The crowd got ugly and started booing the champion, but Roosevelt held up his hand for silence, announced that it was an honest mistake, and shook hands with Hanks before the fight resumed.

~~∾~~

It was his strength of character that led to his developing an equally strong body. His doctor, W. Thompson, once told a friend: "Look out for Theodore. He's not strong, but he's all grit. He'll kill himself before he'll ever say he's tired."

In fifty-nine years of a vigorous, strenuous life, he never once admitted to being tired.

~~∾~~

Roosevelt was always fascinated by Nature, and in fact had seriously considered becoming a biologist or a naturalist before discovering politics. The young men sharing his lodgings at Harvard were probably less than thrilled with his interest. He kept a number of animals in his room. Not cute, cuddly ones, but rather snakes, lobsters, and a tortoise that was always escaping and scaring the life out of his landlady. Before long most of the young men in his building refused to go anywhere near his room.

~~∾~~

Roosevelt "discovered" politics shortly after graduating Harvard (*phi beta kappa* and *summa cum laude*, of course). So he attacked the field with the same vigor he attacked everything else. The result? At twenty-four he became the youngest Assemblyman in the New York State House, and the next year he became the youngest-ever Minority Leader.

He might have remained in New York politics for years, but something happened that changed his life. He had met and fallen in love with Alice Hathaway Lee while in college, and married her very soon thereafter. His widowed mother lived with them.

And then, on February 14, 1884, Alice and his mother both died (Alice in childbirth, his mother of other causes) eight hours apart in the same house.

The blow was devastating to Roosevelt. He never mentioned Alice again and refused to allow her to be mentioned in his presence. He put his former life behind him and decided to lose himself in what was left of the Wild West.

⌁

He bought a ranch in the Dakota Badlands . . . and then, because he was Theodore Roosevelt and couldn't do anything in a small way, he bought a second ranch as well. He spent a lot more time hunting than ranching, and more time writing and reading than hunting. (During his lifetime he wrote more than 150,000 letters, as well as close to thirty books.)

He'd outfitted himself with the best "Western" outfit money could buy back in New York, and of course he appeared to the locals to be a wealthy New York dandy. By now he was wearing glasses, and he took a lot of teasing over them; the sobriquet "Four Eyes" seemed to stick.

Until the night he found himself far from his Elkhorn Ranch and decided to rent a room at Nolan's Hotel in Mingusville, on the west bank of the Beaver River. After dinner he went down to the bar—it was the only gathering point in the entire town—and right after Roosevelt arrived, a huge drunk entered, causing a ruckus, shooting off his six-gun, and making himself generally obnoxious. When he saw Roosevelt, he announced that "Four Eyes" would buy drinks for everyone in the bar—or else. Roosevelt, who wasn't looking for a fight, tried to mollify him, but the drunk was having none of it. He insisted that the effete dandy put up his dukes and defend himself.

"Well, if I've got to, I've got to," muttered Roosevelt, getting up from his chair.

The bully took one swing. The boxer from Harvard ducked and bent the drunk in half with a one-two combination to the belly, then caught him flush on the jaw. He kept pummeling the drunk until the man was out cold, and then, with a little help from the appreciative onlookers, he carried the unconscious man to an outhouse behind the hotel and deposited him there for the night.

He was never "Four Eyes" again.

<hr>

The dude from New York didn't limit himself to human bullies. No horse could scare him either.

During the roundup of 1884, he and his companions encountered a horse known only as "The Devil." He'd earned his name throwing one cowboy after another, and was generally considered to be the meanest horse in the Badlands. Finally Roosevelt decided to match his will and skills against the stallion, and all the other cowboys gathered around the corral to watch the New Yorker get his comeuppance—and indeed, The Devil soon bucked him off.

Roosevelt got on again. And got bucked off again.

According to one observer, "With almost every other jump, we would see about twelve acres of bottom land between Roosevelt and the saddle." The Devil sent him flying a third and then a fourth time.

But Roosevelt wasn't about to quit. The Devil couldn't throw him a fifth time, and before long Roosevelt had him behaving "as meek as a rabbit," according to the same observer.

The next year there was an even wilder horse. The local cowboys knew him simply as "The Killer," but Roosevelt decided he was going to tame him, and a tame horse needed a better name than that, so he dubbed him "Ben Baxter." The cowboys, even those who had seen him break The Devil, urged him to keep away from The Killer, to have the horse destroyed. Roosevelt paid them no attention.

He tossed a blanket over Ben Baxter's head to keep him calm while putting on the saddle, an operation that was usually life-threatening in itself. Then he tightened the cinch, climbed onto the horse, and removed the blanket. And two seconds later Roosevelt was sprawling in the dirt of the corral.

And a minute later, he was back in the saddle.

And five seconds later he was flying through the air again, to land with a bone-jarring *thud!*

They kept it up most of the afternoon, Roosevelt climbing back on every time he was thrown, and finally the fight was all gone from Ben Baxter. Roosevelt had broken his shoulder during one of his spills, but it hadn't kept him from mastering the horse. He kept Ben Baxter, and from that day forward "The Killer" became the gentlest horse on his ranch.

Is it any wonder that he never backed down from a political battle?

～∽～

Having done everything else one could do in the Badlands, Roosevelt became a deputy sheriff. And in March of 1886, he found out that it meant a little more than rounding up the town drunks on a Saturday night. It seems that a wild man named Mike Finnegan, who had a reputation for breaking laws and heads that stretched from one end of the Badlands to the other, had gotten drunk and shot up the town of Medora, escaping—not that anyone dared to stop him—on a small flatboat with two confederates.

Anyone who's ever been in Dakota in March knows that it's still quite a few weeks away from the first signs of spring. Roosevelt, accompanied by Bill Sewell and Wilmot Dow, was ordered to bring Finnegan in, and took off after him on a raft a couple of days later. They negotiated the ice-filled river, and finally came to the spot where the gang had made camp.

Roosevelt, the experienced hunter, managed to approach silently and unseen until the moment he stood up, rifle in hands, and announced that they were his prisoners. Not a shot had to be fired.

But capturing Finnegan and his friends was the easy part. They had to be transported overland more than one hundred miles to the town of Dickenson, where they would stand trial. Within a couple of days the party of three lawmen and three outlaws was out of food. Finally Roosevelt set out on foot for a ranch—*any* ranch—and came back a day later with a small wagon filled with enough food to keep them alive on the long trek. The wagon had a single horse, and given the weather and conditions of the crude trails, the horse couldn't be expected pull all six men, so Sewell and Dow rode in the wagon while Roosevelt and the three captives walked behind it on an almost nonexistent trail, knee-deep in snow, in below-freezing weather. And the closer they got to Dickenson, the more likely it was that Finnegan would attempt to escape, so Roosevelt didn't sleep the last two days and nights of the forced march.

But he delivered the outlaws, safe and reasonably sound. He would be a lawman again in another nine years, but his turf would be as different from the Badlands as night is from day.

He became the police commissioner of New York City.

≈

New York was already a pretty crime-ridden city, even before the turn of the twentieth century. Roosevelt, who had already been a successful politician, lawman, lecturer and author, was hired to change that—and change it he did.

He hired the best people he could find. That included the first woman on the New York police force—and the next few dozen as well. (Before long, every station had police matrons around the clock, thus assuring that any female prisoner would be booked by a member of her own sex.)

Then came another innovation: when Roosevelt decided that most of the cops couldn't hit the broad side of a barn with their sidearms, target practice was not merely encouraged but made mandatory for the first time in the force's history.

When the rise of the automobile meant that police on foot could no longer catch some escaping lawbreakers, Roosevelt created a unit of bicycle police (who, in the 1890s, had no problem keeping up with the cars of that era, which were traversing streets that had not been created with automobiles in mind.)

He hired Democrats as well as Republicans, men who disliked him as well as men who worshipped him. All he cared about was that they were able to get the job done.

He was intolerant only of intolerance. When the famed anti-Semitic preacher from Berlin, Rector Ahlwardt, came to America, New York's Jewish population didn't want to allow him in the city. Roosevelt couldn't bar him, but he came up with the perfect solution: Ahlwardt's police bodyguards were composed entirely of very large, very unhappy Jewish cops whose presence convinced the bigot to forego his anti-Semitic harangues while he was in the city.

Roosevelt announced that all promotions would be strictly on merit and not political pull, then spent the next two years proving he meant what he said. He also invited the press into his office whenever he was there, and if a visiting politician tried to whisper a question so that the reporters couldn't hear it, Roosevelt would repeat and answer it in a loud, clear voice.

〜�〜

As police commissioner, Roosevelt felt the best way to make sure his police force was performing its duty was to go out in the field and see for himself. He didn't bother to do so during the day; the press and the public were more than happy to report on the doings of his policemen.

No, what he did was go out into the most dangerous neighborhoods, unannounced, between midnight and sunrise, usually with a reporter or two in tow, just in case things got out of hand. (Not that he thought they would help him physically, but he expected them to accurately report what happened if a misbehaving or loafing cop turned on him.)

The press dubbed these his "midnight rambles," and after a while the publicity alone caused almost all the police to stay at their posts and do their duty. They never knew when the commissioner might show up in their territory and either fire them on the spot or let the reporters who accompanied him expose them to public ridicule and condemnation.

〜�〜

Roosevelt began writing early and never stopped. You'd expect a man who was governor of New York and president of the United States to write about politics, and of course he did. But Roosevelt didn't like intellectual restrictions any more than he liked physical restrictions, and he wrote books—not just articles, mind you, but *books*—about anything that interested him.

While still in college he wrote *The Naval War of 1812*, which was considered at the time to be the definitive treatise on naval warfare.

Here's a partial list of the non-political books that followed, just to give you an indication of the breadth of Roosevelt's interests:

Hunting Trips of a Ranchman
The Wilderness Hunter
A Book-Lover's Holidays in the Open
The Winning of the West, Volumes 1–4
The Rough Riders
Literary Treats
Papers on Natural History
African Game Trails
Hero Tales from American History
Through the Brazilian Wilderness
The Strenuous Life
Ranch Life and the Hunting-Trail

I've got to think he'd be a pretty interesting guy to talk to. On any subject.

In fact, it'd be hard to find one he hadn't written up.

～❦～

A character as interesting and multi-faceted as Roosevelt's had to be portrayed in film sooner or later, but surprisingly, the first truly memorable characterization was by John Alexander, who delivered a classic and hilarious portrayal of a harmless madman who *thinks* he's Teddy Roosevelt and constantly screams "Charge!" as he runs up the stairs, his version of San Juan Hill, in *Arsenic and Old Lace*.

Eventually there were more serious portrayals: Brian Keith, Tom Berenger, even Robin Williams . . . and word has it that, possibly by the time you read this, you'll be able to add Leonardo DiCaprio to the list.

～❦～

Roosevelt believed in the active life, not just for himself but for his four sons—Kermit, Archie, Quentin, and Theodore Junior—and two daughters, Alice and Edith. He built Sagamore Hill, his rambling house on equally rambling acreage, and he often took the children—and any visiting dignitaries—on what he called "scrambles," cross-country hikes that were more obstacle course than anything else.

His motto: "Above or below, but never around." If you couldn't walk through it, you climbed over it or crawled under it, but you never ever circled it. This included not only hills, boulders, and thorn bushes, but rivers, and frequently he, the children, and the occasional visitor who didn't know what he was getting into, would come home soaking wet from swimming a river or stream with their clothes on, or covered with mud, or with their clothes torn to shreds from thorns.

Those wet, muddy, and torn clothes were their badges of honor. It meant that they hadn't walked around any obstacle.

～❦～

"If I am to be any use in politics," Roosevelt wrote to a friend, "it is because I am supposed to be a man who does not preach what he fears to practice. For the year I have preached war with Spain . . ."

So it was inevitable that he should leave his job as undersecretary of the navy and enlist in the military. He instantly became Lieutenant Colonel Roosevelt, and began putting together a very special elite unit, one that perhaps only he could have assembled.

The Rough Riders consisted, among others, of cowboys, Indians, tennis stars, college athletes, the marshal of Dodge City, the master of the Chevy Chase hounds, and the man who was reputed to be the best quarterback ever to play for Harvard.

They were quite a crew, Colonel Roosevelt's Rough Riders. They captured the imagination of the public as had no other military unit in United States history. They also captured San Juan Hill in the face of some serious machine gun fire, and Roosevelt, who led the charge, returned home an even bigger hero than when he'd left.

⁓≈⁓

While on a bear hunt in Mississippi, Colonel Roosevelt, as he liked to be called after San Juan Hill and Cuba, was told that a bear had been spotted a few miles away. When Roosevelt and his entourage—which always included the press—arrived, he found a small, undernourished, terrified bear tied to a tree. He refused to shoot it, and turned away in disgust, ordering a member of the party to put the poor creature out of its misery. His unwillingness to kill a helpless animal was captured by *Washington Post* cartoonist Clifford Berryman. It made him more popular than ever, and before long toy companies were turning out replicas of cute little bears that the great Theodore Roosevelt would certainly never kill, rather than ferocious game animals.

Just in case you ever wondered about the origin of the Teddy Bear.

⁓≈⁓

Some thirty years ago, writer/director John Milius gave the public one of the truly great adventure films, *The Wind and the Lion*, in which the Raisuli (Sean Connery), known as "the Last of the Barbary Pirates," kidnapped an American woman, Eden Perdicaris (Candice Bergen) and her two children, and held them for ransom at his stronghold in Morocco. At which point President Theodore Roosevelt (Brian Keith, in probably the best representation of Roosevelt ever put on film) declared that America wanted "Perdicaris alive or Raisuli dead!" and sent the fleet to Morocco.

Wonderful film, beautifully photographed, well-written, well-acted, with a gorgeous musical score.

Would you like to know what *really* happened?

First of all, it wasn't *Eden* Perdicaris; it was *Ion* Perdicaris, a sixty-four-year-old man. And he wasn't kidnapped with two small children, but with a grown stepson. And far from wanting to be rescued, he and the Raisuli became great friends.

Roosevelt felt the president of the United States had to protect Americans abroad, so he sent a telegram to the sultan of Morocco, the country in which the kidnapping took place, to the effect that America wanted Perdicaris alive or Raisuli dead. He also dispatched seven warships to Morocco.

So why wasn't there a war with Morocco?

Two reasons.

First, during the summer of 1904, shortly after the kidnapping and Roosevelt's telegram, the government learned something that was kept secret until after all the principles in the little drama—Roosevelt, Perdicaris, and the Raisuli—had been dead for years . . . and that was that Ion Perdicaris was *not* an American citizen. He had been born one, but he later renounced his citizenship and moved to Greece, years before the kidnapping.

The other reason? Perdicaris's dear friend, the Raisuli, set him free. Secretary of State John Hay knew full well that Perdicaris had been freed before the Republican convention convened, but he whipped the assembled delegates up with the "America wants Perdicaris alive or Raisuli dead!" slogan anyway, and Roosevelt was elected in a landslide.

⤳

Roosevelt was as vigorous and active as president as he'd been in every previous position. Consider:

Even though the country was relatively empty, he could see land being gobbled up in great quantities by settlers and others, and he created the National Park System.

He arranged for the overthrow of the hostile Panamanian government and created the Panama Canal, which a century later is *still* vital to international shipping.

He took on J. P. Morgan and his cohorts, and became the greatest "trust buster" in our history, then created the Department of Commerce and the Department of Labor to make sure weaker presidents in the future didn't give up the ground he'd taken.

We were a regional power when he took office. Then he sent the navy's "Great White Fleet" around the world on a "goodwill tour." By the time it returned home, we were, for the first time, a world power.

Because he never backed down from a fight, a lot of people thought of him as a warmonger—but he became the first American president ever to win the Nobel Peace Price while still in office, when he mediated a dispute between Japan and Russia before it became a full-fledged shooting war.

He created and signed the Pure Drug and Food Act.

He became the first president to leave the United States while in office when he visited Panama to inspect the canal.

~

Roosevelt remained physically active throughout his life. He may or may not have been the only president to be blind in one eye, but he was the only who to ever go blind in one eye from injuries received in a boxing match *while serving as president*.

He also took years of *jujitsu* lessons while in office, and became quite proficient at it.

And, in keeping with daughter Alice's appraisal of him, he was the first president to fly in an airplane, and the first to be filmed.

~

Roosevelt's last day in office was February 22, 1909.

He'd already been a cowboy, a rancher, a soldier, a marshal, a police commissioner, a governor, and a president. So did he finally slow down?

Just long enough to pack. Accompanied by his son, Kermit, and the always-present journalists, on March 23 he boarded a ship that would take him to East Africa for the first organized safari on record. It was sponsored by the American and Smithsonian museums, which to this day display some of the trophies he shot and brought back. His two guides were the immortal F. C. Selous, widely considered to be the greatest hunter in African history, and Philip Percival, who was already a legend among Kenya's hunting fraternity.

What did Roosevelt manage to bag for the museums?

Nine lions.
Nine elephants.
Five hyenas.

Eight black rhinos.

Five white rhinos.

Seven hippos.

Eight warthogs.

Six Cape buffalo.

Three pythons.

And literally hundreds of antelope, gazelle, and other herbivores.

Is it any wonder that he needed 500 uniformed porters? And since he paid as much attention to the mind as to the body, one of those porters carried sixty pounds of Roosevelt's favorite books on his back, and Roosevelt made sure he got in his reading every day, no matter what.

While hunting in Uganda, he ran into the noted rapscallion John Boyes and others who were poaching elephants in the Lado Enclave. According to Boyes's memoir, *The Company of Adventurers*, the poachers offered to put a force of fifty hunters and poachers at Roosevelt's disposal if he would like to take a shot at bringing American democracy, capitalism, and know-how to the Belgian Congo (not that they had any right to it, but from their point of view, neither did King Leopold of Belgium). Roosevelt admitted to being tempted, but he had decided that his chosen successor, William Howard Taft, was doing a lousy job as president and he'd made up his mind to run again.

But first, he wrote what remains one of the true classics of hunting literature, *African Game Trails*, which has remained in print for just short of a century as these words are written. (And half a dozen of the journalists wrote *their* versions of the safari to the book publishers, whose readers simply couldn't get enough of Roosevelt.)

William Howard Taft, the sitting president (and Roosevelt's hand-picked successor), of course wanted to run for re-election. Roosevelt was the clear choice among the Republican rank and file, but the president controls the party's machinery, and due to a number of procedural moves Taft got the nomination.

Roosevelt, outraged at the backstage manipulations, decided to form a third party. Officially it was the Progressive Party, but after he mentioned that he felt "as fit as bull moose," the public dubbed it the Bull Moose Party.

Not everyone was thrilled to see him run for a third term. (Actually, it would have been only his second election to the presidency; he became president in 1901 just months after McKinley's election and assassination, so though he'd only been elected once, he had served in the White House for seven years.) One such unhappy citizen was John F. Schrank.

On October 14, 1912, Roosevelt came out of Milwaukee's Hotel Gillespie to give a speech at a nearby auditorium. He climbed into an open car and waved to the crowd—and found himself face-to-face with Schrank, who raised his pistol and shot Roosevelt in the chest.

The crowd would have torn Schrank to pieces, but Roosevelt shouted: "Stand back! Don't touch that man!"

He had Schrank brought before him, stared at the man until the potential killer could no longer meet his gaze, then refused all immediate medical help. He wasn't coughing up blood, which convinced him that the wound wasn't fatal, and he insisted on giving his speech before going to the hospital.

He was a brave man . . . but he was also a politician and a showman, and he knew what the effect on the crowd would be when they saw the indestructible Roosevelt standing before them in a blood-soaked shirt, ignoring his wound to give them his vision of what he could do for America. "I shall ask you to be as quiet as possible," he began. "I don't know whether you fully understand that I have just been shot." He gave them the famous Roosevelt grin. "But it takes more than that to kill a Bull Moose!"

It brought the house down.

He lost the election to Woodrow Wilson—even Roosevelt couldn't win as a third-party candidate—but William Howard Taft, the president of the United States, came in a distant third, capturing only eight electoral votes.

⌒

That was enough for one vigorous lifetime, right?

Not hardly.

Did you ever hear of the River of Doubt?

You can be excused if your answer is negative. It no longer exists on any map.

On February 27, 1914, at the request of the Brazilian government, Roosevelt and his party set off to map the River of Doubt. It turned out to be not quite the triumph that the African safari had been.

Early on they began running short of supplies. Then Roosevelt developed a severe infection in his leg. It got so bad that at one point he urged the party to leave him behind. Of course they didn't, and gradually his leg and his health improved to the point where he was finally able to continue the expedition.

Eventually they mapped all 900 miles of the river, and Roosevelt, upon returning home, wrote another bestseller, *Through the Brazilian Wilderness*. And shortly thereafter, the *Rio da Duvida* (River of Doubt) officially became the river you can now find on the maps, the *Rio Teodoro* (River Theodore).

He was a man in his mid-fifties, back when the average man's life expectancy was only fifty-five. He was just recovering from being shot in the chest (and was still walking around with the bullet inside his body). Unlike East Africa, where he would be hunting the same territory that Selous had hunted before and Percival knew like the back of his hand, no one had ever mapped the River of Doubt. It was uncharted jungle, with no support network for hundreds of miles.

So why did he agree to map it?

His answer is so typically Rooseveltian that it will serve as the end to this chapter:

"It was my last chance to be a boy again."

APPENDIX 6

JOHN WESLEY HARDIN describes his confrontation with Wild Bill Hickok:

I have seen many fast towns, but I think Abilene beat them all. The town was filled with sporting men and women, gamblers, cowboys, desperadoes, and the like. It was well supplied with bar rooms, hotels, barber shops, and gambling houses, and everything was open.

I spent most of my time in Abilene in the saloons and gambling houses, playing poker, faro, and seven-up. One day I was rolling ten pins and my best horse was hitched outside in front of the saloon. I had two six-shooters on, and, of course, I knew the saloon people would raise a row if I did not pull them off. Several Texans were there rolling ten pins and drinking. I suppose we were pretty noisy. Wild Bill Hickok came in and said we were making too much noise and told me to pull off my pistols until I got ready to go out of town. I told him I was ready to go now, but did not propose to put up my pistols, go or no go. He went out and I followed him. I started up the street when someone behind me shouted out, "Set up. All down but nine."

Wild Bill whirled around and met me. He said, "What are you howling about, and what are you doing with those pistols on?"

I said, "I am just taking in the town."

He pulled his pistol and said, "Take those pistols off. I arrest you."

I said all right and pulled them out of the scabbard, but while he was reaching for them, I reversed them and whirled them over on him with the muzzles in his face, springing back at the same time. I told him to put his pistols up, which he did. I cursed him for a long-haired scoundrel that would shoot a boy with his back to him (as I had been told he intended to do me). He said, "Little Arkansas, you have been wrongly informed."

I shouted, "This is my fight and I'll kill the first man that fires a gun."

Bill said, "You are the gamest and quickest boy I ever saw. Let us compromise this matter and I will be your friend."

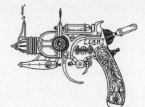

About the Author

MIKE RESNICK has won an impressive five Hugos and has been nominated for thirty-one more. He has published seventy-one novels and more than two hundred fifty short stories. He has edited forty-one anthologies. His work ranges from satirical fare, such as his Lucifer Jones adventures, to weighty examinations of morality and culture, as evidenced by his brilliant tales of Kirinyaga. The series, with sixty-six major and minor awards and nominations to date, is the most honored series of stories in the history of science fiction.